A Glasgow Kiss

Sophie grew up in a town just outside Glasgow and has always had a love for the English language. At a young age, she found herself writing funny stories or poems to friends and family for special occasions, and after high school she undertook a performing arts diploma, flourishing in her creative writing class. Sophie now works full time as a nurse in a busy city hospital.

In 2020, Sophie started writing again as a distraction from the ongoing pandemic, cheered on by fans of her hilarious blog, 'Sex in the Glasgow City'. *A Glasgow Kiss*, her debut novel, shot straight to number one in the erotic charts and has been a word-of-mouth sensation ever since.

A Glasgow Kiss

Sophie Gravia

ORION

An Orion paperback

This edition first published in Great Britain in 2021
by Orion Fiction
an imprint of The Orion Publishing Group Ltd
Carmelite House, 50 Victoria Embankment
London EC4Y 0DZ

An Hachette UK Company

15 17 19 20 18 16 14

A CIP catalogue record for this book is
available from the British Library.

ISBN (Mass Market Paperback) 978 1 3987 0667 5
ISBN (eBook) 978 1 3987 0668 2

Typeset by Born Group
Printed and bound in Great Britain by Clays Ltd, Elcograf S.p.A.

www.orionbooks.co.uk

This book is for any girl who has ever wondered why she isn't enough. Just open your eyes and raise your standards. I see you.

Sophie x

Chapter One

Name: Zara Smith
Age: 29
Location: Glasgow
Interested in: Males
Zodiac sign: Leo

Biography: My name is Zara, I've been single for around five years now. My hobbies include hill walking, good food, and lots of cocktail drinking! No kids, own house, living life to the fullest. I'm looking for someone to share similar interests with and finally settle down!

God, that was difficult, cringeworthy, and incredibly dishonest of me. I never anticipated online dating at this age. I always envisioned myself married in my mid-twenties and to at least be thinking about having kids now. I didn't even contemplate that finding a guy to commit to me would be an issue. Then some clever cunt invented the internet, and now no one in Glasgow seems to want a monogamous relationship anymore. With vast access to so many stunningly beautiful and *available* women out there, I don't blame a guy for not wanting to settle for me,- Zara, the skint student who recently used a scrunchie to wipe her arse because she couldn't afford toilet roll.

I mean, I'm not saying I don't enjoy physical relationships. I absolutely do. It's just that I have the weird female issue that if anyone touches my vagina, it will latch onto them like a fucking Venus flytrap. I admit that whenever I get intimate with a guy, I stalk them for months afterwards on any social media platform I can access, secretly praying for their return to my lonely vagina. Even if they were terrible, deep down, I am willing to settle.

Now, nearing the end of my twenties, reality has set in and the panic has begun. Yes, I'm very much single, with no one to text or sext. I spent ten agonising years of my life completely infatuated with a Glasgow ned who would use me occasionally for weekend hook-ups, well, until he met a younger, prettier model and married her instead. Of course, by the time I finally realised just how pathetic I was being and felt ready to move on I was completely past the 'hot' stage of my life and any confidence I had in regards to speaking to another man was gone. My sell-by date is approaching a lot quicker than I anticipated and the fear of being left on the shelf (having missed out on casual dating, with the skinniest days of my life a distant memory) has officially become my reality.

The continuous pressure from my family to fulfil society's goals of marrying someone before my ovaries freeze over has encouraged me to join the ever-growing trend of online dating.

Ping.

God, it was barely 8am on a drizzly Thursday morning in April and I was already receiving messages on my new dating app, I hadn't even uploaded an image yet. Maybe I wasn't the only desperado left in this city after all.

Ping.

Jesus. I couldn't help but smile at what very little attention I was getting. I had been craving it for long enough. With my usual punctuality problems I left my apartment that morning while beginning the ten-minute journey along the crisp, wet Glasgow street, stepping over the deeper puddles in a desperate bid not to dampen my favourite Primark shoes. I smiled at the occasional familiar face that I recognised from my morning rush to get to work.

'Morning,' I shouted over a loud engine while eagerly waving to my boss as he pulled up beside me in his top of the range Bentley. Trying hard to pick up the pace and get in the door before him to ensure I wasn't last in – again.

Individualise. The sign suddenly lit up the street, and I knew Ashley my best friend, must have got in before me. I worked part-time in a chic aesthetics clinic, which supported me through my degree. I'd be a fully-fledged nurse in a few months, but for now, this was the perfect job.

'Oh my God, so much chat!' Ashley exclaimed as she sprang from the counter, completely ignoring Raj as he walked in behind me.

'Dave didn't come home again last night. I told him if this happens one more time, then that's it. Can you believe that?'

The thing is, I could believe it. Every shift recently, I listened to Ashley's make-up and break-up dramas. I nodded in agreement as she continued her story, though I zoned out occasionally, admiring her long, blonde, artificial locks. She was dressed in a tight black dress good enough to wear on a night out, but she'd look pretty in any setting, with the brightest green eyes and the best set of Turkish veneers you had ever seen. On the other hand, I was in my Individualise printed logo top that was going grey and misshaped from being washed so many times. I didn't have any time for makeup this morning because I got caught up over-analysing my dating profile.

Standing opposite Ashley now, I felt inferior. I knew even on a good day, I was not the best ambassador for this job—given my lack of lip filler and face that moved with every expression. However, I comforted myself with the thought that I was less intimidating for clients as they walked through the door to a chirpy Subo lookalike opposed to a pristine Insta model like Ashley. I found it natural to build great relationships with them and could advise them on the newest treatment packages we had to offer at the clinic with a non-judgemental approach.

Ashley helps promote and market the clinic as she has such a large social media platform herself. When the clinic opened, she saw a vacancy for a receptionist and spoke to Raj about getting me a job. He hired me over the phone, and I'm sure he was expecting a candidate much more glamorous than myself, but I got the job and had been there for three years. Raj and Ashley run the clinic together full-time, and I help out on Thursdays and Fridays on the desk. Raj was laidback, and we all got on exceptionally well. He specialised in Botox and skin procedures and worked for the NHS as a plastic surgeon as well as his private clinic work. His clinic was thriving since Ashley got involved in marketing and promoting his brand. Raj's best friend Doctor Tom Adams, who specialised in lip/cheek fillers, worked in the clinic every Friday. This was undoubtedly my favourite day of the week as Tom was fucking hot! Ashley and I immaturely called him Sugar Daddy!

Sugar Daddy—or Dr Adams or Tom with the Dong—was older than me. Mid-forties I'd say—tall, muscular, kind, quite arrogant, charming, and most definitely single. Ashley and I stalked his social media regularly, and there was *never* any indication of a girl-friend. We attempted to drop it into the conversation at times with Raj, who laughed and called him the Royal Gigolo (a reference to the hospital they both worked in, Glasgow Royal Infirmary, as well as, no doubt, the hundreds of nurses he slept with). My nursing degree couldn't come quickly enough if I could pull surgeons like him at the end of my training. Ashley admired him too, and from the minute he walked into the clinic on a Friday, we'd giggle and pout like Kerry Katona on speed. Tom had such a flirtatious manner you couldn't resist, and the kind of perfect, symmetrical smile that's totally disarming. Not to mention the size of his bulge in the scrubs he wore—that one-eyed monster greeted you at the door. When he was on shift, it was difficult to think of anything else.

The majority of the morning, when we weren't attending to clients, was spent deconstructing and then railing against Dave's treatment of Ashley. When she'd exhausted herself with that topic, I found a quiet time to tell her:

'So, I made an online dating profile.'

'Shut up! Shut up! Let me see!' she shouted, approaching me.

I'd forgotten how loud she could be. I blushed slightly as two clients were waiting only a few metres away, listening intently.

I began to explain while trying to encourage her to whisper.

'I literally created it before work. I haven't uploaded any photos yet. I feel too embarrassed—like I don't want to catfish anyone, but I want a decent picture? I know lots of people do it now but I have never . . .'

'Shut up! Firstly, you're not a catfish at all! Why are you even embarrassed? It's socially acceptable these days,' she replied. 'I'll help you choose your pics.'

Ashley grabbed my phone out of my hand, and I began to feel uncomfortable at my poor selection of photos as she scrolled judgingly through my camera roll. I cringed at a few selfies from over her shoulder praying I had deleted my earlier arsehole pic that was to establish if my piles had returned. Thankfully it was gone, and I instantly felt reassured as Ashley was kindly nodding, admiring my photographs.

'Oooft, look at you! You want to appear approachable but slightly standoffish. Funny but not too funny, like their mate. Aim to look natural and *do not* put unrealistic filters on your pictures.' She spoke another language to me, but as she carried on explaining the rationale behind each statement, I began to understand. The dating scene was most certainly a game. In a world of hearts and crosses, I suddenly realised that first impressions counted more than ever, and it was time for me to be savage with my own standards.

I decided I would wait until I was home to upload my pictures, giving myself time to evaluate Ashley's advice. I had never online dated before; in fact, I had never been on a date with a complete stranger and the thought of arranging to meet and having awkward chat or feeling uncomfortable made me squirm. I was well aware my Facebook profile photos might have looked like showstoppers. But in reality, I showed far too many teeth when I smiled, my stomach wasn't quite so flat and my arse wasn't quite so peachy. So perhaps a few natural pictures were a must. *Mental note: do not upload too many with a duck pout or Snapchat filter.*

I walked home much slower than this morning's journey. The rain had stopped but the streets still appeared damp from before and the sandstone buildings looked soaked through. Everyone seemed to be rushing around but there was only one thing on my mind: men. I suddenly felt like online dating could open up my boring, non-productive life and for the first time in years, I felt confident that I was going to meet someone. I strolled home with an optimistic grin on my face and a new bubble in the pit of my stomach.

After much deliberation, I began choosing a selection of photos from nights out in trendy Glasgow bars, to partying at Ocean Beach. After searching online *'what type of photographs attract men?'*, I chose one of me standing in Central Park. According to Google, this quickly suggested a few important things: that I was well travelled, up for an adventure, and financially had my shit together.

What a lie.

I also began searching vital information into Google *'Interesting topics of conversation on a first date'* and *'the best opening conversations in online dating'*. I was intrigued but terrified at this newfound world I was about to be part of, and after spending almost six hours planning and prepping my online profile, it was complete. As I lay across my sofa, I began swiping, initially feeling overwhelmed but also empowered. I was making cut-throat decisions based purely on someone's physical appearance. I felt powerful, invigorated—and judgemental as fuck. Still, this way of selecting a potential match was strangely fun and highly addictive.

Nope, too short. No. Nice, but shit job. YES, YES. Oh, bald, fuck no.

I was caught up in a world where I was in charge. I felt like Kim Kardashian with the pick of the bunch even though, behind the screen, I was sitting with stained PJs smelling of body odour with a hairy top lip that resembled more Kanye than Kim.

Before I knew it, I began matching with potential suitors, but no one immediately grabbed my attention. For the moment, I was still completely engrossed in the swiping, so replying to any messages seemed more like a hindrance than anything else. It only took a short while before I established which men actually wanted a genuine relationship, to get to know me, as opposed to the 'shagger' variety Ashley warned me about. The shaggers seemed to send heart or wink emojis initially and then made reference to my breasts or blatantly asked, 'What are you looking for on this?'

Not the same as you, thanks. I mean, at least put a bit of effort into it.

Filtering the good from the bad seemed complicated and superficial, based entirely on looks and a few sentences, but I enjoyed the process regardless. Hours passed, and as much as my body wanted to sleep, I continued swiping. I hoped to see someone I knew to immaturely screenshot their profile to my friends, or find love at first sight and call this experiment a success. My eyes felt dry and tired from staring intently at impeccable pecs and grey joggies for most of the night.

Ping.

Mark: *Did you know, some female penguins engage in prostitution, performing sex acts in exchange for pebbles?*

I couldn't help but reply to this message as I was both disgusted and impressed he knew such random facts.

No, I was unaware of this fact, but thank you for enlightening me that penguins are, in fact, dirty wee bastards! I replied, feeling witty and curious.

He was typing . . .

Yes, I would say they are, as here is a more morbid fact, they have been known to rape each other when they die! Anyway, how's things?

Wow. That was some introduction, and already I couldn't help but feel captivated by Mark. He certainly caught my attention. I mean, who could ignore an interesting necrophilia conversation? I found myself replying to Mark regardless of my fatigue with a satisfied smile on my face. I felt sick, apprehensive, but excited with each reply as the night went on. His photos were cute and genuine. There were no enticing dog images or posing with endangered species, only him, on the occasional night out with friends and one of him doing a speech at an event. He had dark hair, pale skin, and large, chocolate-brown eyes. I usually go for tall athletic men, and Mark was 5ft 10, which towered above my petite 5ft 3 frame. Still, I typically prefer men in the 6ft something category. However, something was drawing me to Mark, and I was willing to make an exception.

The thought of arranging to meet up with him was far too much for now, but I knew from the constant message flow we would be heading in that direction very soon. *What if this all went wrong? What if he ends up a serial killer? He did make a dodgy joke about penguins after all.*

I didn't know if this was all a massive mistake, but I had to take a risk for once. The modern world seemed to be evolving into virtual relationships, and there was one thing for sure: I didn't want to be left behind.

Chapter Two

A few days of texting Mark later, he started sending me voice notes. Whenever I heard his voice, I could feel the flutters travel from my heart to my vulva like shocks of lightning. It sounded deep and he had a good range of vocabulary. He seemed well educated but swore quite frequently which made me smile. I always had a thing for a bad boy and with every curse he would turn me on. I was overcome with excitement every time I saw his name appear on my screen, like a love-struck teenager, and I could tell he felt the same. He had invited me for drinks that particular evening at 6.30pm and I had agreed. I was in a love bubble, and I hadn't felt like this for a while—then every so often reality hit: *You haven't even met this cunt, Zara. He could be a murderer.* I knew I had to speak to Ashley.

I spent a little longer getting ready for work that day as it was Sugar Daddy's shift. I wore skinny black jeans and a white crop top, which crossed over at the front revealing minimal cleavage. Raj wasn't too fussed about what we wore as long as we looked clean and professional. My black hair was hanging flat down and as useless as I was with a pair of straighteners, I attempted to add a little wave to avoid looking like Cher for the rest of the day. I headed out the door with my small coffee cup and phone tightly gripped in my hand, waiting not so patiently for Mark to text.

When I got to the salon, Sugar Daddy was sitting on the white leather reception sofa with his long muscular arms hanging over the back, chatting to Ashley. His dark hair looked like silk and was casually pushed back at the top effortlessly. Ashley was dressed up more than usual, and I couldn't help but think she must have got up at 5am, at least, for the amount of makeup she had on. When I put my bag on the desk, both of them smiled and in sync said, 'Morning.'

Tom stood up and gestured to his chair.

'Here, have a seat, we still have a few minutes before our first client. How're things?'

I couldn't help but blush as I sat down. He immediately sat back on the sofa beside me, and I could feel his warm body slightly press against my arm. I made eyes at Ashley, and we both sniggered at one another.

'I'm really well, Tom. How are you?' I said.

'Yes, good thanks. I was thinking about you driving in here today. How long have you got left at uni? It's bizarre I haven't seen you in the hospital on a placement actually.'

Wow. Tom was thinking about me? If I wasn't on such a high from Mark, that comment alone would have been the most exciting thing to happen this entire month.

'Erm . . . I only have a couple of months left. It's quite scary actually.'

When I said that out loud, I realised how close I was to graduating, which made my stomach twist. I had always wanted to be a nurse. My mother is a senior nurse manager for NHS Glasgow and encouraged me to choose the profession. I only took this long to do it because I didn't want her to dictate my life choices. However, she was right, and I absolutely love caring for people. I feel so comfortable and content in the hospital environment. On the other hand, the coursework was more troublesome, I had spent many sleepless nights over the past three years writing essays good enough to pass the course. With the written work completed, I was simply waiting for a date to begin my final placement before being awarded my degree.

Tom was such an enthusiastic listener, sitting there with that intense eye contact. Whenever he spoke to someone, he gave them his undivided attention, and it never failed to make me flustered.

'A couple of months, certainly is soon. We may still cross paths. I'll keep an eye out for you at work.'

His voice sounded sincere, although it had a generic private school tone, which wouldn't usually attract me. However, combined with his cheeky mannerisms and a vast array of compliments, not to mention his high-flying career, he could weaken any girl at the knees. He got up and headed into the clinic room to start prepping for the first client. Ashley and I made small talk until he shut the door, then we both burst out laughing like randy teenagers.

'Is it just me, or is Sugar Daddy getting hotter?' she asked.

I couldn't disagree with her; his confidence just oozed from his masculine frame. He was fucking incredible.

'He was thinking of you driving in? Mate, what the fuck?' Ashley whispered, still giggling.

'Aww, shoosh you . . . If he only knew we think about him every day!' I whispered back.

The clinic had its usual volume of traffic. Ashley was in her element taking before and after photos, revealing each client's new face. When it quietened down, I finally explained to her I had a date that night with Mark. When I said it aloud, it began to feel real, and I suddenly felt like I was going to vomit. I hadn't had a date for over eighteen months, and even then, it was with an ex and it was only a formality as we both needed sex at the end of it.

'What are you going to wear?' she asked.

I suddenly realised how unprepared I was. I had no new clothes or time to buy them. I'd spent longer worrying about that morning's outfit for Sugar Daddy than my actual date. *What do you wear on a casual drink date?* My anxiety started creeping up on me and I began to doubt everything. My face looked puffier than usual. What if he thought I was fat? My thick dark eyebrows had started to grow in, and I was beginning to resemble Chewbacca. *Fuck, I don't think I can do this*, I thought.

'You need to chill out, it'll be fine. Just ask Mark what he's wearing and judge your outfit off his.'

Ashley always knew how to make me feel better, and I sent Mark a voice note asking if he knew what he was going to wear for our date.

Just after five, I began to clear up the clinic as the last client had left. Tom was getting changed in the bathroom when Ashley's boyfriend arrived outside.

'Are you all right to lock up without me? Not wanting Dave to freeze his balls off out there.'

'Yeah, sure, on you go,' I said, waving to Dave through the glass door.

'Okay, thanks. Text me before, during, and after the date! I'm so excited for you! AHHH!'

Ashley always had positive and uplifting energy, she meditated each morning and listened to gratitude podcasts most days. Although it wasn't my thing, her enthusiasm was catching. I immediately had butterflies in my stomach.

'Bye, Tom,' she shouted, walking out the door.

Tom emerged from the bathroom in a pale blue shirt and dark denim jeans. He was adjusting his collar, and I could see the shape of his muscles and broad shoulders underneath. He left the top button undone, and some dark chest hair escaped through. Fucking hell, he looked terrific and smelt even better.

'Why is she so hyper? Spill . . .' His sexy English accent made the hairs on the back of my neck stand up.

'Oh, I have a date tonight, and I think Ashley's more excited than I am,' I blurted out. 'Are we ready to leave?' I tried to sound casual, like it wasn't a big deal, while I counted the till money and avoided eye contact with Tom.

'Oh, a date? We're not going anywhere till I find out the details, Zara. Who is he, and where are you going?'

His strict, assertive tone sent fireworks to my fanny, and I couldn't help but blush.

'His name is Mark, he has his own property company, and we're going to the Sky Bar. Now can we go before I'm late? I have no idea what to wear.'

'Why are you embarrassed? That's great news. Yes, the Sky Bar, good choice. My mate runs it. If you need anything, ask for Robbie. C'mon then, and you can get going.' He ushered me to the door.

Of course his mate runs the fucking bar, I thought. If I have one too many cocktails, Robbie may end up hearing of my undying infatuation with Tom tonight.

We set the alarm and locked up the clinic, chatting as we did so. I turned in the opposite direction to make the short journey to my house as Tom headed to his Mercedes parked outside.

'Oh, and Zara, have a good night! And don't worry about what to wear, you always look amazing.' His smile looked even whiter against the dark night sky.

Jesus Christ, I was not expecting that. My heart dropped to the floor as I mumbled and giggled like a fucking hyena.

'Thanks, thanks, I wish, though. So do you though.' *What the fuck was I saying?* Words were just falling out of my mouth.

I walked faster than usual with my head down, reliving my awkwardness with Tom over and over again until I reached my flat. I had no time to cringe

17

at myself it was now quarter to six and I would be leaving soon. I opened the door and headed straight up for a shower.

I began washing frantically as the clock was ticking. I was going over examples of small talk in my head that I could say if things got quiet with Mark. *'So, how's the property industry these days?'* Or *'Where do you like to go on holiday?'* Occasionally I'd stop dead thinking about my awkward response to Tom tonight, my toes curling. I began shaving my legs to distract my mind as my heart raced in anticipation of tonight's date, but what should I do with my vagina? I glimpsed down to my sad little water-soaked pubes. In the texts and voice notes with Mark, we certainly hadn't got to the stage of discussing sex, and it hadn't made the official schedule for tonight's date. I wanted a real relationship not a one-night hook-up but at the same time, it's not the olden days. I'm a young woman with needs. *Would he see me differently if we had sex straight away?* I was fucking gagging. I'll go prepared, just in case . . .

Off came the pubes, swirling rapidly down the drain.

It was approaching 6.30pm, and Mark had already sent a message that he had left. Nerves were making my stomach flip. I stood looking in the mirror and questioned everything, from my hair, to my outfit, to my weight. I was wearing black leather leggings and a black bodysuit with a white shirt over it. I felt like Sandy from *Grease* but probably resembled more Mick Jagger. My makeup was minimalistic as I am so shit at applying it, and my hair was down straight. *Should I even go?* I started to text Ashley in a desperate bid for reassurance. I could hear a car approaching outside and my phone pinged. He was here. This was it, I thought. I had one last look in the mirror and headed downstairs.

Outside, a massive black Range Rover was parked up in the busy Glasgow street. I approached the car, took a long, deep breath and opened the door.

'Hey, Mark.' I smiled, and so did he.

'Nice to meet you Zara. How you doin'?' His voice sounded softer, less confident than his voice notes, he had his head down while fidgeting with the steering wheel.

'Yea, I'm good thanks. I've been really nervous getting ready but I'm okay now.'

I lied. My heart was going around two hundred beats per minute still.

'Me too, man, I've done this before mind you. I don't think it gets easier. I'm sure we will have a good night though.' He smiled briefly, lifting his head towards me, and began driving.

Mark and I travelled from my home to Finnieston, another lively part of Glasgow, where our date would take place. While he was driving, I was checking him out, and he looked unusually handsome, not my usual type, more indie style than the macho gym guy I would go for, but I was still attracted to him. Mark was exactly like his pictures, only thinner. I couldn't help but feel self-conscious about my own weight looking at him. His hair was dark brown and long, more Bradley Cooper than Ozzy Osbourne, and he looked laidback and chilled. He was dressed in a bomber-style leather jacket, jeans, and black trainers. I wondered if he thought I looked the same as my photos. I asked him about previous online dates he had been on, as suggested by Google as '*Good conversational starters*' earlier that week.

'I went on this date, maybe a month or so ago and the lassie ended up having a really bad twitch. I mean I'm no downing anyone with a twitch, but I had no warning. That was fucking awkward.' We both began to laugh.

'Oh, my, that is a shame though! Poor girl. Although when is an appropriate time to slip that into conversation? ' I replied.

'I'd say not at the date. As I got more drunk I started to imitate it unconsciously. I had a stiff neck for days.'

We both giggled and his comical shy personality eased the tension.

When we got out of the car, I felt incredibly sober as we walked into the Sky Bar. The bar was situated on the top floor of a five-star hotel. It had a glass wall overlooking the Glasgow skyline with a DJ playing music from the corner. The relaxed vibe made me feel comfortable. We sat at the window, one of the best seats which he had reserved unknown to me. After ordering a few gins, the conversation became warm, and we laughed throughout the night. He was drinking vodka and lemonade and I could see his shoulders relax after a few.

I was certainly attracted to him, and we seemed to be on the same wavelength. He owned a property company and had a lot of business trips overseas. At times when he talked, I was zoning out, humming the wedding march in my head. *Could this be the one?* I could get used to travelling around the world with a handsome man on my arm.

I felt burdened each time I was prised away from him to go to the bathroom, but unfortunately, I had broken the seal, and after each drink, I had begun to need the toilet. The drunker I got, the more difficult a trip to the bathroom became. I had to pull down my skin-tight leggings, unloosen my bodysuit and reassemble myself in an acceptable time frame to ensure Mark didn't think I was taking a shit. After the third or fourth trip to the loo, I resorted to hauling down the leggings and shunting the bodysuit to the side of my thigh to pee. I did laugh at how ridiculous I may have looked, but by this time, I only cared about drinking more alcohol as it was approaching last orders.

The night progressed, and we seemed closer.

'You know, Zara, I think this is going really well? I'd really like to see you again soon; I mean so far there hasn't been a twitch in sight.'

Bingo! I felt so relieved as he wasn't over-affectionate towards me and I was questioning my flirting skills.

'Yea, I've had a really good night too, I'd definitely be up for that.'

He paid for all the drinks that evening, which was a massive turn-on. Not only because I was a skint student with thirty quid to my name, but I also believe it set an excellent example of old-school chivalry.

The bar was closing, and it was time to wait in the cold Scottish weather for a taxi. Mark gave me his jacket. I paused for a second as I was unsure it would fit my ever-growing bingo wings, but luckily it did, rather snugly. I could smell his strong aftershave on the leather. We stood outside, and I began to shiver. He came closer, and I immediately felt nervous. There was undeniable sexual tension in the air when he whispered,

'I don't want the night to be over, Zara.'

The hairs from my neck to the stubble on my freshly plucked vagina stood on end. Neither did I, but I knew that this situation only led one way. I was determined not to ruin a potential relationship despite my lustful vagina.

'Me too, but we should really head home separately and go out again soon,' I replied, trying to convince myself as I said it.

'Nothing like that will happen, Zara, I just enjoy your company. But if you're not comfortable, then I completely understand.' He placed both arms on my shoulders, and I could smell some Tom Ford bypassing the nostrils and hitting my heart.

My fuckboy senses were tingling, but so was my clitoris, and in this case, there was only one winner. Before I knew it, I was in a long taxi ride to his home in Lanark. He left his car abandoned in the multi-story and would collect in the morning.

Throughout the journey, I questioned my decision. *What the fuck was I doing?* I didn't even know this man and I was travelling through random woods and fields with him. I quickly took out my phone and sent Ashley a WhatsApp location message, just so my mum had a body to bury if things turned south. I was beginning to sober up, and I knew that I shouldn't have sex.

We eventually pulled up outside Mark's home; a gorgeous three-storey house in a secluded area. *Has this cunt got the full package?* I argued with him briefly about who was paying the taxi fare. He insisted and I pretended to be disappointed. I wandered inside his home, each room was more beautiful than the next. It was open plan and modern. I could see myself fitting in nicely here. *Dun dun da dun . . .*

'Can I get you a drink?' His deep, sexy voice interrupted my wedding march and feng shui redecorating thoughts.

'Yes, please!' I said, admiring his well-stocked alcohol cupboard.

'Rhubarb and ginger gin?' He was holding an unopened bottle of Whitley Neill.

'Good choice!' I was impressed.

We sat on the couch and began drinking more alcohol and chatting drunkenly. We had visited many of the same places. We enjoyed similar music, and each shared memories on previous Ibiza holiday escapades. We laughed and laughed and before I knew it, Mark was getting closer. I could feel he was nervous, and so was I. He leaned over and kissed me lightly. His lips were small and soft, but gentle and shy. I knew I had to take control and began clawing my stick-on nails through his long locks. Things were turning more passionate as we were kissing on his leather sofa, hardly coming up for air, and all that tension was finally being released. I could feel his dick getting harder as he pressed it against my thigh. Things were hotting up, and he was lying on top of me, biting my lip. He began pushing his wandering hand down the back of my leggings and feeling my arse tightly.

'This is really good,' I interrupted, 'but we shouldn't have sex so soon.'

He nodded in agreement as if the thought hadn't crossed his mind.

We continued kissing, and his hands strayed lower down my arse towards my fanny. I felt the pop of my bodysuit unfastening and opened my mouth to speak, but he got there first.

'How long have you had this on for, babe?' he asked.

The question completely took me by surprise.

'Emm . . . I don't know . . .' I whispered. With the pop of the bodysuit, I had also popped out the love bubble I'd been floating around in, and the wheels in my head began turning. *Why was he asking me how long I had my bodysuit on for? Was I dirty? Could he smell it?* I knew I was wet from kissing him, but surely that was a typical female response?

'How long roughly?' he repeated.

Fucking hell, he really wanted an answer.

'A few hours, why?' I replied, attempting to sound more confident this time around.

My response seemed to please him as he had got rougher and more aroused. He pulled the bodysuit out of my leggings, exposing the clipped area. He stared at it for a moment before sniffing it frantically for at least thirty seconds. He then proceeded to suck the exposed clipped area, which had been rubbing into my vagina all night.

What the fuck was going on? He was really going for it too. I sat there uncomfortably, staring at him, hoping that he would be finished with my clothing and start kissing me again. But no, he was in his own little love bubble now, just him and my bodysuit. His eyes began rolling like the fucking exorcist while he was sucking the colour straight out of the material. I was scared I'd lose a button. I couldn't help but think of how it must have tasted as I hadn't unbuttoned it each time I went to the toilet in the club. There must have been some residue of urine in there. I was not wanting to kiss the dirty bastard after that. I allowed him to finish up with my bodysuit, and while the wedding march was getting fainter in my head, I asked myself if I could spend my life with this underwear sniffer. Finally, he sat back, arms perched on the back of the sofa, looking smug. No. I couldn't do it. I yawned awkwardly before making my excuse to head home.

I left in the taxi feeling violated, disappointed, and confused. Perhaps the dating game wasn't for me. Was I just used for a sniff and suck of my dirty bodysuit? Maybe I was being a prude, and this is what dating in the twenty-first century had come to? Everyone had their own kinks, and perhaps if I gave Mark time, I would grow to enjoy his?

Chapter Three

The next morning I woke up later than I intended to. Shit, 11am. I had an online lecture to watch and I was planning to meet my sister for coffee. I turned around and grabbed my phone. I felt a little anxious to see if Mark had messaged, but nothing. Typically, he would have texted by now, a good morning message or a funny meme. I decided to go on and look at his social media and see if his 'last active' was on. *Last active three minutes ago.* What the fuck? He was the one who was sniffing my pants last night, and I don't even get an obligatory '*I had a good night?*' message?'

Maybe he didn't fancy me after all, I thought.

I phoned Ashley and asked her to join my sister and me for brunch that morning.

I lay in bed a little longer, replaying last night's events in my head until I realised, I had to be at the café in twenty minutes. I threw on some Adidas leggings, an oversized hoodie, and a cap. I still had the remnants of last night's makeup on my face but decided that was acceptable, given the fragile state I was in. I ran quietly down the stairs of my close, grateful not to see any of my neighbours after only returning a few hours earlier.

I travelled to my sister's favourite café, Angels. When I arrived, Ashley was already there chatting to my sister Emily. Both of them burst out laughing when they saw me.

'Good night then?' Emily asked.

God, I didn't think I looked that bad. It wasn't until I looked at their fresh faces with natural makeup that I realised how rough I must have been. Emily had already ordered my meal, and she sat like a little impatient child waiting to hear a story.

'Okay, now spill! How was it?' she said.

'I had a perfect night, but he hasn't texted this morning and he usually does,' I replied quietly.

'Maybe he thinks you're asleep if it was a late one, Zara?' Emily said sympathetically.

'No, he's testing you! Take a picture of your food when it arrives and post it, and I'll make my hand look like a guy in the background. I swear it'll work,' Ashley said.

I waited for her to laugh before realising she was being serious.

'Did you pump him? Is that it?' she asked.

I could feel my face go bright red. Emily looked embarrassed and slightly judgemental; she had been married for over five years to her childhood sweetheart. She did not understand the struggle of single life today.

'We didn't have sex,' I whispered. 'But . . . we kissed a lot in his, okay? Then something weird happened. Well, I think it's weird, but I'm not sure,' I carried on.

'Oh, for fuck's sake, what happened? I bet it wasn't that bad,' Ashley roared.

'Ashley, seriously, *shhh*. Okay, so, God, I don't actually know how to put this, but he sniffed my bodysuit and sucked it.' I paused.

The table erupted into laughter.

Emily looked at me in horror before saying, 'And you let him?'

There was a further short pause.

'Yeah, but I was shocked. I didn't know what to do.'

Ashley was wiping tears away from her face, carefully, in case any foundation became misplaced. When she spoke, her voice only got louder and louder.

'I know I've done some kinky shit, Zara, but this is a new level! And you're actually *upset* he hasn't messaged you? He's probably away sniffing park benches or something.'

She was in hysterics, we all were. I realised how ridiculous my night had ended up, no matter how much I'd enjoyed it up till then.

Our food arrived, and I managed to scoff my usual full Scottish breakfast while watching Emily eating a vegan variation. She was incredibly healthy. People often mistook us for twins when we were younger as there are only two years between us. She had long brown curly hair to her bottom, lived in the gym, and despite having two children, her body was perfect.

'I have actually been doing some matchmaking myself, Zara.' Emily's big brown eyes looked at me innocently.

'Oh, go on,' I replied, gulping down my second can of Irn Bru, desperately pleading for it to take my hangover away.

'So there is a guy in the gym who is really handsome, and he's been single for a while, and I showed him some pictures of you, and he wants to take you on a date. What do you think? He's *really* handsome, actually.'

'So, a blind date?'

'You may as well. I promise he won't sniff your knickers. He's recently divorced and such a gem.'

'Do you have any pictures?' I asked, smirking as I considered the proposition.

'Nope, he doesn't have social media, but honestly, he is totally your type. He's like six foot five.'

That does sound like my type, I thought, but as we were discussing it, I felt guilty for Mark. Sniffing and sucking aside, I actually really liked him and thought we had a connection.

'I'm not sure, Emily, I don't think so,' I said.

'Too bad, I told him yes! I said you would text him later.' She sounded serious.

I glared at Ashley for some backup, but she shrugged and said, 'I think you should go for it. You have nothing to lose.'

Emily was holding her phone and smirking. 'I've forwarded his number! Text him!' I took my phone out of my pocket waiting for Emily's message to pop up but secretly hoping I had received one from Mark. Still nothing. *Maybe I should go?* I thought. *Mark clearly isn't interested!*

'Wait, what's his name? Age? Occupation? I don't know anything about him.' I felt overwhelmed. I'd found it hard enough to have one date this year, never mind two in the same week.

'His name's Seth. Ask him the rest on the date.' Emily was wiping down her hands and checking the time. She was always incredibly busy with the kids, husband, and keeping fit. She stood up, kissed Ashley on the cheek, and hugged me.

'I need to run, I have tennis in forty minutes. I'll phone you tonight, Zara, and you better be speaking to him. I mean it.' She threw money on the table and exited Angels.

Ashley and I just sat there in silence for a few seconds. She knew me better than anyone in the world and she could tell Mark was bothering me.

'Do you want to take the arm food picture?'

I laughed.

'Not today, I don't want to do anything,' I replied.

We finished off our brunch and walked along the busy street, talking about anything that came into our heads. The slight distraction was welcoming as I still felt a lump in my heart about Mark not texting. Glasgow was busy and full of shoppers battling their way through the crowds. We paused for a bit at Royal Exchange Square smirking at a group of teenagers attempting to add to the abundance of cones on the Duke of Wellington statue.

'I better go, Zara, Raj will be wondering where I am.'

'Yea, me too. I need to lie down anyway. I'll call you later.' We hugged and separated.

I watched Ashley walk around the corner towards George Square where the clinic was, with the teenagers nudging their friends and whistling as she passed by. While I continued the journey back to my apartment a few streets away with my head down wondering what I done wrong from the night before. I lay on my bed and battled with myself whether to text Seth or not. Best case scenario, he could be the love of my life; worst case scenario he would be a nice distraction.

I felt so needy and pathetic. I was getting so caught up in a guy I had met once. I was refreshing his messenger endlessly, seeing how long he was online and wondering who he was talking to. I was becoming crazy already after one date. Perhaps Seth would help.

Hey . . . I'm Zara. My sister Emily asked me to drop you a text.

Sent.

Okay, I'd made the first move. I lay back in my bed and *ping!*. My heart raced in anticipation, hoping it was Mark but knowing it would be Seth.

Zara . . . I was hoping you'd text. Emily speaks really highly of you, and you look beautiful in your photographs. Would you be up for meeting me?

Fuck, Seth didn't beat about the bush, did he? At this rate, we'd be married next week.

Yeah sure, I'd be up for that. When suits you? I replied.

May seem upfront, but I'm free tonight if you are?

He was undoubtedly a good texter, that was apparent.

I paused and lay back down. Did I really want to do this?

31

Sure? Why not . . . I replied.

We made arrangements to meet that night, and I couldn't help but think of the difference the past twenty-four hours had brought. Last night I was getting ready to meet Mark and wasn't aware Seth existed. Now I was arranging to meet a man I had never seen, only thinking about Mark the entire time.

I was meeting Seth in Ashton Lane, a beautiful part of Glasgow's West End, a little cobbled street full of fairy lights, culture, pubs, and entertainment. It had a relaxed feel to it, and I was looking forward to having some of my favourite cocktails along the way.

I wore ripped black jeans, a strappy V-neck top, and a pair of designer heels. My makeup was minimalistic with a red lip this time, and my hair was brushed down still straight from the night before. I didn't put as much effort into this date as I had the previous night as my heart wasn't in it the same, but I was willing to give Seth a chance. I headed down my shared hallway, out the door, and pulled a taxi over to make the short journey to the West End.

I was a couple of minutes away in the taxi when I received a text from Seth that he had arrived. My stomach began to get butterflies, and I could feel my palms gather sweat from nerves.

I was approaching Ashton Lane, and an exceptionally tall, handsome man was standing there. When my taxi pulled up, he smiled at me. Damn, Emily was right, this giant was incredible. He had black hair, brown skin, the greenest eyes, and an athletic body. He looked Iranian, definitely of Middle Eastern heritage, and I could see other girls checking him out when he was standing there perched against the wall. He spotted me and headed over to the taxi.

'Hello, Zara.' He leaned in and kissed me on the cheek. He spoke with a London accent and seemed very upfront, which I liked.

'Hey, how are you?' I replied nervously. I immediately thought I should have put more effort into my look. *He was hot!*

He wore ripped denim jeans and a plain navy jumper, and he held a Burberry trench coat over his arm. He looked as if he had just walked off the runway, and I was conscious I looked as if I had just stepped off the 240 bus from Easterhouse still feeling hungover from my previous night. His beard was trimmed with precision as if he had used a ruler to perfect the angles. I felt like that amount of dedication to trim a beard when I found it difficult to wash my hair once a week could be a potential issue.

We headed into the cobbled street, found a cosy little bar, Vodka Wodka and began ordering watermelon mojitos. The bar was crowded but there was lots of energy to it. The West End always had such a warm atmosphere. We squeezed into a booth with wooden chairs. Seth looked far too big for the bar never mind the booth and I felt he was a little uncomfortable with his new cramped surroundings. I didn't know anything about Seth, and was keen to hear about his life.

'So, tell me about yourself, Zara?' he said, sitting extremely close to my personal space and giving intense eye contact.

'Well . . . I'm twenty-nine, a student nurse. Hopefully, I'll graduate in a few months, and I work part-time in an aesthetics clinic.'

I took a drink of my cocktail, and he was still staring, looking for more information.

'I've been single for a few years now and recently started dating. That's kind of my life, to be honest, I'm actually pretty boring.' I laughed nervously and took a drink. 'Tell me about you?'

'Well where do I start . . . I was married for ten years, I have two children and recently moved up to Glasgow from London. My mother lives in Bothwell and took unwell so I moved up to care for her. I'm an architect, but to be honest, financially, I don't have to work, I just do projects now and again. My son and my daughter live with me. They are in the best private school in Glasgow. I'm so passionate about education in the young . . .'

Fuck, I was beginning to wish I hadn't asked him anything. I was zoning out. He was talking so much my head hurt from nodding.

'I mean, I spend most of my days at the gym, your sister probably told you about me and my tennis club?'

'No, she hadn't said,' I replied, confused.

'I have the best service in the club, my serve is unreturnable. I travel from club to club just to meet an opponent good enough to play me.'

There was a pause when I tried to determine if he was joking, but I realised he was being serious. Was this cunt for real? *Calm down, Rafa*, I thought. He was utterly self-obsessed. With much strength, I managed to resist an eye roll at his boasting and eventually got a word in to excuse myself to the bathroom.

I took out my phone to text my sister about her poor dating choice, when a message from Mark appeared. My heart raced.

Hey, you okay? I'm sorry if things got odd last night.

I couldn't help but smile. I suddenly felt guilty. I was here with someone else, and all I wanted to do was see Mark.

Hey, I'm good, thanks, just having a cocktail in town. I had a good night even if it did end a little strangely, I replied.

Read. He was typing already.

Ha, ooh, you drunk? When are you leaving?

Fuck, what could I do? I want to see Mark but I have only had one drink with Seth. Would it be rude to bail out now? God, he can see I have read this. Ok.. Ok..

I can leave now if you like. Come to mine?

Send.

Fuck, what was I doing? I was conscious of how long I was spending in the bathroom. Seth had probably chemically combusted not speaking for so long.

Mark's reply came swift:

Sound. See you in half an hour.

Yes! My mood instantly lifted. I needed to get home. I needed to shave my stubbly vagina. I needed to change my underwear in case Mark decides to get hungry later on, I needed to get rid of this fucking chatterbox as soon as possible to zip home and tidy up my flat.

When I returned from the toilet, Seth was standing talking to the couple at the next booth. It didn't surprise me at all. I walked past them, finished my new cocktail he must have ordered when I was at the loo, and allowed him to finish his conversation before he approached me again.

'Wow, you were thirsty! Another drink then?' He smiled.

'Oh, I'm sorry, Seth, I have an assignment due next week and I've stayed out later than I should have already. Can we arrange another time?'

'Of course, let's get you home. Your education is more important, Zara.' He was so sensible and understanding, if only he knew I was actually rushing home to wash my arsehole for someone else.

Back on bustling Byres Road, his long arms flagged down a taxi for me quickly, and he kissed my cheek.

'It was lovely to meet you. I'll text you.'

'Thanks, Seth, yeah, you too. Speak soon.' I jumped into the taxi, distracted and with only one thing on my mind—Mark.

Back home, out the taxi, I raced up the stone tenement stairs into my flat and began throwing bundles of clothes off my bed into the wardrobe. Then I jumped into the shower and frantically scrubbed my vagina.

I looked at the time. Mark would be arriving any minute.

I had just put on clean, sexy red underwear with my jeans shoved back on top and quickly reapplied my red lipstick when the buzzer rang.

I opened the door slightly out of breath from rushing to a cool, calm, smirking Mark holding a wee bottle of gin.

'Drink?' His voice sounded deeper and sexier than the shy Mark who greeted me the previous night.

'Yes, please.'

I giggled nervously and held the door open for him, but as he walked, he pulled my hand back and suddenly we were kissing against the door. Fuck the gin, I wanted him, and I wanted him now.

I led him to my bedroom, and we began undressing one another. I ran my hands slowly down his toned body until I came to his enormous penis. *Jesus, he kept that one quiet!* It was long with a huge girth at the end. I was impressed. Fizzing with cocktail confidence, I knelt down and began kissing and sucking him. Mark was running his hands through my hair moaning while staring at me going up and down on his big dick.

He stopped me after a few minutes and lifted me to the bed.

'Your turn,' he said.

I was in orgasm heaven.

Chapter Four

I woke up the next morning feeling content as I watched Mark sleep beside me. His arms and legs were wrapped around me, and I felt safe, happy—but also a bit suffocated. He was heavy and I had to pee.. The sex was terrific but lying naked afterward made me feel sticky and itchy. I was also aware of a fishy sex smell accumulating inside the room. Gently, I detangled his limbs and headed to the bathroom. I peed quietly, and although I was desperate for a fart, I tried with all my might to keep it inside for now. Washing my hands after, I looked in the mirror and holy shit, I'd forgotten about the red lippy. I looked like I'd been shot in the face at close range. I brushed my teeth and started to cleanse my skin but only succeeded in spreading the lippy all over my face, leaving it bright red. Great, I looked like I had fucking rosacea now. I carefully cleaned my fragile vagina as she was still sensitive from a rough night, then sprayed some perfume and headed back to bed.

Mark smiled at me when he woke up.

'Morning, baby.' His voice crackled, not quite warmed up yet. He gestured for a kiss, and I obliged.

Fuck, his breath stank. I could taste it. I tried to avoid talking directly to him closing my nostrils as I did so. 'Babe, your face?' He sat up, looking concerned. 'Are you okay? Your face is skelping.'

My face became redder with embarrassment.

'Yeah, I'm fine. It's a mixture of sex, lipstick, and friction burns. I have really sensitive skin.'

He leaned over and placed my hand on his growing penis.

'Do you want some more?' I ventured further down the covers. Of course I wanted more.

We continued to have sex and chatted most of the morning. I was relieved that he didn't try and sniff or suck any garments this time around. My stomach felt bloated as I continued to hold the trapped wind all morning, and as much as I wanted him to stay and lie with me, I seriously needed to fart. Any wrong move or change in sex position could blow this cunt to Edinburgh, so I proceeded with caution. We walked through to the kitchen to make a drink, I began pouring water from the tap to fill the kettle as he slowly began gathering his belongings. *Yes*, my stomach would soon be relieved, I thought.

Buzz.

Fuck, the front door buzzer. *Who could that be? Maybe Emily wanting to know how my date with Seth went?* Mark looked at me, smiling curiously.

'Are you not going to get that?' he said.

I walked over to the buzzer, lifted the handset, and said in a worried voice, 'Hello?'

'Hello, don't tell me you're still in bed. Let me in please.'

Fuck, my mother. My face dropped, and I turned back to look at Mark.

'It's my mum,' I said.

He burst out laughing and began squeezing his feet into his trainers. My mother bought the flat a few years ago, and once a month she liked to pop round to check up on me, usually without warning. Today she certainly succeeded with that. It was like she hadn't forgiven me for my teenage years of drinking Buckfast in the park, trying to be one step ahead, knowing I'd be up to something. Despite this, we had a healthy relationship, and I truly admired how she brought Emily and me up as a single parent. She had a strict, occasionally intimidating, matter-of-fact way of communicating and was always immaculately dressed in designer clothes. I knew she would be wanting to discuss the rest of my coursework with my nursing degree looming, and for the first time in my life, I had the feeling that she was about to be proud of me.

'You better get ready, Zara, I'll get that coffee the next time,' Mark said.

I ran to my wardrobe, which, when opened, tumbled an avalanche of clothes towards me. I lifted a floaty dress to shove on top of my naked body.

Buzz.

Jesus Christ, she's at it again.

'That's me, in you come!' I said through the intercom.

Mark walked past me, briefly kissed my forehead, and rushed out the door.

'Text me,' I shouted, feeling stressed. I left the door open, awaiting my mother's arrival.

I could hear the click–click of her Prada heels echoing up the shared stairwell before she came into view on the landing.

'Zara, it's bloody Baltic out there. I was standing in the street for half an hour,' she screeched, greeting me.

The smell of Jo Malone quickly filled the flat, almost deodorising the strong smell of sex and sweat from earlier this morning.

'It was two minutes, Mum. I'd just woken up and needed to get clothes on,' I replied, avoiding eye contact while attempting to tidy last night's mess away.

'And was that the boy?' She raised her voice in disapproval.

I looked up uncomfortably. 'What boy?' I said.

'Oh my goodness, Zara, your face! What's wrong?' She looked at me in shock, raising both hands to her cheeks.

'It's just lipstick, Mum. I slept with it last night and it's stained my face. I'm okay, but my bloody stomach is killing me.' I rubbed my bloated abdomen. 'You could have called before you left you know, Mum, I would have tidied up a bit.'

'I was in town, I didn't realise I had to schedule an appointment in my own property. Oh, will you put the dishes down and come here and tell me about your placement starting, Zara.' She gestured to me for a hug, and as I approached her, I could feel my stomach begin to relax.

I stopped. Relief was coming.

'Oh, Mum, finally . . .' I held my breath with concentration, my face screwed up and—BOOM. I let rip the loudest, most potent fart. But that wasn't all.

I looked down to see an overwhelming accumulation of last night's and this morning's spunk splatland on my living room floor, directly in front of my mother.

'Oh my God,' I said, dropping to the floor dramatically and holding my stomach.

Pretend it's pee, pretend it's pee, I panicked, crouched over the spillage, watching it drip slowly from my leg to the floor. Fucking hell, his balls must have been the size of fucking watermelons.

My mum's pristine black turtlenecked dress towered above me.

'Oh, dear,' she finally said with a disgusted sigh.

'I think you better go for a shower, Zara. You know, when I visit your sister we sit down to a nice cuppa and have a chat, but I never know what I'm going to get with you. Maybe I'll meet this boy properly soon.' She bent over and kissed my forehead.

'I'll let myself out.'

'Bye, Mum.'

She shut the door, and I leaned back not knowing whether to laugh or cry.

I hadn't had sex in months, and of course, when I finally do, my own mother watches me douche on the fucking floor. I sat there for a few minutes, feeling embarrassed but excited. Last night was awesome. My entire body was dehydrated, tired, and tender, but my mind was alive.

I lay back on the hard floor conscious of the spunky spillage below me, reimagining the events of last night and this morning with a broad smile on my scarlet face. *Dun dun da dun*—the wedding march was back!

I spent the rest of the day buzzing around my flat with the radio playing loud. I was tidying up and enjoying my new lease of life. I had an itch that was thoroughly scratched, and I looked forward to the next time I saw Mark. We exchanged flirty messages to one another throughout the day and later that night Ashley came round for some Chinese to get the latest on my newly found sex life.

'So how big was he?' she screeched as she walked through the door into the kitchen, holding the Chinese bags in her hand.

I burst out laughing. 'Fucking big. Like . . . this big.' I pulled a rolling pin out of the cutlery drawer I'd been rummaging through.

'Lucky! And was he generous? Have you spoke today?' She hardly came up for air, seeming even more excited than me. I began dishing the dirt on my night of passion as I was also dishing the chicken balls and fried rice.

I told Ashley everything, and in between our chat would sneakily send naughty messages to Mark of things to come in round two.

'Have you searched for an ex yet? How long has he been single?' Ashley asked crunching another prawn cracker.

'No I haven't searched; he doesn't use social media a lot, but he's been single for six months I think.'

We both paused and looked at one another with a smirk before leaping for our phones.

'Okay, let's find the bitch,' Ashley laughed.

We began scrolling through pictures on Mark's social media, checking tagged images like Miss fucking Marple. Mark didn't have a lot to go on, so we relied mostly on his mum's and brother's pages for old photographs. I was ten minutes into the search when I spotted his parents good old anniversary dinner picture. *Bingo*. My heart raced; there she was. Tagged as well.

Tami Breen.

'Got her! She follows me, Zara!' Ashley sounded proud.

'Me too. Let me see her profile.' I copied her username and started scrolling through her public photos, scrutinising each misplaced hair follicle or slutty dress, which didn't seem too many. *Shit,* I felt ill. She was beautiful. There was no denying it. Ashley remained notably quiet—I knew she was thinking the same.

'I feel sick, Ash, she's gorgeous!' I was disheartened.

'And?' Ashley said. 'So are you.'

She was trying to convince me, but it wasn't working.

Tami had dark hair like me but she was much thinner. She was a primary schoolteacher and in each photograph she wore trendy short dresses exposing her perfect brown legs. I mean, fuck me, I found it difficult to shave once a week and she had those ten-foot pins on show daily. It was unfair. I was deflated. *Why would Mark want someone like me when he's recently had Megan Fox grinding on top of him?*

I couldn't control my detective skills; before I knew it I was on their holiday 2013 to Turkey album. Wow, she stood so confidently in each picture gazing at Mark so lovingly while wearing a miniature thong bikini, I didn't know whether I should burst out crying or report her to the education department for indecent images. I seriously needed to lose weight. I looked at the remainder of the Chinese lying in front of me and felt ashamed.

Ashley looked as if she was regretting suggesting the ex-search. 'Why are you letting her affect your mood, Zara?'

'I just feel ugly compared to her. I'm a size twelve and she's like a six. Her lips are the size of my fist and you could bounce fifty pences off her arse.'

We both laughed. But I felt down, insecure and desperate for reassurance.

'Come on, I've seen enough of Tami's camel toe for one night, what movie are we watching?' Ashley asked.

'You pick.' I was distracted and feeling low. I cleared away the plates and poured Ashley some wine before grabbing a blanket and joining her on the couch.

'You sure you're okay?' Ashley asked, sipping her wine while scrolling through Netflix. I nodded. *Twilight* was a great distraction but in the back of my mind I questioned why Mark would want to be around me when he could pull girls like his ex.

Tami Breen became my top search that week as I watched in envy, carefully checking every like on her pictures just in case Mark wanted her back.

Chapter Five

Mark and I had been progressing well, and my text messages that week were filled with funny banter and sexual innuendoes. I had put his ex to the back of my mind and although she was still my top hit on Instagram, I started to convince myself I was being crazy. If he liked her that much, he'd be with her, *right*?

I struggled to see him as much as I wanted to between working in the clinic and attending uni lectures, but we had made arrangements for dinner when I finished my shift that day. I had taken the entire week to plan my outfit, and I looked forward to seeing his reaction when I stripped down to the sexy lingerie I had got in Love Honey's fifty per cent off sale.

I walked into the clinic that afternoon to find an unusual welcome—Tom and Raj whispering at the desk.

Thank God I had put some tan on, it wasn't Tom's day in the clinic.

'Hey, guys.' I interrupted their conversation while trying to hide my faded clothing and un-ironed top. They turned to acknowledge me and gave distracted smiles. I saw Ashley heading for the staff room, and I took my bag and coat off and followed her through.

'Hey, what's going on with those two? They look very secretive,' I whispered, looking over my shoulder.

'Oh, I was about to text you, I have no idea. Go to the desk and listen.'

Ashley pushed me out of the room, and I stumbled back onto the clinic floor and hesitantly walked towards Raj and Tom. They stopped talking once more. *What the hell?* I had never seen them look so severe. There was a sense of awkwardness in the large, silent white room. Eventually, a client walked in, and the tension was cut.

'Hi, Chloe. It's so nice to see you again!' I brought her to the sofa and began discussing her treatment plan as Raj disappeared into the clinic room to wait. I ploughed through her medical background quicker than I usually would, aware that Tom was still standing at the desk on his phone, and I was keen to join him. When Raj gestured for Chloe to come through, I casually headed back to the reception desk. Tom continued glaring at his phone, looking frustrated.

'You okay?' I asked sympathetically.

'Hmmm . . . Yes. I am now. How's Zara?'

He put his phone in his suit trouser pocket and turned to me. His navy shirt was unbuttoned slightly again, and I could see his muscular frame peek through. He had a scarf hanging from his neck and his suit jacket wrapped around his arm. I blushed at the question.

'I'm good, thanks.'

As I spoke, I could taste the strong smell of his aftershave hit the back of my throat. He stared at me for a few lingering seconds and suddenly gasped.

'Oh, forgive me. How was your date?' He leaned over the desk with his chin in his hands supporting his head.

'Yeah, it was pretty good. I'm seeing him again tonight, actually,' I replied, upbeat and slightly boastful.

'Good, I'm glad. He's a lucky man.' He paused, looked me up and down, then winked. 'See you tomorrow,' and he exited the clinic. Ashley scurried over to the desk like an excited puppy as soon as his car drove off.

'Well? What's the gossip?' she asked.

'I don't know, he didn't say.'

'Yous literally just had like a half-hour conversation, Zara!'

I laughed. 'It was for two minutes, and he just asked about my date with Mark. But . . .'

I paused for a dramatic effect. 'He fucking winked at me. I actually think he was checking me out. '

We both erupted into laughter.

'What the fuck. Sugar Daddy is such a flirt! I'm slightly jealous.'

Ashley paused with her bright green eyes scrunched up, trying hard to think. 'He is definitely a dirty bastard! I get the vibe one million per cent! Think of how much he flirts, his little winks and eyebrow raises, he can't help himself.'

I was holding my mouth, trying not to laugh too loud since Raj looked so pissed earlier.

'What? Do you not think so?' she continued.

I certainly hadn't considered it before now, but now that she said it . . .

'Yeah, I think you could be right.'

'Think? Mate, I'm never wrong about these things.'

Raj interrupted our girly chat by shouting at me from the clinic room.

'Can you assist me, Zara?'

Ashley rolled her eyes, but I trotted in to help him with the procedure. He was subdued and distracted today, which was unusual for him. He seldom made errors in his work, but poor Chloe was bruising like a peach on the table. I helped clean her up, applied some ice to her overly swollen lips, and she left satisfied.

'What's up, Raj? You seem very quiet,' I said when we were alone.

'I was fine until I got in here. I'll be fine, Zara. Thanks,' he replied, sounding agitated.

The remainder of the day seemed longer than usual, and Ashley and I were treading on eggshells with Raj. Usually he was bubbly, laughing with us and having good banter. Not today, he ate lunch alone in the room and avoided coming out to the floor except when he was greeting clients. I was pleased when the day was over, and I began the journey home, attempting to avoid the battle of late-night shoppers and prepare for my date night with Mark. I scurried through the busy streets towards the Italian Centre where my flat was located, stopping only once at a little off-licence to buy some liquid courage.

I stripped down to my underwear immediately as I entered the door and started playing Alexa to get in the mood. I poured a large glass of the cheap white wine

I had just purchased and switched the shower on. The thought of seeing Mark again gave me goosebumps all over. I couldn't wait to walk about town with him, hand in hand, laughing, eating and then getting him home to my bed. I was imagining scenarios of how to greet him and began answering back aloud in the shower.

'I've missed you, Mark.' *Nah too keen.* 'Hey, sexy.' *God too cringe.* 'You look so good tonight, babe!' *Hmm . . . maybe?*

I shaved everywhere from my underarms to my arsehole; any nook or cranny he would get to touch felt as smooth as a fucking dolphin. I wore a sexy all in one bodice underneath a floaty leopard print skater dress, and a pair of killer heels. Taking no chances with the red lippy this time, I opted for a natural look, and my black hair flowed down the dress with a slight wave at the end. I felt pretty and optimistic that he would be pleased. I even took a few selfies and uploaded them to Instagram, and almost immediately, Ashley had texted.

Mate, you look hot! Her reassurance filled me with confidence, and I knew I was in for a good night.

Mark rang the buzzer just after eight. I jumped up excitedly, waited for a few seconds before answering, and let him up.

'Hey, you look nice,' I answered, slightly blushing as he walked through the old tenement door in black denim jeans and a plain black top with leather jacket.

'Mmmm . . . Not as good as you.' He smiled at me and kissed my cheek.

I leaned over and kissed him on the lips. We pressed our heads together for a few moments before he grabbed my shoulders tight, looking sexually frustrated. There was a moment of intensity and then we began snogging passionately right beside the front door. His lips were soft, and his tongue felt amazing against mine. Jesus, my clit was throbbing and he had only just arrived. It had its own little pounding heartbeat, and I could feel my underwear getting wetter and wetter. At this rate, I could join up with the Clyde. He finally pulled away from me, grasping my chin hard, and sniggered.

'Come on, you look too pretty to stay in tonight.' His voice was deep, and he sounded sincere.

'Okay, I'll get my bag.' I bent over the sofa to grab my bag, desperately trying to be seductive as he watched my every move. He stuck his hand out to take mine, and we left the flat.

I walked down the old staircase feeling comfortable, giddy, and unbelievably horny. He looked so handsome with his hair pushed back, and I felt safe with him.

'I've booked us a table at La Vita, do you mind?'

'No, of course not. I love Italian.'

'Good, me too.' He leaned over and kissed my forehead as we left the bottom door.

We decided to walk along to the restaurant as it was a beautiful, dry night in Glasgow. It was getting dark, and the stars were shining so brightly it seemed they were casting shadows along the narrow streets. The regular route I'd walked so many times before had transformed into a romantic, magical place. For the first time, I noticed the architecture of each building along the way. Mark pointed out arches and angel designs imprinted on the tall buildings that I had never looked high enough to notice. He could have made the streets of Cumbernauld sound irresistible.

'You're so lucky to live in the city centre, Zara, you're close to everything.'

I smiled. 'Except you. You seem to live miles away.'

Mark laughed. 'That's true, but I'm always here if you need me. That's us, after you.'

We walked into the bustling restaurant, and the quiet dynamic of our walk changed promptly. The restaurant was cramped and smelt richly of garlic and herbs. My mouth instantly began salivating. I had been calorie counting since Tami came out of the woodwork and was more than ready for my meal tonight. The restaurant had a warm family feel to it, and as I entered the main door, I was surprised to see another two stories towering above us. This place was huge. We walked past the queue of hungry chancers waiting anxiously for a table and headed to the host stand.

'All right, mate. Table booked for Taylor.' Mark was still holding my hand tightly, and I wasn't wanting to let go, so I held on at the back.

'Ahh, follow me, sir, miss.'

The waiter led us towards a small set of stairs only wide enough for one pair of hips, and we were seated at a window table looking down on a hectic Queen Street.

'I love this place, but the waiters' dodgy fake Italian accents are partly the reason I come back.' Mark sniggered.

We both laughed. I picked up the menu and scanned over it to pick a dish that wouldn't give me terrible garlic breath or make a mess when I was eating.

'Have whatever you want. I'm having the carbonara,' Mark said.

Although I pined for the pizza, I knew I would look most unattractive, so reluctantly I replied, 'Yeah, I was thinking the same.'

The evening was going well, and I felt closer than ever to Mark. Occasionally he would lean over the table and squeeze my hand while raising his eyebrows, reminding me how much I wanted to rip his clothes off.

'Tell me about the clinic then. I didn't have you down as a Botox girl.'

I laughed as I had heard this comment so many times. *Why do you work in that industry, Zara? You're so plain and natural.*

'Ha, I haven't actually had anything done to my face, but I just love working there. My boss Raj is amazing and funny, and my best friend Ashley works there too. We're just like a big family I suppose! It doesn't feel like work when I'm there.'

'That's nice. Good for you, but I'll take it you have to leave when you qualify?' He was twirling his spaghetti around his plate with his fork and spoon, and I had a sudden burst of anxiety with that question.

'Yeah, I mean, I suppose I'll have to.'

The thought of moving on and not being part of Individualise made me anxious. I hated change.

'So, what about your work,' I added. 'How's things there?'

Mark let out a large sigh, 'Busy. I have so many projects going on but it's all pretty boring stuff. Investors, contracts. Not as fun as making people better like you will be doing.' He smiled softly at me before resuming his dish.

We finished up our meal, and I politely declined a dessert, worrying that my hips would not fit the shrinking staircase on the way out. Mark paid the bill, and we flagged a taxi down to take us the short trip to my flat as rain had begun to trickle down the street.

I placed my head on his shoulder in the back of the taxi.

'Thanks for dinner.'

'You're welcome.' He shoogled his shoulder, moving my head back upright, and turned my cheek with his hand to whisper in my ear. 'You can make it up to me now.'

I could feel my heart pound, and I giggled with anticipation like a cheeky little schoolgirl. I could feel my thighs getting moist with just the thought of him on top of me.

'Right, pal, that's you,' the taxi driver interrupted my erotic thoughts.

I was suddenly concerned I would be leaving a slug trail of fanny juice behind me. I slid slowly across the leather seats out the door with caution.

Mark followed, and we headed back upstairs with him admiring my arse all the way up.

I opened the door, and he pulled me against him.

'You look so beautiful, Zara.'

I felt sexy and was oozing with confidence as I knew he meant every word. I never replied, only began undressing myself to let him see the sexy bodice I had waiting for him.

'Oh, Jesus. And what's this?' He took a step back, admiring every inch of me.

'Dessert,' I replied and knelt down to unbutton his jeans, exposing his brick-hard dick. I stared at it for a few seconds and began licking him up and down. He tasted unbelievable. The taste of his salty cum was getting stronger the more I devoured his dick and when I glanced up at him, I could see him panting for air. I didn't know whether to stop or pass him an inhaler.

'Jesus, Zara,' he groaned. He stood back, pulled me up to my feet, and began kissing me passionately. 'Turn around.'

I did what I was instructed to, and felt my sexy underwear being aggressively tugged to the side. With a dunt, I felt him enter me. Deep inside.

Fucking hell. I was getting wetter with every hard thrust. 'Is that good for you?' he whispered. 'Yes,' I replied out of breath, grasping the wall while he was pounding in and out of me until he came deeply inside me.

'Fuckin' hell, Zara,' he grunted, still buried inside of me. He was out of breath and shiny from sweat.

I smiled back at him and pulled out of him, still wearing my sexy lingerie—which was slightly stretched at the crotch now—and gave him a peck on the cheek.

'Want to lie in bed for a wee cuddle?' he asked, still out of breath, but slipping his shoes off at the door.

'Sounds good. I'll be there in a minute.' I began picking up my dress and shuffled into the bathroom, attempting to pee and squeeze out the rest of his jizz. I slipped into a T-shirt and comfier pants, put my hair in a ponytail and joined him in the bed. He had turned the television on as I walked into the room and raised his arm up for me to snuggle into.

I felt unbelievably comfortable and content in his arms. We lay there watching *The Office*, both laughing while stroking one another's arms. My phone was lighting up from the corner of the room, revealing messages from an impatient Ashley.

Well . . . how was dinner?

It was lovely, now just watching The Office in bed. Had such a good night.

Awwwwwwww, happy for you! When is our double date? Me n Dave want to interrogate him!

I laughed, holding my phone, and Mark turned to me.

'What you are chuckling at?' he asked.

'Ashley is requesting a double date. She wants to meet you,' I replied, gauging his face for a reaction.

'I'd love to meet your friends, Zara, I'm well up for that.' He kissed my arm and turned back to the television, laughing away at Ricky Gervais. Staring at him, I had butterflies. I couldn't think of anywhere else I wanted to be except entangled in his long, warm arms.

Chapter Six

I was awake early that morning, not contemplating leaving until the last possible second before I really had to head into work. Mark was dragging me back into bed anytime I made a beeline to get up, and I had never exercised such restraint before.

'Phone in sick, just one day in bed,' he pleaded with me, looking incredibly sexy.

'I honestly can't. They all know I was out last night, so they'll know I'm at it,' I replied, briefly considering his proposal but recalling how mad Raj was yesterday. I didn't want to piss him off further.

'Okay, but let me get my hands on you before you leave.' Mark pulled me back into bed. I was laughing as we kissed. His hair flopped to the side, and his lips felt incredibly soft. I could still taste myself on him.

My alarm went off for the fifth time.

'Okay, I'm officially late. I'm sorry.'

I jumped up and threw on skinny black jeans and a top that was lying over the laundry basket.

'Don't feel like you need to rush off, ' I said, gathering my things. 'Post the key through the letterbox when you're organised. I have a spare. Or stay, I know your work's not that important. I could see you when I'm home.' I smiled as if I was joking, but deep down I longed for him to be there on my return. Waiting there with flowers and a lovely dinner and some more great sex on offer. My imagination could run wild.

'Okay, okay, have a good day, Zara,' he said.

I had one last look at the handsome man lying naked in my bed. *Just leaving him is torture.*

I glanced at my watch: *Shit, three minutes to get to work.* I ran out of the building with my arms struggling above my head attempting to secure my bobble, my jacket blowing wide open with the strong wind going against me, and no packed lunch or food provisions for the whole day. I ran for the first twenty seconds of the journey and developed a stitch so proceeded to walk swiftly to the clinic instead.

'Afternoon,' Tom greeted me loudly as I stumbled through the door.

Ashley was photographing the first client and both of them laughed.

'Sorry, traffic was a nightmare.' I made my excuse confidently as I was pulling off my jacket and heading towards the coat stand.

'You don't drive, do you?' Tom replied, sounding smug. *Smart arse.*

'No, no, I don't, yet. But the pedestrian traffic was particularly bad today, maybe a demonstration or something about to start.' I was blushing at the thought of more confrontation, noticing Ashley and Tom smiling at one another.

I walked over to the client and began working immediately. 'Right, Pamela. Let's get you organised. Is it lip and cheeks today?'

Tom retreated to the clinic room, and Ashley hung around the reception desk, patiently waiting to catch up on last night's gossip. Once I'd gone through necessary paperwork with the client, I approached the clinic room door and let Tom know I was finished.

'Pamela, join me.' Tom's smooth voice echoed through the salon, and I scurried over to Ashley as I could eventually approach the desk.

'Last night was fucking amazing,' I yelled. 'Like, I think I may have a boyfriend very soon?'

'Oh my God! No way! I've told you for *years* to get on the bloody internet, see! Seriously though, Zara,' she moved away from me, 'you literally stink of sex.'

We erupted into laughter. Shit, she was probably right. I didn't have time for a shower this morning as I was too busy sucking cock.

'I told him that you wanted to meet him, and he's up for it.'

Ashley gasped and began clapping like a circus seal. 'This certainly isn't just fucking, Zara! Tell him to meet us next Wednesday. You're off on a Wednesday so you'll have the full day to get ready and I can come straight after work. We'll get Dave to meet us there.'

'I'm not sure, I don't want to sound too needy suggesting it.'

'Oh, be quiet. He's basically your boyfriend—ask him.'

For the rest of the day, I daydreamed about our romantic walk, our sexy taxi ride, and how lucky I felt to be sleeping next to Mark, I desperately hoped he was still in the flat when I got home but was conscious of his hectic schedule.

Tom's clients ranged in every way from young to old, some classy, others trashy. It seemed all of Glasgow's WAGs and influencers adored him, as did all women in general. I smirked throughout the day, noticing how his clients got just as overdressed to see him as I did. The charm and respect he gave to each and every client ensured their return.

Towards the end of the day, Tom had a break and joined me at the desk. He was wearing his scrubs and a pair of white trainers.

'Did you have a rough night last night?' He smiled while flicking through some client photos Ashley had taken earlier.

'Is it that obvious?' I began to giggle. 'I'm just a little hungover today.' I wasn't really, I was just exhausted from a late night shag-athon and keen to see if my flat was still occupied.

'Oh, I've been there, Zara. Don't worry, Raj and I are not exactly on speaking terms, so I won't be telling tales.' He sounded deflated.

'Yeah? What's going on with you guys?' I asked.

'It's complicated. It will take considerably longer to explain than a ten-minute no show.'

He smiled and walked back towards the clinic room.

'I'll get set up for the last client. You two can start locking up if you like?'

Thank fuck, that was a long day. I shouted on Ashley, and as she went outside to pull the shutters down, I began counting the till money.

'You can go, Zara, I know you'll be dying for your bed, I'm sure Ash can deal with the paperwork for Mrs Massey,' Tom shouted out.

'Do you mind, Ash?' I replied, sporting a petted lip in an attempt for her to feel sorry for me.

'Shut up, of course not. On you go.'

I dashed through the back for my belongings, threw on my coat, and walked home in the crisp, cold evening.

When my flat was in sight, I was disappointed to see it in darkness. Mark must have left. My walk became slower and when I eventually reached my home, I opened the door to the key and a small white business card with Mark's name on, I turned it over and it had a little note at the back:

Had a great night, smell your pants later?

I laughed at his weird sense of humour and lifted the card to my face, hoping I'd smell some essence of Mark. Instead I got a waft of lavender Zoflora as it had been lying on the clean floor all day. However, I knew the note was the perfect excuse to text him.

Just got home and seen your romantic note, I hope you weren't going through my laundry basket when I left?

I sat with my phone and the note in my hand, waiting for him to reply to my witty message. *Ping.*

Absolutely not, but where do you keep your dirty washing? I'm just curious. How was work?

I peeled off my work clothes, stripped to my underwear and crawled onto my bed, smiling as I replied to him. The bed smelt so masculine like every inch of him, with a delicate hint of body odour which I weirdly enjoyed. I lay on my pillow, holding the one he lay on to my chest, sniffing it occasionally between messages. I was keen to talk about the double date again but felt nervous bringing it up. Maybe this was casual for him? Perhaps he only agreed because he felt under pressure. I drafted a few messages before deleting them, wondering how I could ask without sounding too full on.

Ha! I'm not telling! Work was okay, slightly hungover but got away a little early, Ashley asked me if you are free on Wednesday for the double date?

Sent. Fuck I felt sick. I was putting myself out there. He's typing . . .

Next week's a bit mental at work, but I'll try to move some things around. Shouldn't be an issue.

Okay, so I think that was a yes. I am seeing him again in five days. God, that felt like a lifetime away. I couldn't wait to show him off. This was it for me. I had that fantastic flutter again.

My body was so lazy, but my head was alive, making plans. I had to secure this relationship somehow. My dreams that night were magical, romantic, his and her moments all of which contained *my* Mark.

Chapter Seven

Five agonisingly long days passed. I managed to fill them with continuous sexting, receiving the odd dick picture and daydreaming of how perfect life was with my new handsome date. Finally the night I had been waiting for arrived: the one that would seal the deal and secure my relationship status with Mark. According to *Cosmopolitan* magazine, *'Double dating indicates a healthy relationship bond, which shows a significant connection between couples and a willingness to accept the other person's friends.'* It wouldn't be long until we were an official couple, and I was pulling out all the stops tonight to make it happen. I had been envisioning all the romantic ways Mark could ask me to be his girlfriend, maybe he would send flowers to my work with the card inside reading, *Zara, be mine forever?* Or perhaps something less extravagant, like lying in bed and whispering in my ear while we made love.

I travelled into Motherwell by train to get my hair done at the luxury Bombshell Salon at 11am. The salon was high-end and unbelievably active for a Wednesday morning; the atmosphere felt friendly but chaotic. I enjoyed sipping my expensive complimentary latte while watching the bustle of the place, the makeovers, the discussion of latest trends and the abundance of women all taking time out of their busy schedules to be pampered. The smell of hairspray and the noise of dryers filled the salon and I almost forgot at times how vital tonight would be. But then I'd remember, and would attempt to get lost in the magazines rather than clock-watching and letting my anxiety build. *In eight hours, I will be with Mark.*

'I'll have a root touch up and a loose wave please, Sarah,' I confidently asked for my usual style and two hours later, my hair looked voluminous and alluring.

'Thank you, girls. You really are miracle workers.'

I glanced at my watch for the fiftieth time that day and paid for my new locks. It was a quick dash from the salon to the train station to head back into the city centre, but I made it without any disruption to my new do.

I sat on the train, grinning as I caught a glimpse of my hair in the window reflection. I took out my phone and felt slightly disheartened that Mark hadn't texted me yet.

He does have a very important job, Zara, stop being needy. Maybe I should text him first?

I typed out a quick, casual message:

Hey you, I hope you're having a good day. Looking forward to seeing you later X.

Okay, sent. I don't need him to text me first every day. I was trying really hard to convince myself. I sat my phone on the small green table, screen upward. Any notification made me pounce from my seat and snatch it up, but none were from Mark.

The train was approaching Glasgow Central, and as I stood up my stomach rumbled. I weighed up if I had enough time to devour a sausage roll before my makeup appointment, and with a scurry off the platform I headed towards Greggs, before making my way to the House of Fraser department store. I walked over to the MAC counter where my appointment was booked, running only five minutes late. A crowd of extraordinarily glamourous girls were standing around the desk, looking more porcelain than human.

'Can I help you?' the tallest girl of the bunch called out.

'Yes, I have an appointment at two for makeup,' I replied, feeling self-conscious that I was under-dressed in my unbranded hoodie and leggings, compared to the stylish black leather fitted uniforms all the MAC girls were sporting.

'Oh, that's with me!' A small brunette popped her head out of the crowd. She looked about eighteen and was very beautiful. I especially couldn't fault her makeup; it was very precise and incredibly bright.

'I'm Kayleigh, come sit here.' She patted the tall black bar stool, and I followed her around.

'I'm Zara, by the way.' I felt awkward and uncomfortable despite how cheery Kayleigh was.

'Zara, you have some pastry flakes on your mouth. Do you mind wiping them before I start your consultation?'

'Oh, sorry. I had a quick sausage roll before I came in.' I giggled as Kayleigh nodded gravely.

'Okay, what can I do for you?'

'I just want my makeup done really, just make me look pretty I suppose!' I paused.

'Oh, perhaps slightly less bright than your makeup— although it is lovely. This is more of a formal occasion.'

Kayleigh laughed.

'Don't worry, Zara, this is mainly for the younger clients, I'll make you look beautiful. Let's get started.'

Ouch, *I thought I was still considered a younger client. I am in my twenties, after all. Okay, the late twenties but even so* . . . Kayleigh began, and as I sat there with my eyes shut, I was eagerly twitching for her to move on to my skin so that I could grab my phone out of my pocket to check if Mark had responded to my text.

'So, where are you going tonight, then?' Kayleigh asked.

'Oh, just on a double date, my boyfriend's meeting my best friend and her partner.' I felt smug calling Mark my boyfriend even though he technically hadn't asked me yet.

'Cool, sounds fab!' Kayleigh continued working on my face as she discreetly hinted about the number of products she recommended for my skin, she finally finished my makeup and turned me around.

Wow. I was flawless. Every pore was smoothed over, and my fake eyelashes were dramatic and full, setting off both golden bronzed smoky eyes. I had never felt so good.

'Kayleigh, wow. Thank you so much.' I beamed at her.

She took me over to the till, where I dipped into my overdraft to purchase my new look, as well as buying the eyeshadows and lipstick I almost certainly would never use.

'Have a great night, Zara, I'm sure all your friends will love your new boyfriend!' Kayleigh shouted as I reached the door, and I smiled. *It has a ring to it, having a boyfriend.*

As soon as I was outside, I retrieved my phone and noticed Mark had texted—finally.

Days a bit mental. Speak soon.

Oh, that was incredibly dry. *Never mind, he must be having a stressful day. Still, I will be able to cheer him up when he sees how much effort I've put into tonight.* I marched back up a hilly Buchanan Street and made my way home to get ready. I waited precisely the same number of minutes *(forty two)* he took to text me back and replied.

Hope your days got better. Are you still OK for 7? Ashley and Dave meeting us there.X

I began washing at the bathroom sink just after five, avoiding any mishaps with the shower encountering my new face and hair. I was pristinely polished and well organised for a change. Mark, *again*, was taking his time to reply to my text, so I decided to call him instead.

No answer.

Shit, maybe he's driving? God I wish I hadn't phoned him so quickly.

Zara, I'm caught up. I can meet you at the bar just after 7??

Ah, fair enough. He was a very important businessman, after all. I supposed relationships were all about compromise, and at least now Ashley and Dave would get to see his reaction when he saw how good I looked tonight. I typed a message back:

Sure, see you there, can't wait!! X

For once, I was running early, so I necked a glass of wine and took a few selfies while waiting before it was time to leave. After much deliberation with what to caption them, I chose no words, only two girls and two guy emojis. Post! Everyone would know that I *finally* had a man. *Queue the DMs!*

Ashley called me as she was walking to the bar on her way out of work. I filled her in with my busy day and she was just as enthusiastic as I was about tonight. I slipped into an oversized white lace shirt dress, accentuating my fake golden glow, and attached a chunky black belt to match. I felt classy and trendy. My hair looked angelic, and my face was perfect—*time to go*. I quickly made the bed to ensure it looked clean and presentable for the night of passion I had in store on return from the pub, before toddling down the street to meet my friends.

I entered The Social, the bar we were meeting at, and gave my surname to the kind waitress. It was always really busy, though tonight there were a few empty tables around. Still, I had taken no chances and made sure I had a reservation. Ashley and Dave were already waiting for my arrival; when they saw me, they both stood proudly from a little booth in the corner. Ashley was wearing a black knee-length tailored dress and her makeup was as perfect as mine, even after a full day at work.

'Zara, you look amazing!' she gasped.

'Aye, you scrub up no bad.' Dave's deep voice echoed around the walls, and he reached over to kiss my cheek. He was wearing dark Armani jeans and a black Vivien Westwood jumper. He was always dressed well; I doubt I have ever seen him in an unlabelled outfit.

'Thank you guys, you both look amazing as yous always do.'

'Well, where is he?' Dave continued. 'I'm no listening to work chat all night, ladies. And more importantly, what team does he support?'

Ashley and I exchanged a smile.

'He's running a little late so he's meeting us here,' I admitted. I took my phone out of my bag and refreshed the home screen. Nothing.

'Dave, get Zara a drink! She's had a busy day,' Ashley instructed.

Dave stood up from the booth, carefully manoeuvring the feature lamp hanging down.

'What you drinkin', Zara?' he asked.

'Boë Violet Gin and lemonade, please, Dave.' I smiled at him gratefully as he went to the bar.

'You look so amazing, Zara, honestly the best I have ever seen you look,' Ashley confessed.

'Thanks. I feel sick. Mark's running so late,' I said.

'So what? He's busy. Make him pay for it later. It just means we can have more drinks before he arrives. Just wait till he sees you.' Ashley was pulling out all the stops to make me feel reassured.

'Drinks, ladies.' Dave delivered the first round of gins before returning to the bar for more shots.

'Oh my God, I'll be pissed for him coming!' I started to giggle before offering cheers to my friends. We all took a shot of Sambuca.

I glanced around at the bar. No sign of him. Every time the door opened my heart raced and anytime it was a guy on his own, I jumped in anticipation. I gulped down my gin and announced, 'I'll get this one,' before making my way to the bar only a few minutes after the first round.

The bar gave me a better lookout onto the street while I gripped my phone. No sign of him and no messages either, only Instagram likes and comments from my unusual selfie activity. I decided to send him a text as it had just past 8pm.

Hey, hope your OK. Will you be much longer? We're all here;-)

I brought the second round of drinks and shots to the table, conscious of any phone activity along the way. I was distracted and nervous.

'So are you sure this guy exists, Zara? I mean, if you brought us here to get with Ashley and me when you're looking like that, I mean I'm totally game,' Dave teased, and Ashley slapped his arm to tell him off. I was too distracted to reply.

I felt a buzz on the table.

'Oh, finally. That's him texted.' I sighed in relief and quickly unlocked my phone to get into his message.

Do you mind if we rearrange, I'm fucked. Been busy all day. Won't be much company tonight.

71

The eager smile drained from my heavily made-up face. Dave and Ashley stared at me, waiting for a reaction. I slipped my phone back into my bag and shrugged.

'Ah, well he's not coming. God. I'm really sorry you guys are here for—'

'Are you fucking serious!' Ashley interrupted. 'Do NOT text back, Zara. I mean it. What did he say?'

'Ash, calm doon. The guy's maybe just nervous.' Dave was playing the devil's advocate, but it was too early for Ashley to give him the benefit of the doubt.

'Look at the effort she's made. Do you think that's acceptable?'

'Guys, honestly, it's fine. I'm going to go to the toilet. Another drink would be good if you don't need to rush off?'

'Course not, Dave?' Dave stood up as Ashley demanded, and I followed behind him, making my way into the ladies'.

I didn't need the toilet. I needed five minutes alone. I felt humiliated. I knew this was too good to be true. I sat in the small cubicle, wondering if I should respond to Mark, holding back the tears from my heavily painted eyes.

'Zara?' Ashley called out. 'Are you okay?'

'Yep, I just feel like such a dick. He's totally embarrassed me.' I opened the door to her, leaning on the cubicle door frame.

'Why do you feel like a dick? He should be the one feeling like a fucking dick, Zara. He's the one that's let you down tonight. And why do you feel embarrassed? It's Dave and me.'

She was right. Mark had totally messed this up, not me.

'Let's have another drink,' I grunted, still dabbing around my eyes, trying to contain the wandering tears.

Six Boë Violet Gins and ten shots later, last orders were called, and the three of us stumbled out of The Social.

'I'm walking you home, Zara,' Ashley mumbled.

'No, you're not, I live two minutes away. Take her home, Dave,' I insisted.

'Are you sure?' he called back, but I had already crossed the empty street towards the Indian before making my way towards my lonely flat.

When I stumbled through the door, I remembered how much I had Hinch'd my home before expecting a night of passion, but instead, it was only me and some chicken pakora returning.

I had kept my phone in my bag after receiving Mark's text, hoping that when I took it out I would have umpteen apology messages and some missed calls. But instead I had nothing. I poured a glass of water, took it through to the bedroom and lay on top of my bed, re-reading the earlier text messages.

What a cheeky fucking bastard!

My hurt was turning into anger, and I turned to my Instagram likes. I scrolled through every person who liked and commented on my earlier selfie, and he wasn't one of them. *Dick.*

Next, I made the drunken decision to stalk Tami Breen's Instagram. *What did she have that I didn't?* Besides half my body weight, I couldn't think of much else.

I wondered how many likes her latest selfie had and went to it. Then like a red rag to a bull: Mark had liked hers. *No. No.* My heart raced. I started frantically flicking through all her posts and sure enough, he had liked them all.

Was he back with his stunning ex? *Maybe they hadn't separated at all.* He did always come to my house, except for that one time. I felt my drunken penny drop as I started jumping to possible conclusions in my head.

I wasn't fucking standing for this. I clicked off Instagram with a fury of anger behind my intoxicated fingers and headed straight to my earlier text messages.

Soooooo I actually did mind that you didn't come earlier. I got my hair and makeup done for you and felt like a complete dick when you didn't show. But lets face it u suold b the one feling like the dik. Maybe you were too busy spending time liking Tami's pic coz you clearly aren't over her! See ya!!!

Sent.

My room was spinning, and my heart ached. *Please text back and say this was a misunderstanding.* My eyes were heavy, and I was falling asleep with dark desperate thoughts. *Why am I never enough?*

Chapter Eight

I woke around four the next morning with a migraine and feeling woozy. Within a few seconds of opening my eyes I had the dreaded fear to lift my phone as the realisation of my late-night trolling came flooding back. I slowly sat upright paying special attention not to move my fragile head too much, praying that last night was all a bad dream. But I knew I would have to face my fate today at some point.

Maybe I can delete the message if he hasn't seen it yet?

I immediately jumped for my phone. Low battery. *Shit.* I began scrolling down, around twenty notifications from Instagram, I continued and yep, one text message from Mark. I stared for a brief moment, attempting to recall the exact message I had drunkenly sent, and eventually opened it up. Nerves floated around my already sensitive stomach.

It wasn't a text message at all, it was a screenshot. A screenshot of his schedule from yesterday. I zoomed in and glanced over his day. It was more jam-packed than my pamper day, from meetings with lawyers, visiting companies and skyping head office to check out new potential premises, all the way through to a late-night conference call. My name was also at the bottom.

Shit. Maybe I had jumped the gun a little. I didn't know if I was relieved or worried, but he hadn't written one word. I lay back in bed and stared at the ceiling swirling above me until my alarm went off for work. I sat up, and reluctantly made my way into the bathroom. *Holy shit*, I looked like Gene Simmons. I went through my early morning cleansing ritual then made a strong coffee to go. I threw on plain denim jeans, a black shirt and a warm jacket and headed to work earlier than usual. I didn't want to be alone in my flat feeling like this and I needed advice from Ashley as soon as.

I walked along the dull road, which had large dark puddles lying from the night's rain. The weather felt as depressed as I was. As I crossed over into George Square, I began narrating possible messages I could write to Mark to explain my reaction. I skimmed about my bag in search of the keys to the clinic, but they were gone. *Shit, wrong bag.* I was too fragile to walk home so instead I sat on the cold, wet step staring at the ground with my cold hands wedged between my knees, waiting. I was in my own little world, examining each pair of shoes that passed by when the rain started pouring down densely. *Great.* I pulled my large tartan scarf from the bottom of my bag and shoved it over my head to protect my new hairdo from the rain, watching it fall onto the filthy Glasgow pavements instead.

Suddenly I felt a scatter of money hitting me and tinkling over the concrete. I gasped and looked up to find a handsome Dr Tom staring at me in amusement.

'Oh, sorry, you really did resemble one of the Romanian beggars Zara. Are things that difficult as a student nowadays?' His cheeky sense of humour insulted me, and I jumped up immediately.

'No, I thought I would start early and forgot my key. What are you doing here?' I replied.

'Mini Raj has been vomiting overnight, so I said I would do today for him. But there was one condition.' He stopped at the door and gave me a serious look before turning the key.

'What?' I asked, attempting to dust myself down.

'You bring your Romanian accordion or at least the little harmonica. I do love a bit of music when I'm working.' I rolled my dry eyes at his childish sense of humour and he laughed as he walked into the clinic, and I followed behind, resetting the alarm.

'You look very tanned, Zara—sunbeds?' he asked, taking off his suit jacket and hanging it on the coat stand.

'No, it's fake. I was out last night with Ash,' I replied, trying my best to sound calm while frantically searching for some lipstick from the bottom of my bag. *Bingo*. I had the products from yesterday's pamper day.

'Oh, on a Wednesday night? Any occasion?'

I felt a stab of anxiety in my heart as he asked, but instead of admitting the truth, I shrugged.

'Nope, you don't need an occasion when you're young, Tom.' I smiled teasingly at him.

'Touché, touché!' He laughed as he walked into the clinic room. My eyes followed, and I watched him unbutton his shirt, exposing his broad shoulders and chest.

He pulled on his scrub top, and I stared patiently hoping he'd pull down the bottoms.

'Morning!' A bright Ashley came bursting through the door. How could she be so alert when I still felt shaky from last night's alcohol?

Tom heard her loud tones and came out of the room, fully dressed in his navy scrubs. *Damn, I missed the strip.*

'How are you feeling today?' Ashley asked sympathetically, but I shut her down with a shake of my head, hoping she wouldn't mention last night's events in front of Sugar Daddy.

'Just a bit hungover. I'll be fine.'

'Ha, yes. You will, indeed, be fine. She's young, Ash, she'll bounce back.'

Ash looked confused at the handsome doctor and made a face before strutting into the staff room with her six-inch heels.

'What time does Raj usually work to on a Thursday, Zara?' Tom asked.

'I'll check the diary, but usually about half six.' I began logging onto the white iMac to verify, when Ashley overheard us.

'Why, Tom? Hot date tonight?' she asked.

'Ha, that would be telling now.' He winked over to me.

'Yep, around half six.' I smiled back.

'Let's get started then, ladies! Woo!' His energy was electric and seeing him unexpectedly that morning had wholly lifted my mood.

The morning was busy, and Raj's clients enjoyed a new, more sculpted surgeon attending to their beauty needs. Tom was flirting with every customer, male and female, and his charming attentive chat allowed Ashley and me more time to discuss last night's events.

'He hasn't written one word. No apology whatsoever. Do you think a screenshot from a diary can excuse him for standing you up?'

I gestured for her to keep her voice down as even the sheer memory of the event made me feel nauseous.

'But I was a complete psycho with my last text, and my spelling was atrocious,' I replied, trying to justify his lack of apology.

'So? You were drunk. And it's justified. He fucking waited until the last possible second to cancel, he basically stood you up.'

I paused for a second. I knew Ashley was entirely right. However, my heart was aching, I wanted to speak to Mark. I decided to request an olive branch.

Hey, apologies for my drunken message last night, was just a bit gutted you didn't show. Hope your days less chaotic:-).

Send. Instantly I felt relieved.

'How many likes did you get on Insta last night with that picture? You blew up the Glasgow internet, Zara, you really should selfie more often.' I could tell Ashley was being kind as I only had a fraction of how many she got per day.

I blushed slightly. 'So I had a few messages from guys trying to chat.'

'Eh, anyone we know?' Ashley sounded shocked that I was only just informing her of this information.

'Barry Jones messaged.' I burst out laughing like a fangirl.

'No way! As in Barry Jones from school?! Is he still as adorable?'

She hurried over to me, eager to stalk his profile, and while I lifted my phone, I was conscious there was still no reply from Mark. I proceeded to go on Barry's Instagram and shuffled my way through his most recent pictures. He was still the same old 'it' boy from school. His perfect blonde hair, blue eyes, and muscular trim frame hadn't changed.

'What did he say?' Ashley stood clapping her perfectly polished nails together.

Hey stranger. Hows things? Your looking great wee yin. Baz XX

'Did you not go with him before?' I asked, trying to recall a decade of chubby childhood, late night parties dressed in shell suits with a bottle of MD down the local parks.

'Hmm, pretty sure I gave him a blowjob at a party one night. Still one of the best nights of my life,' Ash said, and we both erupted into laughter. 'You should message him back—even for a distraction. Let's face it: he's one million times better-looking than Mark.'

She was right. I couldn't argue with her superficial statement, and I did need something to take my mind off Mark. I typed a message back to Barry, enjoying the attention:

Hey, I'm really good. How are you, stranger? X

'Oh my God, can you imagine you guys got married! And he's been in your life all along, shit like that happens every day.' An unrealistic Ashley was daydreaming already.

'No, imagine we got married, and you had given my husband a blow job, that would be tragic!'

'Good point. If this ever goes anywhere, let's not tell Dave about that.'

I giggled as I saw my phone ping.

Barry.

'Already a better texter than Mark.'

I'm good man. Keeping quiet. Would be good to catch up with you one day if your up for it? You look really well Z.

We read the message together, Ashley standing just behind my shoulder.

'Obviously, I'm not arranging anything. Don't get too excited. There's plenty of time for Mark to reply to me and for us to sort things, surely?' I said.

'Well, my Granny Scott always said, the best way to get over a guy is to get under a new one.' She walked away with an *I told you so* twang to her voice.

'Ash, I know your gran, she would never say that,' I laughed, still glaring at my previous messages to Mark.

'Well . . . she might have done. But seriously, google it. It's an actual saying! Give Mark twenty-four hours, and if you don't hear anything, then fuck him!'

Chapter Nine

I gave Mark twenty-four hours, and then forty-eight, and even extended it to one hundred and sixty-eight more hours with still no reply. I was miserable, continuously uploading selfies trying to flood his newsfeed with my filtered face. Instead, it only filled my mailbox with undesirable men that I didn't want to communicate with. My weight was skyrocketing as I lived off a diet of kebabs, deep-fried Mars Bars and Doritos, only drinking coffee and Irn Bru to keep my body functioning. At night my eyes grew tired and square analysing Tami's social media, trying to distinguish imperfections on each over-filtered selfie. I was like Columbo trying to figure out whose hand was in the background of shots, desperately hoping she hadn't been wining and dining with Mark. I had only been to his home once and he lived so far outside the city that I had no idea how to get to it or a late-night drive by with Ashley would have occurred.

I hated this. He was the one who stood me up, and yet I was the one being punished for it.

More than ever, Barry Jones, my teenage crush, was becoming more and more desirable. His chat was basic and boring but at the end of the day, he was Barry fucking Jones.

Ping.

Ashley.

Are you dressed today?

I sat up slightly to reply, pulling my hard, matted dressing gown out my arse. I caught a whiff of fish and screwed up my face. *Oh God*, I must have pissed on the rope tie while sitting on the loo last night.

Nope, still here. If your passing I need more crisps! X

Ping.

No, This is ridiculous. Get up get dressed or I'll seriously text your Mum. He wasn't your BF Zara you need to be strong and get over this. I'll come round tonight. GET WASHED!

That was harsh. Surely she wouldn't call my mother? I sat up and looked around the flat; it really was a midden. Maybe I did need someone to distract me from this heartache. Maybe I did need to get a grip. Maybe I did need Barry? I wiped my crummy fingers on my already minging robe and texted him.

Sorry for the late reply, been swamped at work. I'd like to meet up at some point, absolutely. When are you free?

Done. Ashley couldn't say I hadn't tried.

How about tonight? Im working the rest of the week, you could show me your fancy city gaff?

Jesus, was I ready for this? I sat at the edge of the couch, not knowing if this was a good idea. *But what was I waiting for?* Mark clearly wasn't interested.

Sounds good. What about 9pm give me time to tidy up. I can text you the address.

My heart paused in anticipation as he read it instantly. *Sound, See ye soon wee yin.*

I chuckled at the 'wee yin' as he hadn't seen the size of me during this week of turbulent emotions. I quickly phoned an understanding Ashley to cancel her slot and update her with my latest plans for this evening. I had the same butterflies from fifteen years ago when passing him in the school corridor, but this time, he actually knew who I was.

I began to scrub the flat. I needed him to think I had made it in life. Own flat in the centre of town, practically a nurse, a good number of friends, okay, *one* friend, and my puppy fat had gone. *Mostly.*

I bleached the floor, changed the bedding, and scoured the toilet. *Not a skiddy in sight.* In the shower, I scrubbed my greasy hair and around three rinses later I began feeling clean again from my week of depression. After the deep clean I was ready for him remarkably quick. Wanting to look effortless and casual, I wore a pair of black leggings and a plain white V-neck top. My makeup was minimal. I placed a pack of chewing gum at the side of the couch, praying that if the night would turn passionate, I might get an unexpected kiss.

This was it. Barry Jones was coming to my house. I had spent countless hours of my life dreaming that this would happen, and here it was. If only the popular girls could see me now. I began pacing the floor at around half eight, glimpsing out every window at any sight of a car light from the busy street below.

Buzz.

Barry.

I walked up to the handset.

'C'mon up.' My heart was pounding, my breathing was shallow. I opened the door to greet him, and as he approached me, I examined him. He still had the golden blonde hair, athletic body, and sparkling white teeth I remembered. He hadn't aged much apart from growing a light-coloured beard now. *Damn, he looks hot.* He was wearing grey jogging bottoms and a hooded jumper; he'd obviously gone for the casual look too.

'Awright, stranger, nice to see yeh.' As confidently as ever, he opened his mouth, and I remembered how slang he spoke. His deep neddy voice hadn't changed, but he seemed warm and happy to see me. When he got close enough, he kissed my flushed cheek.

'Fuckin' crackin' house, Zara.' He looked around my home in wonder.

I stood behind him smiling, slightly awestruck that he was in my house. Eventually I produced enough saliva to be able to speak.

'I can't believe you're here, Barry,' I said. 'Drink?'

'I know, fucking random man, eh. I'm okay, hen.' He sat down on the sofa and smiled over towards my open-plan kitchen. I poured a glass of water for myself and watched my hand tremble as I carried it over to the living area.

I sat down beside him, and he immediately put his arm around me.

'So wit have you been up to for fifteen years?' He laughed too much at his piss poor patter and then stared at me.

'Well, I'm almost a nurse, graduate in September. I've been working too, with Ashley actually. We're still pretty much inseparable.' I laughed nervously and sipped my water, not wanting to move too much to disturb his lingering hand. 'What about you? Where are you working?'

'Aye, well, still in the chippy, hen. I'm one of the head fryers now.'

'Oh. Well, good for you. So do you, like, run it?' I asked, trying my best to sound optimistic.

'Well aye, and naw. Got a cracking wee motor last month, was saving up for months. Done it up, and she's fly as fuck. If you behave, I might let you have a wee shot on our next date.' He laughed and gave me a cheeky wink.

'Oh nice, what kind of car do you have? Do you still see anyone from school?'

'A wee blue Fiesta, Zara. Honestly, that's my baby. Eh, I still see everyone more or less; Dean, Kim, Wee Kev, Ryhzo, all still my best mates. We were all camping out the Black Bridge last weekend actually.'

Okay, was this cunt still fifteen? He hadn't grown up at all, whatsoever. I had traded a Range Rover for a Fiesta and felt cheated.

I tried to smile politely as Barry slid deeper down in my estimations with every chavey sentence he spoke. We reminisced about high school and people we knew,

86

but in the back of my mind, I began to miss Mark. *What the fuck was I doing?*

I took the TV controller and started flicking through Netflix, welcoming any distraction to the situation I had put myself in.

'Any suggestions?' I smiled at him.

'Eh, what about *South Park*? Me and my ma buckle at that.'

I laughed, 'Aw that's nice, do you still see a lot of her?'

'Nah, I stay there. Ever since my last bird done the dirty on us.'

Jesus, I felt like I was on *Jeremy Kyle*.

He began spilling his life story and I was nodding along while paying more attention to *who killed Kenny*. I was not particularly listening to his story of adultery when he decided to show me his tattoo of his ex's name.

'Do you want to see the cover-up, Zara?'

'Sure.' I sat back and he pulled his jumper over his head disclosing a hot toned muscular body. He had two red roses going over his chest. He lifted my hand and gently skimmed it over his tattoo.

'Looks good, eh?'

It certainly did look good. Chat aside, his body was remarkable. He must have had an eight-pack at least. I began to wonder how heavy the chip barrels are these days because he was fucking buff.

'I always fancied you, Zara, do you know that?'

I smiled, but I knew that was a lie. 'No, you didn't,' I replied teasingly.

'No, honestly, you were always funny and goofy. I liked that. But we were in different circles, hen. Maybe I've no missed my chance, though?' He stared at me, seductively edging closer.

Oh shit, what should I do? I knew there was no future; he was as dull as old dishwater with no prospects, but at the end of the day, he was *Barry fucking Jones*, and he was in my living room hitting on me.

'Maybe you haven't,' I replied quietly, and his pearly white teeth came closer until we were locking lips.

Damn, he *was* a great kisser. All those rumours at school had been true. He ran his chip frying hands through my freshly washed hair and I was surprisingly horny. I leaned closer to his body, almost straddling him, as he continued kissing me. My face was red raw from his bristly beard, but he still wasn't progressing to the second stage. Soon enough we were dry humping.

Feel my fanny, feel it. Move your hands down Barry. C'mon to fuck! I thought.

'Do you want to just go into my room?' I eventually blurted, coming up for air from the thirty-minute snogging session that seemed to be going nowhere.

'Oh. Are you sure, hen?' His face lit up as he replied unexpectedly.

I grabbed his hand and led him into my bedroom. It was pitch black. I immediately began stripping, feeling more confident as there was no way he'd see any unsightly lump or bump in the darkness.

'Wow, you are amazing,' he whispered and proceeded to take his jumper off and join me on top of the bed.

We started kissing again, and I could feel my legs become damper as he was grinding on top of me.

'Let me lick you everywhere, Zara.'

Finally. I couldn't complain. He had eventually got the fucking message.

He went down towards my vagina and lightly started kissing the surroundings. My body squirmed and jumped at each gentle touch as he got closer to the clit, I wasn't sure if he was deliberately trying to tease me or needed a road map to my clit but I enjoyed the interaction.

'Mmmm, you like that, hen?'

'Yes, keep going, slightly to the left.' I held his head until he was deep in-between my legs hitting the jackpot.

It finally felt amazing. Barry wasn't coming up for air, and he was devouring every fold of my pussy. I pushed his head deep inside me, running my hands through his perfectly fair head of hair. He was eating me like he was going to the electric chair. *Fucking hell, maybe I could see him again! I could get used to this!* My back was arched, and I could feel myself repeatedly cum in his mouth.

'Come up here,' I said after the fourth orgasm. My trembling legs couldn't handle another one.

'You just taste so fucking good man. Mmmm . . .'

I glanced down to see the whiteness in his big, beautiful eyes staring up at me. I had to physically prise him away from my fanny to come up and kiss me. We pressed our heads together briefly, panting but smiling in the darkness as he began to loosen his jeans.

'Kiss me,' I whispered, and he obliged.

89

Ewww, God. His breath tasted rancid. I seriously needed to start eating pineapple for breakfast or invest in some Femfresh if that was how I tasted down there. But even so, it hadn't seemed to put him off.

'Do you want a shot?' he mumbled during the kiss and my thoughts suddenly changed.

He pulled his boxers down and I eagerly put my hand down to feel and *shit, it's tiny*. Smaller than I ever imagined. Why didn't Ashley give me a heads up on this chipolata? I pretended to be impressed, groaning as I made my way down towards it. I stopped in the darkness, scrunching my eyes up, trying to differentiate the ball sack from the dick. *Holy fuck*, it looked like a stuffed mushroom. Still, I had a job to do. I began sucking it and pulling back the small fold of foreskin, repeatedly repaying his earlier oral favour.

Within a couple of minutes, he blurted,

'I'm gawny come, hen.' I jumped out the way and let him finish, half on my fresh duvet cover and half on my thigh.

We lay there silently for a few minutes, catching our breath.

'That escalated quickly,' I said, then laughed and reached for the bedside lamp.

As I pulled the duvet cover up trying to cover any unsightly folds, I gasped. Lying there, completely unaware, was Barry drenched in dried-in blood, a satisfied gory smile all over his face. The blood had clung onto the blonde beard hair, and he looked like Hannibal fucking Lecter.

I discreetly put my hand down towards my fanny and glanced under the covers.

Please don't be my blood. Please be that he has a cut or a spot that's bled with the severe fanny licking he has just given me.

Nope. It was indeed my period. I had bled all over the poor cunt. *So that was the taste.* Now that I thought about it, there was a metallic tang to it.

My heart was thumping. I stared at the mirror on the other side of the room, hoping he wouldn't catch his reflection. He was turning my stomach, and I was starting to panic. He looked as if he had stepped out of *The Walking Dead* and broke into the fucking blood bank.

'God, what time is it?' I began yawning, trying to figure out how I could get Barry out of my house immediately.

He looked at his phone. 'It's almost twelve, darlin'.'

'Shit, I'm up soon. I better get organised for bed.' Rummaging through the covers, I found a pair of abandoned pants and made my way to the edge of the bed. I leaned over, pulling on some PJ bottoms and prayed my bleeding wouldn't leak through.

'I better go then?' Barry followed me to the edge of the bed and attempted to kiss me.

I pecked his dry lips instead, which were now crumbling with my menstruation.

'I'll text you, Barry. I had so much fun,' I said, smiling, and made my way out towards the living room.

Shit, shit. Should I tell him? What if he goes home and his mum thinks he's been slashed?

'I'll call you tomorrow. I get out the chippy about ten?' Barry said, fully clothed now and bearing a dull red smile. *He's eager now, wait until he sees the state of his face,* I thought.

'Yeah, sure.' I paused, still thinking of what to do, then gave him a large hug, carefully avoiding any contact with his crimson grin.

Once he was gone, I locked the door. I was in shock.

I scurried to my bedroom, searching for my phone to call Ashley, but instead noticed that the place looked like an episode of *CSI*, and I was both the victim and the perpetrator. I paused to take it all in. I had really made an arse of myself again. I began stripping off my bedsheets and remaking my bed for the second time that day, only returning when I was washed and sporting a super jumbo tampon. There was no way I could see Barry again after this, *was there?*

The following morning, I woke up early with severe menstrual cramps and mortifying anxiety from the previous night. I lay wide-eyed, recalling how inno-cent Barry looked while unknowingly sporting his gory new look. I had to forget all about it. I needed a fresh start and to get out of my depressive slumber. Taking a deep breath, I pushed the night behind me.

There were a few uni books lying around, so I collected them and decided to return them to the library. I was planning to enjoy the last few weeks of freedom before my final placement began.

I grabbed my skinny black jeans, warm grey hoody and a denim jacket, threw my hair in a ponytail and began marching through the city towards Glasgow Caledonian University. The contemporary building was crammed with prospective students, who were visiting the large lobby full of pop-up tents advertising clubs and social events. Walking through the campus, I saw students enrolling, so vibrant and excited. The atmosphere was uplifting and friendly. I had a pit at the bottom of my stomach. God, this could well be the last time I'm in this building. I had so many positive memories here, from enrolling in my course, attending lectures, to receiving placement allocations and getting my grey student nurse tunic. I loved being a student and found studying nursing so natural. I continued making my way through the crowd and headed for a coffee before attempting the library rush.

'A white coffee, please, oh, and wait . . . sorry . . .' I began edging my way back into the line pushing through the queue to examine the cake and pastry options that the café had on display. I paused as I considered my options. I hadn't had breakfast and was certainly not full from last night's sausage fest.

'Ah, a balanced diet, Zara?' said a familiar pretentious English voice behind me. My heart stopped with a bang.

'Tom!' I turned around in shock to find him a few metres away waiting in line.

'Hello, fancy seeing you here,' he replied, grinning at me. He was dressed in a crisp white shirt with a grey suit jacket and matching trousers. Jesus, I could smell his masculinity take over the room.

'Do you want a coffee?' I gestured to the till as there was a queue accumulating behind us. *Please say no, please say no, I have about £4 on my card.*

'Why not. I'll have the same. Minus a cake.' He made his way towards me, edging in between the crowded tables. 'I'll find us a seat.'

'Two white coffees, please. No cake.' I smiled sheepishly at the cashier. I couldn't risk the fucking cake now since I wasn't overly familiar with the prices, and I was not risking insufficient funds in front of a bloody surgeon.

I grabbed the coffees and nervously walked over to a table where Tom sat staring at his phone.

I sat down opposite him. 'Here you go.'

He placed his phone on the table and took a sip of his coffee. 'Mmm . . . Thanks, Zara. This is a nice surprise.' He paused, staring into my eyes.

'Yeah, I know. What brings you here?'

'I was speaking to the head of media, actually, for a new project I'm launching. All very hush at the minute. Anyway, how's life? How's the dating going actually?'

Shit, he remembered.

'Hmm . . . oh, not too well. We're not together, honestly far too difficult for me. We wanted completely different things.' *Like he wanted his ex, and I wanted him.* I laughed lightly and sipped at my coffee as if I had made the decision to end it with Mark.

'You're as well finding out now before it's too late,' Tom said.

I nodded in agreement. 'So, are you not working in the hospital today?' I asked, hoping to change the subject.

'Yes. Well, I'm on call.' He flashed his other phone from inside his jacket pocket, slightly exposing his broad chest.

Jesus, he is fit.

'Remind me, when do you return to practice?' he asked.

'I start my final placement in six weeks, but I don't find out where it is until two weeks before. I'm actually only here because I have some books to return, the academic side of my degree is complete.' I sat back, feeling pleased with myself, conscious of the attention Sugar Daddy was attracting in the cafeteria.

'What a clever little nurse you are, eh.' His eyes widened suggestively.

Tom's on-call phone began to ring, and he checked the time on his watch.

'Excuse me.' He walked to the slightly less occupied end of the café, looking extremely important with his arms gesturing in frustration as he listened to his call. *God, he looked even sexier when he was mad.* I watched on in amazement.

A few intense minutes later, he slipped the phone back in his designer pocket and came back to the table.

'Apologies, Zara, looks like duty calls. Some idiot locum can't do a simple laparotomy.' He rolled his perfectly round brown eyes.

I laughed as if I could efficiently perform such a procedure too, and nodded in understanding. 'That's a shame. I'll see you Friday anyway.'

'Yes, you will indeed, and perhaps I'll be returning the coffee favour.' He paused and winked flirtatiously at me.

I laughed nervously. 'You better.'

As soon as he began to walk away, my shaking hands reached in my pocket to retrieve my phone.

'Oh, Zara.' He came back to the table as if he had forgotten something.

'Yeah?' My eyes were skimming our surroundings to see what he had left behind.

His voice was deep and quiet as he said, 'You look very attractive today with your comfortable clothes on. I've always had a thing for student nurses you know.'

'Ha, yes, so have I.' *What the fuck am I saying?*

He raised his eyebrows and smiled. 'See ya.'

'See you Friday,' I spluttered.

So have I? Since when have I had a thing for students? My awkwardness was slowly paralysing my excessively sweating body. But I sat there grinning like the Cheshire Cat until he had left the café. *Does Sugar Daddy actually like me-like me?*

I wasted ten minutes attempting to get a hold of Ashley with no reply until my fingers finally gave up, and I began making my way towards the library. As I walked through the large doors, I looked around, avoiding the librarians and my overdue fees.

Ring ring.

Ashley, great.

'Guess what? ' I began. The room of ostentatiously eager students started to stare.

'Oh, for fuck's sake, hang on.'

I tossed the books on an unused shelf and made my way to a more appropriate place.

'Tom and I met in uni and had a coffee, and basically he said he has a thing for student nurses and I looked really good.' I could hardly breathe from excitement as I shared the gossip. Ashley screamed like a teenager down the handset.

'He obviously wants you, Zara. Ooft, honestly, you are in high fucking demand this week, hen.' She sounded as pleased as I was.

'I know, this has never happened to me before. I don't know what's going on, but I'll bloody take it. He looked so fucking hot, Ash.' My stomach flipped at the thought of his sexy wink.

'Well, I know exactly what's going on, it's your period that's attracting them all!'

I chuckled as I walked slowly down the corridor.

'He's not a fucking dog, Ash, that doesn't happen to humans,' I whispered.

'He might not be a dog, babe, but I'll guarantee you one thing, you will be doing it doggy by the end of the week.'

We giggled for the remainder of the call and as I began the long walk downhill to my flat, my mind stayed in the café where the fannyworks went off. '*Dr Adams and Staff Nurse Smith*' did have a ring to it, didn't it?

Chapter Ten

That week I had a whole new lease of life. *Yes, yes,* I still checked the viewers on every Instagram and Snapchat post I uploaded, secretly hoping Mark had seen them and they suddenly reminded him of how much he had missed me. *But no luck.* Maybe he would never forgive my psychotic behaviour, or perhaps he'd simply moved on and found someone else's panties to sniff? I thought about him often, but at the same time, I felt happier, excited even. I was washing regularly and getting on with my days.

I spent a lot of nights dreaming about Dr Tom. I'd played down our earlier run-in and put it down to his flirtatious nature, but if there was even a slight chance he liked me then I was prepared to go for it. It was a week of crash dieting, tight tops, chicken fillets, and creating a fake love interest to make Tom jealous. Operation Sugar Daddy was on!

I woke early that Friday morning and headed straight into the shower to rinse off the cheap tan I'd plastered on my skin.

My period was still flowing, so I popped in a tampon and dressed in my pre-planned outfit I had carefully laid out the night before. I was wearing tight, high waisted black jeans with a loose, low-cut white shirt. Underneath I wore a red lace bra, making sure it was slightly visible when I moved. I brushed my long black hair on either side and straightened it. My makeup was simple but looked slightly more glamorous because of the tan. I looked at myself one last time in the mirror, took a deep breath, and left the flat.

Outside, it was pouring down. I couldn't risk any unplanned hiccups to my incredibly thought-out plan, so I called a taxi and had it drive the three-minute journey to work. When I saw Tom's car out the taxi window, I immediately felt sick. *What the fuck am I doing? I'm literally trying to seduce my boss.* I was so preoccupied and self-conscious of how overly done up I was, I got out of the taxi forgetting to pay.

'Have you forgot something, hen?' the overweight driver called out from his window.

'Oh, sorry. I did, here you are.' I handed him a fiver and watched him rustle about a small tin, trying to pick up the change with his chubby fingers. I was getting drenched from the bucketing rain falling and realised there was no actual benefit to getting a taxi after all.

'In fact just keep the change.' I turned around and plodded into the clinic, soaked through and shivering.

'Morning,' I said distractedly while examining my wet hair in the mirror behind the desk.

'Jesus, Zara,' Ashley called out.

She gestured to my shirt, and I looked down to find the only thing visible was my red lace bra. The rain had saturated the white fabric to a thin lining. I gasped.

'Shit. Oh shit. What will I do?' I looked at her frantically, then scanned the room for clients or worse—Tom—but I was too late.

'Ding dong!' Tom popped out of the staff room and immediately began approaching the desk. 'And when people ask why I moved to Scotland, and I say the weather, they think I'm joking. But this is precisely what I mean.' He was entertained, smiling, still staring at my breasts.

'I got caught in the rain. I didn't mean it.' My voice was trembling as I tried to position my arms over my chest.

'Have you got a change?' Ashley was trying her best not to laugh, remaining serious for my sake.

'Nope,' I replied. 'I'll get a taxi home. It won't take long. I can't spend the full day like this.'

'It's a real shame you can't,' Tom said. 'Although I don't think I'd be able to concentrate.'

Ashley laughed. 'Stop being a perv!' She pushed him jokingly.

He smiled at me. 'Here, Zara, take my shirt. I need to change into scrubs anyway. Your shirt will dry quickly if you stick it on the radiator.'

'It's fine. I only live a few minutes away,' I said, feeling my face burn with embarrassment.

'I'm not taking no for an answer. Here.'

Tom began unbuttoning his shirt right there on the clinic floor, his hairy, muscular chest proudly on display under the bright shop lights. Ashley and I stared in amazement. When he threw the striped shirt to me I grabbed it out of the air, and automatically sniffed it.

'Did you just smell my shirt?'

Shit, shit, shit.

'What? No!' I replied, with my face now as red as my bra.

He smiled before walking into his room. 'Who's the perv now?' he called out.

The remainder of the day passed quickly. We didn't see much of Tom due to his vast clientele, but I enjoyed wearing a high-quality expensive shirt. I imagined this was precisely how I would feel with him wrapped around my body. His strong cologne suffocated me throughout the day, he smelt expensive and warm. I didn't want to take it off, and kept it on long after my own shirt had dried out.

The day was wearing on, and around six Tom finished with his last client. He had a full day of lip and cheek augmentations which seemed to require a lot more concentration than the skin care and Botox Raj special-ises in. Ashley and I were counting the tills when he came out of his room.

'You guys all set?' He sounded tired.

'Yep! Home time?' Ashley batted her extra-long, semi-permanent eyelashes at him, and he smiled.

'On you go. Zara, what about you?'

I was still analysing receipts, and I paused. 'I'll be literally five, ten minutes max. You guys can go, I'll lock up.'

'Well, you don't have to ask me twice,' Ashley said. She pulled her jacket and bag out from under the desk and secretly nudged my leg, I glanced down to her squatting at my legs and she winked cheekily at me then stood up and began walking out the glass door. 'See you two.'

Tom laughed. 'Looks like I need to wait on you anyway, shorty.'

'Oh, sorry. Your shirt.' I dropped the receipt roll on the desk and quickly marched through to the staff room where I had left my own shirt drying. Suddenly, I became aware of Tom behind me.

'Sorry, Tom, I'll be one minute.' I felt flustered and could feel my heart begin to pound.

'I can help you with that. I mean, if you want?'

I turned to see Tom standing behind me with his strong arms folded. He was staring at me seductively.

I nodded. 'Okay.' It was all I could say.

Tom strolled towards me, his warm brown eyes taking in every inch of my body.

'Lift up then,' he said.

He placed his hands on my wrists, tightly, and raised my arms to the ceiling. Then he pulled the shirt upwards over my head and tossed it to the floor. My bra was the only thing covering my breasts, and I could see my heart pounding out of my bare chest. He lifted his own arms up, and I began pulling his scrubs upwards and off him. He brushed his hands up and down my body, and I felt the blood rush to my fanny instantly. He walked around me, running his large hands gently over my shoulders and back, but stopped again as he came to my face.

'You're so fucking sexy,' he whispered. He grabbed the back of my hair tightly in his hands and pulled me towards him. We began kissing. His lips were soft, but I could feel the hard bristle of his stubble against me.

He was incredibly passionate. Anytime I thought the kiss was ending, he would bite my lip and not allow me to finish it. His hands came down to squeeze my boobs hard as he edged us against the wall. His huge hands started caressing my stomach and they began to wander lower with every second. I wanted him inside me so badly, I could feel my underwear getting wetter and wetter. *Shit, my fucking period*, I remembered. I could not have another night like last week. I couldn't fuck this one up.

'Wait. We should stop,' I managed to mutter.

'Should we?' Tom laughed and took a step back with his hands on his hips.

'You're basically my boss, Tom.'

'No, Raj is, and besides,' he edged towards me and began kissing my neck again, 'I won't be here much longer.'

I was in a trance from his touch, and it took me a second to register what he said.

'What? What do you mean?' I stood back, trying to understand the handsome surgeon.

'I mean I'm opening my own clinic. That's why there's so much shit with Raj, but it's also why I can finally pursue you.' He leaned towards me.

God, I wanted to fuck him so bad. I had to play it cool and try not be so needy for once.

'Pursue me? In the back of a staff room? Hmm . . . Maybe you need to try a little harder, Dr Adams.' I reached over and kissed him on the lips before swivelling away from him and putting my shirt back on.

'What? Is that it?' He looked shocked.

I laughed. 'I guess so. I think we should head home. See you soon?'

'Zara, Zara, Zara. Yes. See you soon.' Tom looked frustratedly down at his manhood as I walked out of the room, grinning.

It took all my willpower not to turn around and start humping him like a dog on heat, but I was here for the long game. Plus, my jumbo tampon felt heavier than Tom's wallet from all my vaginal juices that day. I placed the till roll back in the drawer, still shaking but feeling ecstatic, and walked home in the drizzle, happy to cool down.

Ping.

Tom: *That was hot*.

Yassss, he's got my number. A huge smile beamed across my damp face. *Should I wait to reply?* I paused briefly, overwhelmed with the situation. There's no way I could wait, my fingers were twitching, eager to respond. He was online and I knew he would see the blue WhatsApp ticks appear on his phone indicating when I had read his message. I had to reply immediately.

Yes, it really was. How did you get my digits?

Tom: *We were once in a Christmas group chat I believe. You almost had my digits tonight Zara but you declined. What you doing Sunday?*

My stomach flipped. He wanted to see me out with our working week. *What did this mean?* Before I even dared to reply I scheduled an early morning breakfast with Ashley and Emily for advice. I couldn't fuck this one up. I got off the phone from Emily and had another message from Tom.

Well . . .?

After recalling my behaviour with Mark I decided to go for a laidback, take-it-or-leave-it reply.

Yea, I'm free Sunday. What you thinking?

Tom: *Good, you can help me with a few things. I'll pick you up at 12?*

Cool :-)

The only thing I wanted to help him with was emptying his balls, but, I knew I should really wait for that to happen if we were to become anything more than fuck buddies. *God, I felt sick.* Sunday was only a couple of days away and I didn't have much time to prepare for this momentous occasion. I lay on my bed restlessly that night, tossing and turning as I recalled our semi-naked kiss. I fantasised about what could have happened if the kissing didn't stop, and I couldn't wait to feel his warm body against mine once again. I genuinely felt like the luckiest girl in the world.

Chapter Eleven

Waking up to a text from Tom felt surreal. I clicked on the message, timestamped 4am. I was always so sleepy in the morning, but not today. My eyes were bright, and my palms felt sweaty in anticipation of what he was going to say.

Is it just me who can't sleep thinking about that kiss?

A smile instantly spread across my cheeks. I wanted to send a reply immediately but decided to hold off for now. I had to keep Tom interested somehow and didn't want to appear too eager straight away.

Breakfast was booked at 9am at Coia's Café in the East End of the city, and I left the house in plenty of time to walk and feel refreshed. It was almost June; outside, there was a hint of sun peering through the grey clouds and it was warm enough that I was wearing just leggings and a T-shirt. Taps-aff weather if ever I've seen it. I popped in some earphones and strolled through the city, thinking of how happy my mother would be if I married a surgeon and how amazing my life could be. My walk became a familiar daydream as I imagined my creative kids being educated at a top private school. I could cut my hours down at work or stop altogether. Our offspring would take school trips to Africa and Europe, not scrimp to afford the Burntisland and M&D's trips I endured. All in all, I had my life pretty much mapped out from that one simple, sexy kiss and I couldn't wait to elaborate on it with my friends.

After at least thirty minutes of fantasising, I reached the busy café with aching calves and a sweat rash. As I walked through the familiar glass doors, the smell of sumptuous Italian food hit me.

'I haven't seen you girls for a while! Come sit at your table.' Marco, the waiter, greeted me by pulling out a chair at our usual table. I sat patiently, waiting for the rest of my party to arrive with my phone glued to my hand. I was scrolling through it, writing and editing potential replies to my note section that I could send back to Sugar Daddy.

'Hi, sis.'

I looked up to see Emily standing in a mint crop top and matching gym leggings. We hugged for a second before Ashley came in almost immediately behind her. She was dressed in a black maxi dress with a stylish denim jacket hanging off her shoulders and huge sunglasses that took up most of her face.

'Hey, Ash.' Emily embraced her too, and we sat down.

'God, I've missed the breakfasts in here,' Emily said, taking a deep inhale of the smells while examining the menu.

'I've missed the waiters,' Ashley replied, giggling.

'Right. Enough. Guys, last night.' I paused for dramatic effect.

'Yes, she's going straight in there. Tell me exactly what happened.' Ashley slammed her hands down on the table.

'Okay, so basically I had the best night of my life,' I exclaimed.

'You won the lottery?' Emily suggested sarcastically, still more interested in the breakfast range.

'More than that. Emily, stop. Listen to me.'

She looked up, and I finally felt pleased I had everyone's attention. 'Okay, so, I fucking kissed Sugar Daddy.' My face beamed with pride.

Emily and Ashley looked at one another in shock.

'Shut. The. Fuck. Up!' Ashley yelled out. 'Like properly tongue snogged?'

'Yes! Okay, so you know I had the whole shirt situation? Well, I walked through the back to change and return it to him, and he followed me through and asked if I needed a hand to get undressed. Then, before I knew it, we were kissing against the fucking wall. Like so passionately.' I had vaginal tingles just reminiscing about it.

'And you didn't do anything else?' Ashley sounded impressed.

'No, I couldn't. Period was kind of there, but basically away this morning!'

'So, hold on,' Emily piped up, 'is this the guy you've both been fascinated with since starting that job? The hot old surgeon?'

'Yes.' Ashley nodded.

'He's not that old, I don't think,' I replied, defending him. 'But anyway, he's asked me to do something tomorrow! Like, I am *officially* going on a date with Sugar Daddy!' I couldn't stop smiling.

'Are you ready to order, ladies?' Marco interrupted.

'Yes, eh, could I have the eggs Benedict and Diet Coke, please, Marco.' I decided to stick with a slightly healthier option today as I could potentially be shagging again soon.

'I'll have the same,' Emily said, closing her menu.

'I'll have the waffles please, and coffee. Thanks, Marco,' Ashley said.

'Thank you, ladies.'

'So, right, where are yous going?' Emily asked.

'No idea. He text me as soon as I left work and asked if I was free, and when I said yes, he replied, great, I could help him with a few things?'

'Aye, I bet you could.' Emily smirked.

'What like? Polishing his dick?'

We all began laughing, and I was suddenly conscious of the tables around us. I lowered my voice to a whisper, and said, 'But let's be serious, guys. I don't want this to be just sex, so I genuinely need help.'

Emily looked at me sympathetically.

'Zara, you can't have sex then, for at least a few weeks. Make him chase you. Flirt, kiss, maybe feel, but do *not* have sex. Get him to respect you, that's the secret.'

Ashley nodded in agreement.

'I mean, I had sex on the first night with Dave, but he stalked me for years. I knew I'd never get rid of that cunt, but Sugar Daddy is from another generation. I think you should try and refrain. Be strong. Keep away from the dong!' She pointed her finger towards me as if she was a schoolteacher telling me off.

What they said made perfect sense, but I'd fantasised about having sex with Tom for years. Just imagining his face made me soaking wet; resisting sex when it was being offered on a plate seemed like an impossible task.

'I honestly don't know if I'll be able to do it, man, you have no idea the sexual chemistry that was there last night.'

'Do the trick!' Emily gasped.

'The trick?' I was confused.

'Don't shave anything. Keep your fanny permed, legs hairy, and underarms wild. That way, you won't be tempted to let him touch you,' she explained.

'And wear the ugliest granny pants you have on your dates,' Ashley suggested.

'Good one,' Emily agreed.

Marco approached the table once more with our drinks and food order. The food was presented beautifully, and I could feel my mouth salivating as he set it down in front of us.

'Here you are. You not have the full breakfast normally, Zara?'

I blushed slightly as his broken English still managed to fat shame me. 'Yes, normally I do.'

'She's off the sausage, for now, Marco, don't encourage her!' Ashley called out.

We all began laughing, and Marco looked more embarrassed than me.

'Enjoy, ladies.'

The healthier selection went down almost as well, and I sat in the café a little longer with Emily as Ashley rushed off to begin her shift.

'Think how happy Mum would be if you married a surgeon, Zara.'

'I think I'd maybe be the favourite after that,' I said.

'I mean, I wouldn't go that far, but she would like you a little more than she does now.' Emily laughed as she teased me.

'Want to head?' I asked.

'Yeah, sure. You know your niece and nephew haven't seen you in forever, Zara.' She looked at me with the same disappointed face our mother used.

'Well.' I grabbed onto her shoulders from behind, walking out the café. 'Their mum and dad know where I live too. Bye, Marco, thanks.'

Emily rolled her eyes at me as we emerged onto the street.

'Do you want a lift?' she asked.

'Nah, I'm going to walk again. Need to be a size zero for tomorrow,' I insisted, patting my bloated stomach.

'Okay.' She got into her large Audi estate car. 'Zara, please don't shag him. You will regret it.'

'I can't hear you,' I called out as I put my earphones in and began walking back to the city centre.

Once I was sure I was out of Emily's sight, I took my phone out and took a deep breath. I was finally ready to reply to Tom.

Hope you finally managed to get to sleep and stop thinking about our kiss?

Send.

God, maybe that was too forward? I hoped he hadn't changed his mind about tomorrow. Perhaps the kiss was a random spur of the moment thing. I started sweating in anticipation of a reply, but it came quicker than I had hoped for.

When I said I was thinking about the kiss, I was being polite, Zara. I was thinking about your tits in that red bra. Jesussssss.

Phew. Not the most romantic of messages, but at least I knew Tom was thinking of me. *Oh God, a sexless date will be impossible if this is his tone already*, I thought. *Okay, I just need to divert the subject away from sex.*

Cheeky! Where are we going tomorrow? I need to know the dress code.

Sent. Read. He was typing already.

You have no idea. Casual!

Okay, somewhere casual. Maybe bowling or the movies? Perhaps a stroll around Kelvingrove Park hand in hand? I continued the journey home, contently listening to some nineties RnB, carefully prepping tomorrow's outfit in my mind. How would I pull off a date with the Nelly to my Kelly without letting him touch me? My mind was switching from thought to thought so quickly I felt nauseous, anxious, excited, and overwhelmed. I replayed the kiss over again in my mind.

And then it hit me. Tom was leaving the clinic. In all the excitement of our kiss, it had completely slipped my mind. I would be leaving soon too when I graduated, but that wasn't for a while. My brisk, bright walk became slower and more of a struggle as my mood flipped with the thought of losing that guaranteed time with Tom each week.

As I reached the stairs to my flat, my legs were tired and weak. I gripped the banister, pulling myself up each step until I spotted a large package sitting on my doorstep. I racked my brain wondering if I had ordered anything but nothing sprung to mind. It was bulging, with a cover placed carefully on top, discreetly hiding the contents. I pulled back the cover, and a stunning bouquet of flowers was revealed. I was shocked; no one had ever sent me flowers before. There was a small card tucked between the leaves. I opened it and read:

The shirt looks better on you. T.

For a few seconds, I paused. What did he mean? I looked down at the cover I had excitedly thrown aside and found the same shirt I was wearing yesterday at work. I felt overwhelmed and emotional. Slouched against my close wall, I held the shirt to my face and inhaled, hoping for a trace of Tom's spicy vanilla scent. I looked back at the bouquet, admiring each individual flower, from thistles to roses, how the colours perfectly complemented each other. The man had good taste in flowers. I was just glad I hadn't seen him when he delivered them, not in my Primark legging that were bobbling at the thighs or my date proposal would have been out the window.

Eventually, I opened my door and immediately sent pictures to Emily and Ashley of my unexpected delivery. This was so kind. So thoughtful. So keen. Oh God, he was smooth, incredibly charming, and seemed to tick all my boxes. Keeping my legs shut tomorrow was undoubtedly going to be a challenge.

Chapter Twelve

My eyes opened widely at the sound of my alarm clock. It was the morning of my date, and as I stretched I let out an excited screech. Sunlight cascaded through the blinds. This was going to be a good day.

As I sat up I patted around the bed to retrieve my phone, which had slid down my silky bed sheets over-night—no notifications. Damn, I kind of hoped he'd send the obligatory 'good morning' message. I yawned and stretched again, catching a whiff of my freshly fake-tanned arms which still smelt strongly from the night before. *Two hours until my date.* I plopped back into my pillows and let out another scream.

Today was the day.

My first official date with Sugar Daddy.

I felt like a kid on Christmas Eve. Was this going to be as amazing as I hoped? Would I get everything I had wished for? Would he even turn up? My head was doing overtime, questioning every decision, and my stomach ached with nerves. I had to focus.

I walked into the kitchen and made a strong coffee then retreated to my bedroom to get ready. There, I perched my bottom on the side of the makeup table and slowly drank my coffee, taking in how vital today could be. It was Ashley's only day off, and I wondered if it was too early to call her for moral support. I decided to wait for at least half an hour.

I glanced over to the wardrobe where the pre-planned outfit I'd chosen hung neatly from a hanger; looking at it now filled me with doubt. *How casual should I be?* Tom didn't specify where we were going. I'd picked out an oversized black T-shirt dress with a Tenerife-special 'Gucci' belt and slip-on pair of Vans. *Perhaps the Vans are too casual?* He was considerably older than me, and I hadn't seen him wearing anything other than a shirt or scrubs. Maybe his idea of casual would be a fucking kimono, I had no idea. Come to think about it, I didn't have any idea about Tom at all. Yes, he was a surgeon. Yes, he was charming. Yes, he was unbelievably fucking gorgeous. But realistically, I didn't know him one bit.

I was starting to talk myself out of the date when my phone pinged, and a message from Tom appeared.

Are you up? We have a busy day. See you at 12.

Instantly, I felt better.

I had the Mark stand-up in the back of my mind, but now that I knew today was definitely going ahead I felt relieved. I had one last stretch and went into the shower to rinse away the excess tan from my mahogany body. I looked down at my dull-looking vagina. Emily and Ashley were adamant I shouldn't shave if I wanted this to be more than a quickie. So, I reluctantly shaved my legs and underarms and left my bristly garden wild and untamed. There was no turning back now; I couldn't have sex with this amount of pubes.

As I dried myself off, I clocked my monobrow in the mirror. The amount of hair I seemed to accumulate right before going on a date was unreal. Edging myself closer to the mirror, I realised that my moustache was in full bloom too. Jesus. I looked like fucking Big Foot. It was far too late to make an appointment for waxing without being red raw for the date. I reluctantly reached over and shaved the moustache and monobrow clean off. *That's better.*

Next, I proceeded to tackle my hair. I untangled last night's loose plait, hoping that it would fall effortlessly into some sort of loose wave this morning. But I soon realised it was too loose, practically non-existent. I ran my hands through it frantically, hoping it would pick up some volume, when Ashley began facetiming me.

'Hey, what's going on? Oh, you look so lovely and tanned, Zara!' Ashley said, smiling at me from her cosy-looking bed.

'Ash, I have had a nightmare. I've basically shaved my full coupon. My hair is completely flat, it looks shit, I'm gonna need to put it in a ponytail,' I said, the words coming out at roughly a hundred miles an hour as I tried to shove my hair up into something presentable.

'Right, calm the fuck down. Do not put it in a pony. It looks fine and it'll be sexier when you can run your fingers through it and play with it. And your face looks fine. Just don't stay too long, or you'll get a twelve o'clock shadow.' She began laughing, and so did I.

'Listen, Zara, you know him. He knows what you look like, and he's asked you out, so relax. He fancies you the way you are, just try not to stress and you'll be fine.'

I nodded in agreement. She was right. I had patches of red skin blooming all over my face and neck from the nerves. I needed to calm down.

'Just go get ready and take pics when you're done. You're going to have a great time, and if you don't, then fuck it, you're almost qualified and don't have to work with him for much longer.'

I got off the phone from Ashley and felt immediately guilty. I hadn't said about Tom leaving the clinic. I didn't know enough about the situation to tell her, and I knew she would instantly take Raj's side. I tried to put it to the back of my mind and continued getting ready. The hours had flown by, and with some foundation smoothed onto my face and eyelashes dipped in mascara, I was ready. I sprayed my body in Chanel Chance and stared hard in the mirror. *Please make him fancy me. Please, please, please.*

Ping.

Outside.

I glanced outside at his sleek car parked up on the kerb. I couldn't believe this was actually happening. I took a deep breath, locked up the flat, and began walking down the close stairs.

As soon as I stepped out, butterflies consumed my stomach and chest. I felt dizzy with nerves. I could hardly breathe. My heart was pounding so hard I could feel it radiate to my fists. I needed a nervous poo. But I was committed, and he had already seen me.

He leapt out of the car and came up to me.

'Hello, beautiful,' he said and kissed my cheek lightly before opening the passenger side door.

What a fucking gentleman, I thought as I slid into the car and he closed the door behind me. I sat alone for a few seconds as he made his way around to the driver side. I could hear my lungs panting for air as the butterflies continued to erupt in my chest. He opened his door and sat beside me, turning his head with a smile.

'Nervous?' he asked.

'A little,' I replied with a smirk.

'Don't be, it's only me.' He placed his hand at my seat's headrest. I could smell his aftershave. Potent and masculine. He was wearing a pair of dark denim jeans, trendy Armani trainers, and a plain black jumper with a white polo neck collar sticking out from it. I had never seen him look so casual, but I liked it.

'So, where are we going?' I asked curiously.

'Aha, that's the question. It's only up the road but trust me, you're about to get sweaty.' He raised his eyebrows suggestively, and my nervous belly returned with a vengeance.

Oh no, he thinks we're going to have sex, and I have the hairiest fanny in the world. Play it cool, play it cool.

'I don't get sweaty on a first date, Tom,' I replied, giggling and blushing.

He stared into my eyes briefly. 'I'm sure you could make an exception, Zara.' The car journey continued as

I made small chat nervously staring out the window in apprehension until he finally announced, 'We're here.'

I paused and looked around; we were still in the city centre but at Blythswood Square, an affluent, up-market area in town.

'C'mon then.' He jumped out of the car, leaned into the back seat, and began rummaging around in a briefcase for something.

I wondered what we were doing. Blythswood did have a beautiful hotel and spa. *Oh shit*, maybe he's taking me for a swim, and I'll have spider legs escaping out. He didn't ask me to bring a swim suit? *Shit*, what if it's a skinny dip!

'Got it, this way.' He gestured down a small street just off the square, and we walked together. 'You look nice, Zara,' he said, checking me out.

'Thanks, so do you,' I replied, unable to take the compliment.

'In here!' He lightly gripped my forearm and pulled me towards a large sandstone building. It was beautiful from the outside with ten stone steps leading up to a grand entrance. I walked up behind Tom while he rustled about with many keys, looking up, admiring the other buildings on the road.

'Here we go, after you.' He opened the large, heavy door to a beautiful white hallway. As I entered, the penny dropped, and I realised where he had taken me.

'So, this will be your clinic?' I asked, still staring around the beautiful building we were standing in.

'It will. Welcome to Ageless, Zara.'

'Ageless. I like it.' I smiled briefly at him, still admiring the high ceilings and the elaborate cornicing carved from decades before.

'Let me take you on a tour—follow me.' He was like a child eager to show me his project, and it was awe-inspiring. This clinic was more than double the size of Raj's shop. He was walking around, pointing expressively, explaining his ideas of expensive chandeliers and high-value artwork he was investing in. Individualise, on the other hand, was beautiful but minimalistic, and I'm pretty sure Ikea was the most expensive place Raj went for décor.

'So this is clinic room one, then you walk into here and clinic room two.' My eyes were examining every inch of the enormous rooms, imagining how luxurious they would look once Tom had finished them. 'So are you working with someone else too?' I asked, wondering why he needed such large spaces.

'Yes, an amazing Doctor Finn is starting too.' He smiled. 'What do you think?'

'I honestly love it, Tom. It's so impressive. And so extravagant.'

'Extravagant? You have no idea, this is just the shell.' His deep voice echoed throughout the empty building. 'There's more.' He opened a set of double doors, and another sizeable white room appeared. In the centre was a picnic blanket and a bottle of champagne.

'Oh shit, sorry, I must have left that there last night, forgive me,' he teased.

'This is nice!' I smiled, pushing his arm slightly. I hadn't been expecting such a gesture.

'You get comfy, have some champagne. I want you to pick your favourites, okay?' He walked over to a large pile of wallpaper samples while I sat on the blanket.

'I'm murder with these types of things, Zara. I want this place to look expensive, perhaps some black and gold—everything must be extra. Designer wallpaper, curtains, sofas, et cetera. This will be completely high-end. What do you think?'

I had no idea what to think. I had never seen Tom so enthusiastic about anything and felt honoured that he wanted my advice, but I couldn't help but feel guilty for Raj losing Tom and what looked like potentially half his business.

'I mean, I'm impressed. A little lost for words, it's all so flamboyant. You must have planned this for such a long time.' I didn't even think Tom was listening as he was being distracted by each detail, eager to share it with me.

'Pick the ones you like.' He passed me over a pad with some of the wallpaper samples. Each one was incredibly thick and heavy; some of the pieces felt like leather.

As I flipped them over, I saw that the price was on the back of each sheet: £155 per roll. *What the fuck?* I dreaded to think how expensive this project would be with the sheer height of the ceilings. I scrutinised each one, picking out my favourites.

'I love this one.' I held up an intense emerald-green sample that had an art deco design with gold trim around the dramatic edge.

'Oh, yes! I loved that one too, I was thinking of that in the bathroom with some exotic plants?'

I smiled. He seemed relieved to get all of this off his chest and have someone to share it with.

'That will be an expensive bathroom, Tom.' I laughed.

'Tell me about it.' He came over to where I was sitting on the blanket and looked down at me, smiling. His perfect eyes were bright with excitement.

'I hope you don't mind coming here, I was just desperate to share it with someone.' He was staring directly into my eyes, and I wasn't taking any information in, just sheerly mesmerised by him.

'I don't mind. I love it here. It's going to be amazing, Tom,' I replied, trying to look up at him but blushing as I did.

'Please don't say anything to Ash about this, Zara—I can't deal with more animosity with Raj. He knows I'm moving on, but I don't think he realises it's my own company and only a stone's throw away from his.' He pushed the palms of his large hands against his forehead.

'I won't,' I said, even as my heart began to feel heavy. *God, poor Raj.* I totally understood why he would be upset. Surely Tom could have gone to the other end of Glasgow at least? But I didn't want to add to Tom's worries and ask questions, so I decided to be supportive instead.

'Thank you.' Tom smiled and knelt down on the blanket.

My anxious heart began to beat faster as he started edging towards me. We were facing one another, and I could smell him more powerfully than ever. He began crawling over my legs, coming towards me, but he paused before he reached my face. We both smiled. He closed the distance between us, placing his soft, warm lips on mine. I shut my eyes, feeling the blood pulsing through my clit. The kiss deepened, his large muscular arms supporting his weight as he held himself a few inches off my body. I wanted him more than ever. He gently moved my tongue around his mouth, and I felt as if he was hypnotising me with every turn. He teased me occasionally, biting on my lip, reminding me that this was not a dream. When I thought the kiss was about to end, I pushed into him, begging him for more.

He began groaning as he kissed me more passionately. I felt one of his large, wandering hands slowly stray down my torso. I gasped as he gently brushed by my nipples. He proceeded to get lower until he was rubbing my trembling legs. My body felt stiff as I was tensing my muscles to begrudgingly keep my legs closed. He stopped and smiled at me. His smile looked cheeky. He opened my legs and began rubbing in between my thighs, stroking my vagina. My underwear was getting wetter with every hard rub. I could tell he was getting more excited as we locked lips again, when suddenly I remembered I hadn't shaved my fanny. *Shit!* I wanted him more than ever right now. My forehead was sweating, and my body was thirsty. Still, I somehow reluctantly broke away from the kissing and started to giggle.

'Wowwww, this is going too fast, Tom.' Who was I kidding? I was desperate for a good pounding but

I had to pretend to be classy with every inch of my exceptionally horny body.

Tom smiled and slid off me, sitting up. 'Really, Zara? You drive me crazy. We're both adults here. Why not?' His large eyes were full of mischief, and I wanted to join him desperately. Still, I didn't want our first time to be overshadowed by him struggling through a forest to find the opening to my secret garden.

'I mean, of course I want to, but not so quickly,' I replied, pulling down my dress and securing the premises in case he decided to undertake a second attack.

'Have you not shaved, Zara, is that it?' He looked at me disappointedly.

What the fuck, can this cunt read my mind.

'What?' I was lost for words. He must have felt the bristly Brillo pad escaping through my pants. The blood was rushing from my clit to my face at an alarming rate. I felt incredibly warm, trying to deny the truth.

'Why would you think that? I always keep a tidy vagina.' *Jesus, I'm such a liar. He obviously knows. This will be me officially dumped*, I thought.

'No, I'm just saying I know some girls who need to be completely bald to go to the next stage, whereas right now, I would happily poke a hole in that wall and shag it. You have got me very hard, Zara.'

He raised his eyebrows, and I automatically looked at his jeans. I could see how aroused he was, and I wanted to feel him inside of me. He reached over, grabbed my hand and started gently rubbing his bulging jeans. His dick felt thick, and I wanted to see it.

'Let me fuck you, Zara,' he whispered, allowing me to continue to explore above his fastened jeans.

God, this is torture.

I looked down and re-evaluated the situation.

I didn't want this to be a quick shag. I wanted to be Mrs Tom Adams. I stopped frisking the sexy surgeon and lay back on the blanket, facing the ceiling. I let out a huge sigh.

'Not today, Tom.'

He also laid back, parallel to me. *Have I fucked this whole thing up?*

Maybe this will be it now, and he'll go fuck someone else. I was anxious and full of regret. Until I felt a warm hand on mine. I looked down to see him pick it up and gently kiss it.

'Whenever you're ready, Zara.'

We spent the rest of the date deciding where his furniture would be in his new clinic. Tom had a fantastic imagination, and his body came alive when he was showing me his ideas. He was full of life, sticking samples to walls and describing sketches of interior design ideas. He kept the champagne flowing for the afternoon and I loved being around his energy. I loved being around him. I loved being part of his dream, as he was now, most certainly, part of mine.

Chapter Thirteen

The days that followed my first date with Tom were filled with fantasising about sex, taking numerous over-filtered selfies and staring at my phone, pathetically counting how many minutes he was taking to respond. Overall, he was good at replying; his read receipts were on, which I came to realise was a good indication that he was not a fuckboy. I spent a lot of time popping out to the shop, continually purchasing batteries for my favourite vibrator, trying to combat my rampant sexual desire to fuck Tom. We would text throughout the afternoon, exchanging our daily updates; he would describe life-changing surgeries he was part of whereas I filled him in on Khloe's latest dilemma in *Keeping Up with the Kardashians* with a handful of pickled onion Monster Munch scattered across my chest. We phoned every night before bed and it was never long before some sexual innuendoes were slyly traded, leaving us both turned on and wanting more.

We hadn't worked together at the clinic since our date but had arranged to go for dinner on the Thursday night before our shift together on Friday. It couldn't come quick enough. He asked me to stay at his that night, which could only mean one thing. Sex!!!

On the evening of the date, I was more ready than ever before. I was shaved from my tash to my toes. I had plucked my right hairy nipple and chosen the smallest silk thong and bra set I could find. My black hair was straight down like a Russian dominatrix. I decided on a super short satin cream dress with ruffles at the sides that disguised my muffin top nicely. My legs were bronzed and my makeup was on. I felt confident.

Tom was picking me up at seven, and around half six I started stretching around my flat in preparation for the only physical activity I would willingly participate in. I felt like a fucking contortionist, forcing my legs up over my shoulder, giving myself a good warm-up.

I had my nineties RnB music on with a gin in my hand when my buzzer went. I glanced out the window and saw Tom's car outside. My overnight bag was ready and waiting at the door with my work clothes packed for the following day.

'Hello, Doctor,' I answered, trying my best to sound sexy.

'Zara, it's me. Head down,' Tom replied in a more serious tone.

I slurped the last mouthful of my drink, spritzed some Jo Malone on my neck and up my dress, and headed down the old stone steps to be greeted by Tom. He was standing with his back to me, but turned when he heard the clip-clop of my high heels. He raised his eyebrows, looking impressed.

'Fuck. You look amazing.' He kissed my forehead. 'There's been a change of plan.'

I looked at him in confusion. *Please don't cancel!*

'Is everything okay?' I asked.

'Yes, it's just . . . I ran into an old friend and his wife today, and I happened to mention I was out for a meal tonight, and they've asked to join us. I hope you don't mind?'

'Oh. Eh, no, I don't mind,' I answered, trying my best not to sound disappointed.

'If you do, we could go somewhere else and do a no-show!' He smiled.

'Not at all. Let's do it.' We began walking to his car when I paused. 'I do think I should change for dinner with your friends though. I look like a prostitute.' I glanced down at my outfit in disgust.

Tom reached out, held my chin, and moved it upward to look at him.

'That's why I like it so fucking much,' he said. He pulled me in till our bodies were pressing, and we kissed passionately outside my flat. I was on my tiptoes with heels on, trying to match his tall frame. I could feel my dress ride up at the back, and Tom's hands were all over me.

'Get in,' he demanded with a slap of my arse.

I giggled like a teenager and got in his car. My eyes followed him in the mirror as he circled round to the driver's side, and as he opened his door, the light inside shone on his clean white shirt with a black blazer. He had some stubble which now had a shine from my lip gloss, and he was staring at me intently.

'I can't wait to get you home.' He moved his large, warm hand up my smooth thighs, rubbing directly on my underwear. This time I allowed him to, keeping my legs open for him to feel every part of me. My body was squirming as he teased me.

'Do you like that, baby?' He positioned his body towards me with his mouth whispering in my ear. With every groan he made, I felt goosebumps travel down my quivering body, my nipples felt hard and erect while I nodded in enjoyment.

Suddenly, Tom's phone received a text message through the car's hands-free system, and we both jumped.

'Simon's there.' He rolled his eyes in disappointment and started the engine.

'I don't think I'll be able to keep my hands off you tonight, Zara.'

'I don't think I want you to, Tom,' I replied, tugging my micro dress down to at least cover my fanny. His white teeth shone brightly in the dark, and we set off to Miller & Carter.

We arrived in the city centre and parked outside the clinic, which was only a short walk from the restaurant. I felt nervous meeting Tom's friends, but part of me was excited. Surely he wouldn't introduce me if I was only around for sex? Perhaps this meant something more to him as well.

We walked into the steakhouse and I immediately felt self-conscious. My outfit was entirely over the top. I looked like I should be going to the Savoy, not a fancy restaurant. We continued walking through the grand entrance, Tom's hand on my lower back, and we paused, waiting to be led to our table.

Tom squeezed my shoulders. 'Are you okay?'

I must have looked every bit as uncomfortable as I felt.

'I'm good. I feel very naked, though.'

He laughed and took off his blazer and wrapped it around my shoulders.

'You have no idea how much I love that dress, and I can't wait to pull it off you tonight,' he said quietly.

Still, my face went red with embarrassment in case anyone passing by could hear him.

'Tom, Tom.'

From the midst of the restaurant, an overweight, balding man waved to us. Tom walked over to the table, with me following anxiously behind. Both men shook hands, and I watched Tom greet the woman sitting at the table.

'Simon, Anne, this is Zara,' Tom said.

'Hello, lovely to meet you both,' I said as Simon came over and kissed my cheek. I waved across the table to Anne as she nodded back.

Tom pulled my seat out chivalrously and sat down beside me. I decided to keep his jacket on for a bit longer. Anne was dressed in a floor-length Aztec dress. She had ice-white hair and a solemn face, and Simon wore a pair of brown cords with a matching jacket. He seemed older than her and from first impressions appeared to be a lot more friendly. She was exceptionally poised, and while the men made small talk about their jobs, we sat in silence, examining the menu.

'So, how did you two meet then?' Simon asked, kindly breaking the silence between us.

'We work together.' I smiled at Tom as he nodded in agreement, glancing down the menu.

'Oh, at the hospital?' Anne chirped up in her posh West End accent.

'Oh no, in the clinic. I work on the reception desk.' I was about to elaborate when I felt a hand begin to sneak up my thigh, and lost concentration; I quickly grabbed Tom's hand with mine and gave it a squeeze. I could see him smirk to himself as he was discreetly trying to get out of my grip.

'What about you guys? How do you all know each other?' I asked, still deciding what I was going to order.

Tom let out a laugh.

'Well, Simon and I went to uni together. He now lectures medicine at the university, and Anne is one of the senior charge nurses at the hospital too, so we see each other quite often. We've known each other for years.'

'Yes, many, many years, Tom. Probably before you were born, Zara.' She grinned.

Our conversation was interrupted by the waitress. 'Are you ready to order?'

A few nods later, our fillet steaks were ordered, and the drinks had arrived. I was so grateful for another item on the table I could fidget with.

'Tell me, Tom, how do you find the consultants in the Royal?' Simon asked.

The three of them chatted and laughed while I smiled politely, sipping away at my gin and pretending

I knew the people they were gossiping about. I could feel myself getting slightly tipsy as I had nothing else but my drink to keep me entertained.

'So, Zara, do you get facial treatments? Filler and whatnot?' Anne asked, finally including me in the conversation. But her question surprised me.

'No, I don't. Well, not yet,' I answered, smiling across the table to her.

'Not yet?' she asked abruptly.

'Well, I'm still young, but I'll definitely get some when I need it,' I replied politely and sipped my drink.

She laughed. 'You certainly are young, yes. Never too young for Thomas though, eh?' Anne smiled at her husband as the table fell quiet.

What the fuck was this bitch's problem? I glanced at Tom, who was giving Anne a warning stare.

'Anne, forgive me, but have you ever had any work done?' Tom asked.

'You know I haven't, Tom. I certainly won't either,' she replied, shocked at the question.

'Zara, if Anne came into the shop and you wanted to enhance her beauty, what would you recommend?' He placed his hand on my knee and gestured me to go on.

I started to laugh at the awkwardness while everyone at the table waited on my input.

'Ehh . . . What, really?'

'Yes, on you go. I'm intrigued,' Anne said as she sat back in her chair with her arms folded. I also sat back analysing her face shape. She did have a lot of movement when she spoke, and would totally benefit from some anti-wrinkle injections but I felt unsure how to inform her with such an audience. I paused and looked at the group egging me on.

'Okay, so I would start with some Botox, three, maybe four areas for the lines around your forehead and eyes. The middle frown line in the centre on your brow is a little deeper, so you would need filler to even that out. You have perfect lips and a very straight nose, I wouldn't touch them. But to give your face more structure, I would recommend some cheek filler—not a lot, just to add some definition.' I glanced at Tom, who began to clap and laugh as Simon made a face at Anne in an attempt to make her smile.

'Bravo, eh. So Raj lets his receptionists do the consultations?' Anne snapped back.

'Just this one, she's special.' Tom winked and placed his hand back at the top of my thigh.

Our meal arrived just in time. I'd ordered a medium steak, triple-cooked chips and peppercorn sauce, and I began devouring it immediately, sloshing it all down with as many gins as I could order. I was nearing the end of my dinner when I excused myself to go to the bathroom.

'I'll walk with you. I'm needing the little boys' room too,' Tom added, dabbing his napkin off his perfectly juicy lips. We headed to the bathroom and stood outside in the hallway.

'I'm sorry if you're having a shitty night, Zara, I should have told you Anne could be a complete arsehole.' He ran his hand through the front of my hair, moving it out of my face.

'I think she hates me. I don't know what her problem is,' I replied, shrugging.

'I'm sorry, I should have told you—I was engaged to her sister many years ago. We split up amicably, but she seems to hold a grudge.'

I was speechless. I couldn't believe he had left such vital information out. Still, years had passed, it was no excuse for her to treat me so badly tonight. How could Tom have kept that from me. I suddenly realised there was so much about him that I didn't know.

'I did like how you noticed that disastrous line on her forehead. I've told her to get that fixed for years.' He laughed and put his hands on my shoulders.

'Oh, come on, Zara, smile. It's almost time to take you home.' He came closer and whispered in my ear, 'I want those little panties off.'

I began to smile and looked up into his playful eyes.

'You have some serious making up to do, Thomas.'

I pulled away from him and entered the ladies' bathroom.

Sitting in the cubicle, I replayed Anne's frostiness towards me. *What a bitch.* I wondered what her sister looked like or if I could somehow get her to name-drop her so I could run through her social media. Why was I letting this bitch upset me? I was determined not to let her ruin my night.

The toilet was spinning as I had overindulged in my alcohol quota, and suddenly my thoughts turned to sex as I could smell Tom's scent off his blazer still draped around my shoulders. I wiped myself then had an idea. *You can't wait to get my pants off eh, Tom?* I pulled my underwear off, slipping it down past my golden thighs, I then held the tiny thong in my hand, thoroughly examining it in the light. It looked clean. I gave it a little sniff; it smelt okay. I walked out of the bathroom, commando style, gripping my under-wear in my hand tightly. Tom was waiting patiently for me in the corridor outside. We started walking back to the table.

'Tom,' I called out.

He was slightly in front and turned around briefly. We were almost at the table.

'Yes?'

'Here you are.' I passed him the underwear discreetly.

He glanced at his hand. His eyes bulged and he began to laugh loudly. I overtook him and sat back down at the table.

'Is that what I think it is?' he whispered into my ear as he took his seat next to me.

'You said you wanted them off. They're off,' I replied, giggling.

Simon and Anne were chatting to one another, looking over curiously at us, whispering like teenagers. Tom slipped my underwear into his pocket.

'Simon, Anne. It has been a real pleasure. But we have to go,' Tom announced.

'But you haven't even had a coffee,' Simon said.

'I know, I know, Simon, and I'm sorry. But some-thing has erm . . . come up.' Both Tom and I burst into laughter while Anne tutted, unimpressed.

'Shall we?' Tom turned to me, and I nodded in agreement.

It was the happiest I'd been all evening, and I had a feeling it was about to get better. I stood up to adjust my dress and gather my things.

'Oh shit, let me get this,' Tom pleaded with Simon. He stood up and began digging into his trouser pocket to retrieve his wallet, only to bring out my stringy white thong entangled with it.

My mouth opened wide. Simon and Anne tried to hide their shock. Tom's face went red.

'Ahh, well, now you understand the urgency. I can only apologise. Anne, I will see you at work. Simon, keep in touch.' Tom placed money on the table to cover the meals.

'Erm . . . lovely to meet you, Zara,' Simon answered, smiling as he admired me up and down.

'You too, and you, Anne, see you.'

Tom took my hand and began leading me from the restaurant as we sniggered.

Outside he said, 'You are fucking filthy, Zara!'

He pulled me enthusiastically down the street towards the car. I was struggling in my heels a little, quickly moving through the dark streets in an attempt to follow him closely. We continued cutting through the busy city, and I could feel the late-night wind ride up my skirt, hitting my naked vagina. Tom continued like a man on a mission until we reached his car.

'Get in then,' he demanded. His sudden lack of manners shocked me, but I couldn't help but like it.

I opened my own car door and sat down on the seat. He looked at me for a few seconds and licked his middle finger, then pulled my legs open wide and stuck his finger deep inside me.

He leaned over, whispering in my ear, 'Do you like that, you dirty girl?' He was pulling his fingers in and out of me like he was decoding WikiLeaks. Still, my body felt sensational, weak, and unlike I had ever felt before. He was rubbing my clit, not caring if any passers-by could see through the tinted windows, and I was allowing him. After fingering me aggressively, he stuck his fingers in my mouth to suck.

'You've wanted this so bad, haven't you, Zara?'

I was nodding in agreement, feeling overwhelmed but intrigued about what else was to come. He continued stroking my clit. My legs were trembling, and my body felt stiff to the seat until I suddenly turned warm and tingly and began to cum. When he felt me cum, he kissed me passionately, keeping his fingers inside of me. I was groaning and jerking as he continued to play with my clit. Finally, he stopped and smirked.

'Time to get you home. Now.'

Chapter Fourteen

Tom drove towards the West End of the city like Lewis Hamilton and parked his car opposite Kelvingrove Park.

'This is us.' He pointed to a large period sandstone building.

'Wow, best location in the city,' I said.

'You better believe it; would you like to see inside?' He winked and got out of the car to open my door.

I fumbled about for a second, gathering my overnight things that had scattered around his car from driving, then followed him inside. The impressive building was the end block of the iconic Kelvingrove strip. He opened the private entrance and kindly took my bag out of my hands.

'After you.' His deep voice echoed in the stairwell.

'So well-mannered, Thomas, thank you,' I teased as I began walking upstairs.

'Who says I'm well-mannered? I just love this view of your arse.'

I looked back, rolling my eyes at him.

'One more floor up, keep going.' We reached the top floor, and Tom opened the door to his large open-plan home. It looked newly refurbished but still had those periodic statements I loved; the living area still had the traditional fireplace standing proudly in the centre surrounded by modern artwork, and the skirting boards were three times the size of mine but had been sanded down and painted. The kitchen and dining areas were behind the living space, so everything was flowing and open. Subtle lighting glowed behind each appliance. The entire place was white and smelt of fresh linen.

'This is beautiful, Tom, it's so clean!' I was spinning around the vast space.

'I'm afraid I have a cleaner to thank for that, but yeah, it's been a lot of work to get this place the way I like it. Downstairs, on the other hand, is like a building site. Would you like a glass of wine?' He walked through to the kitchen area and opened a large wine cooler, scanning the selection of bottles he had purchased.

'I'm good with water, thanks, I've had a bit much. What's downstairs?' I asked, still gazing around the features of his immaculate home.

'I bought this place first, about five years ago, then a year later the middle floor went up for sale, so I bought that too. I didn't want some arsehole neighbour moving in. Then a couple of months ago, I bought the downstairs apartment. I still haven't got round to that one yet.'

He poured some bottled water into a glass and joined me in the living area, handing me the drink.

'So, you own the entire building?' I responded, still processing the information.

'Yes, I guess I do,' he laughed as he offered a cheers with his water.

'What are you going to do with it all?'

'Well, I haven't really decided yet. I could turn it into one large home or lease out the bottom floors when they're renovated.'

'You could have put your clinic at the bottom. This location would be ideal,' I said.

'I like my clinic in the city centre where the competition is,' he said, laughing loudly.

He approached me. His face was incredibly close to mine, and I could feel his breath on my skin.

'Would you like to see my bedroom now?'

I leaned forward to kiss him, but he pulled back, smiling, grabbed my hand and led me away. The room he took me to was dark compared to the others. He switched on the sidelight, revealing navy walls and décor just as immaculate as the other rooms. A large bed centred the bedroom, neatly dressed in designer bedding and pillows.

I suddenly felt nervous. *This is it. No turning back now.*

I took a deep breath and unzipped my dress. Tom was staring at me, subtly biting his lip as he leaned against the wall. I stood there with only my bra on.

'Turn around for me, Zara,' he ordered.

I did as I was instructed and turned around slowly, folding my arms, trying to hide my stomach. I felt incredibly self-conscious as he observed my every move.

'You're beautiful. Stop folding your arms.'

He walked towards me, examining every inch. When he reached me, he kissed my neck, gently running his hands down my body as he did so. He stopped at my bra, and with one flick unclipped it. He began rubbing my nipples, making them hard as I groaned, then suddenly squeezed them tight, making me flinch.

'Am I hurting you?' I nodded, smiling curiously at him as he whispered, 'Good.' He moved down to my stomach and slowly put his fingers inside me for a second time. 'You're still wet, baby.'

I nodded again, feeling too overwhelmed to speak. He pushed me onto the bed then slowly pulled off his shirt. I took in his tanned, toned body, the dark hair at his chest.

Next, his trousers and boxers were lying on the floor, and he joined me on the bed, naked. I couldn't help but stare at his penis. It was rock hard, medium-sized but had a huge girth. I was finally ready to put it inside me. Lying side by side, we started kissing, getting hotter by the second. I put my hand out to feel his dick, but he stopped me.

'Not yet,' he muttered.

Then he slid his fingers inside me over and over again. He was moving his hands so quickly, I wasn't sure what was going on, but I was enjoying it. My legs were jerking and my breathing became heavy, but he continued like he was solving a fucking Rubik's Cube in my cervix when suddenly—boom!—an almighty release of fluid came flooding out.

Jesus! What the fuck.

'Aaaaahhhhh.' I felt warm, tingly and euphoric as I screamed loudly, releasing the biggest orgasm.

'Oh my God!' I screamed.

'I knew you were a squirter!' he whispered proudly into my ear.

I officially was a squirter, wow! Aka a dirty bastard. I couldn't believe it. My time for celebrating was cut short as Tom mounted me and slipped his dick inside my over-lubricated vagina. As soon as he was inside, he began pounding in and out. His eyes were shut, and he was breathing heavily, squeezing my tits as he did so.

'Are you ready to suck it, Zara?'

I didn't have time to answer as he leapt off my body, knelt up on the bed, pulling my face forward and shoving his dick in my mouth. He started fucking my face, frantically pulling in and out. I could feel the tears stream down my face from holding back my gag. He was running his hands through my hair, I could taste him at the back of my throat, and suddenly I felt an explosion of cum. I reluctantly took one for the team and swallowed it as the hot lava spurted out, not wanting to disappoint him and cause any mess in his pristinely clean home.

'Wow, Zara. That was wonderful,' he said, panting.

He lay back on the bed with his arms wide. I joined him and cuddled in.

'That *was* wonderful,' I added.

The time passed and I felt our warm, sweaty bodies turn cold.

'I'm going to have a quick shower before bed. Feel free to use the bathroom here, I'll use the main one,' Tom said. He kissed my forehead, and I watched his perky bum strut confidently out of the room.

I gathered my things together for bed, carefully unpacking a matching set of silky shorts and top, then retrieved my toothbrush from the bottom of my bag. I waddled through to the en suite, trying not to empty my jizz on the expensive bedroom carpet. The en suite was so incredibly bright and spacious that it took my eyes a few seconds to adjust. I examined the spotlessly clean room with a smile on my face. *Wow, I could seriously get used to living here.*

I sat down on the toilet, gently perching my tender fanny at the side of the pan to minimise any squelching noises. I walked over to the sink to wash my hands and gave myself a fright as I looked in the mirror. The light showed up every pore and blemish on my face, which was now red and excoriated from all the kissing. *Great, a fucking stubble rash.* I carefully dabbed a wet cloth on it and headed in for a shower.

As I stood under the hot water, I replayed the magical moments that had just happened. *He really is the full package.* The house, the job, the looks, the personality and the sex. *This is it for me, I know it.* I couldn't take the grin off my face when I realised: I had to fix myself in time for bed. I scrubbed my fanny, making sure it smelt fresh just in case he decided to go down for a little nibble later tonight. My mouth tasted like dick, and I didn't want anything to jeopardise more kissing so after my shower I rummaged around the bathroom cupboards, searching for some toothpaste.

Opening the middle cabinet, I not only found a tube of Colgate but behind it a pink bobble and small stud earrings. They were carefully placed at the back of the shelf, and on seeing them I immediately felt sick.

Whose the fuck are these?

My heart froze and my body went heavy with shock. Was it too early on to ask about this?

I could hear Tom moving around the flat and began brushing my teeth. I finished up, closed the cabinet, and returned to the bedroom. He joined me on the bed with a glass of water.

'You need to replace those fluids you've lost, Zara, that was some squirt!' he said, handing me the glass.

'Thanks.' I smiled politely, taking the glass from him.

'Are you okay?' he asked, putting his arm around me.

'Yeah, course,' I lied. I wanted to ask him, but it was none of my business.

This was only our second date. God knows how many people he was seeing besides me.

'Come over here then.'

I laughed as he pulled me in towards him.

It was the first time in my life I felt special and truly happy. Maybe if I asked him, that would all change. Maybe I didn't want to know the answer at all. I'm sure there could be a reasonable explanation for the items in the bathroom, it could be the cleaners? Or his sisters? I snuggled up for the night, wide-eyed and full of questions as I lay beside the man I had dreamt about since the moment I met him.

Chapter Fifteen

I woke the next morning with the light peering through the wooden blinds. Remembering where I was, I turned around to find Tom out of bed. Footsteps came from the other room. *Excellent, at least I have time to sort myself out.*

I stood up and examined the master bedroom in more detail, now that my brain wasn't clouded by sex. He had large mahogany furniture and a heavy circular mirror opposite the bed. I ran my finger over the spotless table, which felt incredibly smooth and expensive. Careful not to make any noise, I opened his wardrobe to find a coordinated colour system, with cufflinks and watches sitting on a glass shelf within. *No signs of female clothes, phew.*

Next, I headed to the window and pulled the blinds to the side, eager to admire the view from his room. It was stunning. His home faced directly onto Kelvingrove Park, which was already bustling with morning commuters. Above the trees, I could see the top tiers of the art gallery, only slightly visible. The weather was dry and bright, and for a city flat, the view was magnificently green.

'Zara, are you up?' Tom called out from the other room.

I jumped back from the blinds and bolted towards the mirror to fix myself before welcoming him.

'Yep, just. I'll be out in a minute.'

I threw my hands through my sweaty, tuggy hair, wincing as I came across some unwelcome knots. I glanced at myself in the mirror. *Fuck.* My red stubble rash had turned into a large scab on my chin. *No, no, no!* I looked like I had the fuckin' plague. *Shit.* I frantically started trying to pick the scab off, but flinched in pain when I touched it. *Okay, too sore, plan B.* I marched over to my overnight bag and began raking through the contents. Some cheap foundation and a concealer stick would have to do the trick. I started applying it to my face like a bucket of wallpaper paste and only succeeded in making it look like someone had chucked a cornflake at me. I admitted defeat as Tom called out again, and sheepishly walked through to the kitchen.

'Morning.' I was holding my chin in my hands.

'Good morning. Breakfast?' Tom's kitchen worktops were packed full of fresh foods, the chopping board piled with cherry tomatoes and diced onion. A plate sat next to the hob with grated cheese, and he was frying an omelette while sipping on a protein shake.

'Wow, this is some breakfast. I'm okay with a cup of tea, though, thanks.' I smiled up at him.

'Why are you holding your chin?' Tom sniggered, looking at me with curiosity.

'You gave me a stubble rash, Tom.'

'Ha, let me have a look then. God, maybe I should have shaved before our date.' He walked towards me and held my temples, carefully examining my face. Then he scrunched his face up, looking disgusted.

'Fuck, the makeup's made it worse. As long as it's not impetigo.' Tom shuddered at the thought, and I felt my face turn as red as his tomatoes.

'It's not impetigo, and I had to try to cover it up— we have work soon.'

'Put some Vaseline on it. There should be some in the bedroom.'

I smiled at my handsome doctor's advice then made my way back to his bedroom and found the Vaseline sitting on the bedside table. After applying a generous layer, I shoved on the black jeans I'd packed along with a tight top and a shirt hanging over for my shift that morning.

'Zara.' Tom was shouting from the kitchen again.

'Yes?' I reappeared, laughing at his demands, fully dressed this time.

'Your tea. That was quick.'

'Yeah, we'll need to leave in like twenty minutes.'

'Are you sure you don't want anything to eat?'

'No, thanks, I'm not a big omelette fan. I'm good with a cuppa.'

'There are other things besides omelette you know. What do you normally have?'

'Hmmm, occasionally toast, but honestly, I don't normally eat in the mornings.'

I didn't want to admit that my most common break-fast dishes consisted of left-over Chinese or a roll and

Thai sweet chilli crisps when I was standing opposite Gordon fuckin' Ramsey.

'Okay, okay.' He came over to me. 'You look lovely today, Zara. Ah, glad you've put the Vaseline on.'

'Yeah, I did. And thank you. You look very handsome too.' I smiled, looking up at him as he approached me. 'Tom?'

'Yes?'

'Why do you keep the Vaseline at your bedside?'

He roared, laughing, and walked out of the room to get dressed. *Ewww. That answers that question.* Suddenly my chin felt violated.

I waited on Tom, drinking my black tea while flicking through my phone. *No messages from Ashley today, that's weird.* I was excited to see the dynamics in the clinic when Tom and I were together. How would he act in front of clients or when we were alone in the staff room? I wasn't sure how I'd be either.

'Let's go, Zara,' Tom called out from behind me, and I watched him spray the fanny-tingling aftershave over his face and neck. I sat back in a daze, admiring him and inhaling the spicy scent as it passed by my nostrils.

'Okay, I'm coming.'

I followed Tom out of the flat and we headed downstairs.

'You smell amazing,' I said, unable to keep it in as the scent wafted around me, tantalising.

'So do you.'

'Me? I haven't brought my perfume or had a shower since last night,' I admitted.

'That's what I mean; you smell filthy.'

'Tom!' I laughed, forgetting he didn't have neighbours.

'It's fine, neither have I. I'll be smelling your pussy off me all day.'

Oh. My. God. I blushed with embarrassment—*what a dirty bastard.* As we continued down the stairs I subtly sniffed away at myself, wondering – did I really smell filthy?

We walked to his car before making the ten-minute journey across town towards work.

'Do you want me to go in before you?' I asked in the car.

'It's only Ashley, and I'm perfectly aware that she'll know within ten minutes what happened last night, so I don't think there's any need, is there?' He smiled over at me, and I blushed.

'That's true.'

As we approached the clinic, prowling for a parking space, Tom's finger started wagging as he spotted a car parked up on the street.

'That's Raj's new car. What's he doing here?'

I shrugged, but Tom seemed anxious about him being at work.

We eventually got parked around the corner, and Tom walked on before me while I was still loosening my seat belt.

'C'mon, Zara,' he ushered.

I still had my overnight bag to carry and felt weighed down trying to rush behind him. We walked into the clinic to find Raj and Ashley looking severe at the desk.

'Morning,' I called out, smiling to them both.

'Are you seriously fucking leaving, Tom?' Raj walked across the floor, pointing his finger. 'Tell me this is all bullshit.'

'What? What are you on about?' Tom stuttered.

'I had a client yesterday who said she received a text message from you last week to say you would be leaving next month and setting up shop at Blythswood?'

Tom stood speechless, shaking his head.

'When I asked you a couple of weeks ago about leaving, you told me it was only an idea and it would be years down the line. But then you go and steal confidential records to poach my fucking clients. You're supposed to be my best mate.'

I looked over to Ashley, who was shaking her head in disgust.

'Ohh, piss off, Raj. It was a couple of my regulars. Don't pretend you wouldn't do it either. They're my fucking clients.'

'Well, why don't you take your shit, leave now and go set up your fancy fucking clinic,' Raj snapped. His face was red and he looked furious, he was getting closer and closer to Tom's face with every word.

'Guys, please, stop this. Clients will be arriving any minute,' I pleaded.

'You're right, Zara. Get him out of here. I don't want to fucking look at him again.'

'Ha, gladly. I was the one who put this place on the fucking map, Raj, and you know it. This is just pocket money for me.' Tom shrugged his shoulders, then looked at me and Ash.

'Ladies, I apologise, and I will speak to you both soon.' He glanced over to me, rubbing his forehead, and walked out.

'Aye, don't count on it,' Ashley snapped.

Tom laughed as he pushed out of the clinic. The door slammed shut behind him.

'Raj, I'm so sorry. Are you okay?' I asked.

Ashley looked at me disappointedly.

'I'm sorry you girls were a part of that,' Raj said, bent over the desk. 'I can't believe it. Please, can you contact all his clients today and tell them he won't be back. I'll work an extra day and late night to cover the extras if they're happy with me doing there treatments. Please. I'll stay today, and we can sort this mess out.'

Ashley put her hand on his shoulder, consoling him as his eyes watered. Eventually, he went through to the clinic room to prep for the first client, leaving Ashley and me alone. She marched over to stand behind the desk, her stilettos the only sound she made.

'What the fuck?' I said.

She ignored me, just attempted to raise her eyebrows, which looked difficult to do with the amount of Botox she had in her forehead.

'What's up with you, Ash?'

'You knew, didn't you? You didn't even look surprised when Raj just pulled him up.'

'What?' *Oh God, I feel sick*. My heart began to pound heavily.

'You knew he was leaving. You knew he had bought

another clinic and was planning to take Raj's clients, and you didn't say anything?'

'Wait, what?' My neck felt hot, I was turning red and blotchy, and I started to stutter, trying to defend myself.

'Admit it.' I had never seen Ashley so angry. She stood with her hands on her hips, not giving me a chance to explain.

'Okay, I knew he was leaving, yes. But I didn't know anything about the clients, Ash, I swear.'

She tutted and shook her head.

'How can you even look Raj in the eye knowing that you didn't warn him? Fuck, you probably gave him the clients' details. I mean, you're so desperate for him to like you. Maybe you didn't want to tell Raj but at least tell me, Zara. Just because you'll have a new job in a couple of months doesn't mean you fuck this place up. I work here too you know. This is it for me.'

I felt sick, shaky, and unbelievably gutted. *I am a horrible person.* I never thought for one minute that keeping Tom's project to myself would cause so much drama.

'I never knew anything about the clients. I swear. But how can you say that? I'm so, so sorry I didn't tell you, Ash, but it wasn't my secret to tell, that's all . . .'

'Forget it. You're just lucky Raj doesn't know about your weird relationship with Tom, or you'd be out on your arse as well.'

Ashley stormed back across the floor towards the clinic room. I stood trembling, with all my might holding back tears of regret.

What have I done?

The rest of the day, we continued business as usual without any personal chat in between. Raj would come out of the procedure room occasionally for a friendly ear or some support. I felt incredibly two-faced, offering him reassurance while Ashley tutted to herself. I was too anxious to check my phone around her, worried she'd make comments about Tom. At lunch, I snuck into the bathroom, checking if he had messaged to explain all of this. He hadn't.

I concentrated more than I ever had before as I phoned Tom's entire client list and encouraged them to change their slot to Raj instead. I promised he was a more experienced practitioner as he was both the owner and the clinical director of the practice. Most were happy with the swap, but a few had already contacted Tom and wouldn't go elsewhere.

The day was going on, and with a tremendous amount of work complete, Raj approached the desk, amazed.

'Zara, I can't believe you've managed to do all of that in one day. Thank you.'

I smiled at him sympathetically, feeling an overwhelming amount of guilt.

'Don't be silly. That's my job.'

'Come here.' He came behind the desk and gave me a hug.

I closed my eyes tightly, embracing him and wanting to tell him the truth. But I couldn't. Not today.

'What the fuck's that on your chin, by the way? You better not be rubbing impetigo into my good scrubs?'

I started to laugh and hit his arm jokingly.

'It's a dry patch. Made worse with makeup.'

'Ouch. Get some Vaseline on it.'

I couldn't help but smile at him. We closed the clinic together while Ashley walked off with Dave.

Raj waved me off. 'Thanks again for today, Zara.'

I walked home in the cold, dark night. I retrieved my phone to find that Tom had finally sent a message.

What a piss-take. Gutted I can't bend you over in the staff room, that's about the only thing I'll miss there. Hope work wasn't too unbearable.

I slid my phone back into my pocket, not wanting to speak to anyone.

I was torn between my friends and my heart. I didn't know whose side to take, both friends had equal points. I didn't want to fall out with Raj or Ashley, but I also didn't want to break things off with Tom.

This morning had started so perfectly, but was ending with me roaming Glasgow's streets alone, with only the feeling of cold tears trickling down my cheeks for company.

Chapter Sixteen

Ten days of feeling incredibly isolated passed quicker than I imagined. Ashley was still giving me the silent treatment. Even when we were working, she would respond to me only when absolutely necessary by the way of grunts or nods. I found myself helping Raj more with setting up injectables, initial consultations, and participating during his procedures. He was swamped with the extra workload since Tom left, and I felt partly responsible, so anything extra I could do to help him made my conscience ease a little.

I spent a lot of time reaching out to my sister, but she didn't understand. She was the popular one married off early and seemed to have the perfect family life. She tried to support me but only really offered an ear to vent and encouraged me to speak to Ashley. On the other hand, Tom seemed to be the only thing I had that was going well. He had more free time now that the clinic had dismissed him, and most days were spent wrapped around one another's naked bodies. I hadn't had this much sex since, well, ever. My clit resembled a throbbing tinned tomato with all the external rubbing. Still, I managed to battle through it for the sake of my thirsty vagina. I was utterly fascinated with my Sugar Daddy: his chocolate-button eyes, his bright symmetrical smile, his dry sense of humour, his thick dick, and his magic fingers. I was completely and utterly in love, with hardly anyone to tell. I didn't seem to find any other evidence of women in his flat and I felt ridiculous I was even worried over a bobble and a cheap pair of earrings. Things were progressing and I could hear the wedding march ring in my ears whenever I thought of my new man.

On Monday I'd looked forward to meeting Emily for a coffee, desperate to boast about my new excellent relationship while Tom was working. I threw on some blue jogging bottoms with a strappy top and made the short walk to the Wilson Street Pantry at Merchant City. Emily was already waiting for me when I arrived, sipping away on her complimentary water.

'Hey, sis.' I hugged her tightly, happy to see someone who wasn't as involved in all the drama at work.

'Hi, you look nice. Have you lost weight?' Emily checked me up and down, smiling like she was impressed.

'Probably. I'm doing *a lot* of cardio now.'

We started giggling together.

'Sit down, shh.' She looked over her shoulder, still laughing, making sure no one could hear. 'What are you having?'

'I love the scrambled eggs in here,' I said, finally taking a seat.

'Me too. Maybe with cheese or avocado.'

I made a disgusted face.

A young, hippy-looking waitress approached our table. 'Ladies, are you ready to order?'

'Scrambled eggs, toast, avocado, with a latte for me, please.'

'Can I have the same minus the avocado, thanks.'

'Sure, it shouldn't be too long, girls,' she said, collecting our menus and returning them to behind the counter.

'Okay, tell me what's been happening?' Emily asked as soon as we were alone again.

'So I basically have a boyfriend. We're with each other every night, have sex, watch movies, have sex, have dinner, have sex.' I started to blush thinking about him. 'He's so handsome, Emily.'

'I don't doubt it if he has you! So what's his story? Does he want kids? Marriage et cetera?'

'For fuck sake, we've not spoken about any of that yet.'

'You're as well getting that out the way just now. The sooner the better.'

'For God's sake, you're so black and white.'

'And you live in a fantasy!' Emily hit back.

'Hey!' I blurted, taking offence.

'It's true. You're getting carried away and you have no idea what this guy's intentions are.' We paused the conversation for a few serious seconds until Emily rolled her eyes. 'Okay, tell me about the sex.'

'It's amazing. Best sex I've ever had. He does this bizarre thing with his hands though: he like puts a few fingers up me, rummages about for a while then boom—I've squirted like a burst pipe all over him.'

'Oh my God, eww!' Emily burst out laughing. 'He must have got that from his anatomy class because that doesn't sound normal, Zara.'

'It's not. It's like some sort of Harry Potter shit going on, I swear.'

'So no negatives?'

'Hmm. Nope. Well . . . maybe one. But it's not a biggy.'

'Spill.'

I paused for a second while our lattes were placed in front of us.

'He doesn't go down,' I whispered.

'What, like, with his mouth? Like ever?'

'No. He's never ever licked me.'

'I hate guys like that. It's so selfish. When I was pregnant with Leo, Andrew done the same to me for nine months! Wouldn't go down. I was distraught. If I didn't have his child inside me I probably would have filed for divorce.'

'Oh my God, too much info! But why when you were pregnant?'

'He said he was frightened he tickled the baby's toes or something weird. Pure drama queen! So, do you go down on him?'

'Emily, that's disgusting! And, yes, till I have fucking locked jaw.'

'Maybe he's just nervous about it. It's a skilled technique. You should ask him about it?'

'No way! How embarrassing. I just miss it. It's my favourite thing ever. I'm starting to have a complex—worried in case I stink.'

'Yeah, you should check your pH, invest in some Femfresh or something.'

She laughed inconsiderately as our breakfasts were served. I glared at her and picked up my fork.

'What about Ashley?' she asked once she'd calmed down again.

Ping.

I was happy with the interruption as my heart felt heavy the second Ashley's name was mentioned. I scrolled through my phone, reading an email from the university carefully.

'Ahhh, oh my God. I start my final placement on Monday! Ward Seventy-six at the Royal.'

'What? Zara, that's amazing! What kind of ward is it?'

'Surgical receiving!'

'Surgical? Isn't that where Tom works too?'

'Yes. Well, not like confined to one ward, but I'm sure I'll see him there.'

'How long are you there for?'

'Six weeks! God, I'm excited to get back out there.'
I felt the blood swoosh around my body in excitement, I felt ecstatic.

'So, in six weeks, you'll be a fully qualified staff nurse?'

'Yep. Hopefully. Just need to pass this placement!'

'Amazing, Zara. Mum will be buzzing!'

'I can't wait to tell Tom.' I was bopping up and down in my chair, unable to contain myself to one spot.

'I'll tell him tonight actually. He's making me dinner. He's away to an event all weekend for a new skin-tightening procedure he's going to offer at his new clinic.'

'Oh cool, do you think he'd give me a discount?' Emily started pushing her face around, making me giggle.

'Where's he going?'

'Down south somewhere. I know it's sad, but I'm dreading being away from him for so long.'

'You're right, it is sad. Now eat your eggs, you madwoman. They'll be Baltic.' I lifted my cutlery and started nibbling at my scrumptious breakfast,

'So, tell me about the kids and the holidays. What have you all got planned?'

'We booked Turkey again, so plenty of kids clubs to keep them occupied, I can't wait to get away from here. They are out playing most nights around the estate now with their wee pals! You should come see us one night this week?'

'I'd love that!'

I scoffed the rest of my food, eager to walk home and prepare for my evening with Tom.

'Let me get breakfast, Zara. In six weeks, it'll all be on you.'

'God, I know. I won't be able to play the skint student card for much longer!'

Emily left money on the table and we went back out into the sunshine. She had parked outside the café, so we hugged quickly before she got into her car and merged with the mid-morning traffic. I turned for home, walking in the warm weather.

I was excited and nervous at the thought of being back in the hospital. I didn't realise how much I'd missed it till now, but I did. The responsibility seemed real as I was almost qualified and didn't have someone to fall back on, but the pleasure of really making a difference to someone's life outweighed any second thoughts I was having.

I almost pulled my phone out to text Ashley for reassurance, forgetting for a split second that I couldn't. I decided to text Raj instead, determined to keep my secret from Tom until dinner later tonight.

Hey, guess who starts the Royal – surgical receiving on Monday? May need to swap a few of my days at the clinic when I get my hours x

Ping.

Ah, amazing. Plastics are a bit away from that ward, but I will still see you. Almost there, Zara, well done. Swap any shifts you like. R x

Ping.

The ward manager there is a tyrant, but I'm sure you will win her round, R x

I smiled at my friend's optimism and walked through the bright Glasgow streets with ambition, purpose, and, finally, something to look forward to.

Chapter Seventeen

Dinner at Tom's had been arranged for six o'clock. Having only £7 to my name, I decided to get the subway along to his flat, leaving in plenty of time to guarantee us as much quality time together as possible before he left for his event. I hopped on the subway at Buchanan Street and travelled the few stops down the line to Kelvinbridge.

The subway was dark and noisy. I was sure the seat felt wet, and I spent the short journey constantly adjusting myself, making sure I wouldn't dirty my outfit. I felt remarkably overdressed and clean-looking compared to the other commuters, wearing a white floaty midi skirt, a short white top, and a pair of Converse. My stop was called, and with a whiff of hot air and sprinkle of dirt to the back of my throat, I climbed out of the subway and continued my journey along the beautiful, warm, cultured street to Tom's home.

I rang the upstairs buzzer and sprayed some Jo Malone while I waited to be let in, keen to get the subway smell out of my hair.

Buzz.

I let myself in and climbed the stairs. When I got to the top, I found Tom's front door slightly ajar.

'Hi,' I called out, the smell of rich food hitting my nostrils.

'In here.'

I followed Tom's voice to find him in the kitchen, pouring two glasses of champagne. Sitting on top of his white worktops were two large Paesano Pizza boxes.

'Wow, what's all this?'

'I have good news, Zara!' He handed me a champagne glass, briefly kissing my forehead as he passed by.

'Me too!' I said excitedly.

'Okay, my clinic has had the approval with all the necessary bodies and will officially open in two weeks.'

'Oh, amazing! That's so soon, Tom, well done.' I hugged my handsome man proudly.

'Your turn?'

'Ah, yes. As of Monday, I will be starting my final placement—in the Royal!'

'Oh. In the Royal? The Glasgow Royal?' he replied.

'Yea, of course I mean the Glasgow one. I wouldn't be celebrating if it was the Edinburgh Royal. You know I'm not a morning person and that would involve me getting up far too early.' I laughed, but his face remained serious.

'Okay, well done, Zara. Do you know which ward? Medical or surgical?'

'Surgical receiving!' I yelled, raising my glass for a toast.

'Oh.' He paused.

'What's up?' I asked, disheartened, slowly bringing my glass back down to earth.

'Absolutely nothing. Ignore me. I'm sure you'll do great.'

'What is it?' I laughed and took a step back. 'I feel like there's something you're not telling me.'

'It's not that I'm not telling you something, Zara, it's just . . . it's my work. We can't act the way we did in the clinic. I can't be the guy fucking the student.'

'Oh. Okay. I wasn't going to start dry humping your leg during a ward round, you know. I know how to be professional.'

'I'm sorry. Come here.' Tom came closer, embracing me, and I rested my head on his warm chest. 'You took me by surprise. That's all, kid.'

'It's okay, I just thought you'd be excited about it the way I was.'

'Zara, of course I am. It's just a different dynamic. Hey, it might be fun keeping a dirty little secret from the rest of the ward.' He laughed, still hugging me. 'Oh, did you realise whose ward it is?'

'What? No?' I looked up at his serious face.

'It's Anne Murphy's ward. As in, Simon and Anne, who we were out for dinner with?'

'You have *got* to be joking me.' How would I survive six long weeks with the ice queen?

'Nope, runs it like Hitler too. You'll be fine though, you've met her. Come, let's eat.'

'I met her once, Tom, and she hated me.'

'She didn't hate you. But she did see your knickers. Come sit down. Here you are.'

He opened the pizza box, grinning, and for a moment the delicious smell of cheese and red onions distracted me from my thoughts.

We munched away at the pizza, but I couldn't help but feel a heaviness in my chest. *Why wasn't he excited? Was he annoyed that I will be working in the same place?* I didn't want to be anyone's dirty little secret. I wanted people to know I was Tom's girlfriend. I wanted him to elaborate on the subject but I was worried any questions I had about us would push him away.

Instead, we spent the rest of the night watching *Titanic* and sipping on the remainder of the champagne. We cuddled on his sofa with a fleece blanket draped over our legs, me lying in his muscular arms. It wasn't long into the movie before he started twiddling my nipples, pulling them as they grew harder.

'Tom, we have yet to watch a full movie together. Stop.' I was patiently waiting to see Leo pumping Kate in the car scene and didn't want him to ruin my fix.

'Who wants to watch a movie when I can watch you bounce up and down on me?'

I started to laugh.

'Thomas!'

'Or I could always let you watch it, and I could do all the work? How does that sound, babe?'

He slid off the couch to the floor, then knelt in front of me. *Oh yes*, was he hinting he was about to lick me out? My thighs felt moist in anticipation as I lifted my arse slightly, allowing him to pull my pants to the floor. He slid his hand between my thighs.

'You're wet already.'

I nodded guiltily. *Oh, yes I am, baby. I've been waiting for this!*

'Let's get you even wetter then, eh?'

Finally! This was it. I opened my legs willingly, smiling down at the most handsome man kneeling before me. I waited eagerly for his head to move closer to my fanny when, instead, he slid his large, talented fingers inside me, vigorously turning and churning. It began the same as always, a strange, rough movement. I even questioned what he was doing up there as it felt more like he was giving me an internal, a severe, concentrated look on his face. Still, after a couple of minutes, I started panting and groaning, and with a sudden pop, I distributed an overwhelming amount of fluid all over his sofa.

'Oh my God,' I groaned as I came.

'Mmmm, Zara. Was that nice?'

'So nice.' My thighs felt shaky.

He stood up, took his trousers off, and smiled down at me.

'You're going to cost me a fucking fortune in dry cleaning. Look at that sofa.'

I started to blush. 'I'm so sorry.'

'Show me how sorry you are, Zara.' He took my hand and pulled me to my feet, then turned my body around, bent me over the sofa, and with a hard hit, spanked my arse cheek.

'Ohh, Tom, fuck sake!' I gasped.

'You move an inch, you're getting spanked, okay?'

'Hmm . . . Okay.' I was smiling with bubbly confidence, feeling open to a little role-play.

He gently took his dick and slid it inside me. I cringed at the squelch of my super-lubricated vagina as he picked up the pace, getting harder and faster with each thrust. I was grabbing onto the sofa, determined to keep my body upright to avoid a hard spanking.

'Do you like that, you little slut?'

Oh, wow. I certainly did.

'Yes, yes, I do.'

'Do you want Daddy to keep fucking you?'

Oh my God! Did he know that we called him this? My eyes widened as I pretended not to notice his daddy patter.

'Yeah, keep fucking me,' I whispered.

I felt unbelievably horny. His posh English accent made me feel like I was starring in my own porno. I didn't know if it was the champagne or Leonardo on the TV, but I enjoyed the filth. He carried on fucking me until he came powerfully inside me, squeezing his large hands into my hips as he did so.

'Jesus.' He grunted, sliding his semi out of me.

I turned around and kissed his soft lips.

'Water?' he panted, out of breath.

'Yes, thanks, I'm just going to the bathroom.'

I had learned my lesson from Mark and knew to douche immediately after sex now.

'I'll bring it through to the room.' He gestured for me to go, and I tried to look ladylike as I waddled out of the living room and through to his en suite.

I sat on the pan for a while, catching my breath. *Jesus Christ,* he must have had some force behind his ejaculation—nothing was coming out. I bopped up and down on the toilet, encouraging it to fall. *Come on . . . come on . . .* I could hear him switching lights off in the hallway. He'd wonder why I was spending so long in the bathroom. *Come on!!* I squeezed my stomach muscles to help de-gunk, struggling and straining, when suddenly the loudest fanny fart came echoing around the pan and out of the bathroom.

My heart froze. I stopped dead. I closed my legs immediately to try and minimise the sound. But it was too late.

'Zara?' Tom called out.

'Yep?' My face began burning up as I was panicked.

'Did you hear that?' He sounded confused.

'Yes, I heard something.' I was rubbing my forehead, dying of mortification.

'What do you think it was?' he asked curiously.

Do you not know a fucking fanny fart when you hear one!

'A loud bang, I think, maybe something's fallen. Or perhaps they're working on the subway line again?'

'Come quickly. I think some bastard is trying to break in,' Tom said.

No, no, hun, that was just my massive fanny fart, I thought.

I wiped away the remaining jizz and headed out to the bedroom to find a naked Tom holding a baseball bat at his shoulder.

'I think we should call the police. Someone tried on the door,' he whispered. He looked genuinely afraid.

'What? Tom, we can't call the police. Why don't you check out the stairwell, and I'll stay behind you and call them if anyone is there.'

He nodded, too terrified to speak. His naked figure started tiptoeing about the flat like Inspector Clouseau, with me hot on his tail, pretending to go along with him rather than admit the truth: that my vagina is as big as a hippo's yawn. He stood at his front door, gently opening it to avoid any screech that would warn intruders off. I watched on in silence as he checked the staircase from right to left, moving slowly down the steps one at a time like a fucking marine. Any slight move I made, he'd look up and put his finger over his lips, signalling for me to be quiet. Once the area was clear, he returned to the flat.

'They must be away. People know the bottom two flats are empty and think they can try their fucking luck. Look, I'm shaking.' He held out his trembling hands.

'Yeah, God. I thought this was a good neighbourhood too.'

'Zara, it's Glasgow.'

'Yeah, I suppose.' I walked behind him, smirking. How could he mistake a fanny fart for an attempted break-in? I didn't care, as long as he didn't think it was me.

We headed to bed, and I snuggled into Tom, warming up his cold body.

'I'll miss this when I'm away for a few nights,' he murmured into the top of my head.

'Me too,' I said, hugging him tighter. 'We can always call when you're back in the room.'

'Yeah, well, Dr. Finn's coming too. We have lots to sort for the opening party, but I'll be able to drop you a text or two.'

'Aww, okay. I didn't realise you were having a party! That's so exciting.'

'Yes, it's good publicity. Invite the papers et cetera. I've been thinking a lot . . . I'm not sure if I should invite Raj and Ash, extend an olive branch?' Tom sounded sad, and I couldn't help but feel for him.

'That would be nice. Even do a generic one for the clinic, and I'll encourage him to go.'

He smiled back at me and kissed my forehead. 'You're amazing, Zara.'

That night I lay awake for longer than Tom, terrified to adjust my position in case another firebolt came bursting out my vagina. When I was convinced he was in a deep enough sleep, I turned cautiously to face him. I was actually lying next to my Sugar Daddy. Weeks later and I was still pinching myself. I continued to observe him while he slept—his breathing, his skin, everything about him was just perfect. I lay there thinking of how fortunate I was to have someone so clever, so interesting and insanely handsome who was interested in me. I stared, feeling content, until my own eyes felt heavy and I fell asleep, meeting Tom again a few minutes later in my dreams.

Chapter Eighteen

The next morning, I woke up to Tom kissing my forehead. I opened my eyes slowly while they adjusted to the light. Tom was fully dressed in a suit and crisp white shirt with a few buttons undone at the neck.

'I've got to go, Zara,' he whispered.

'What time is it?' I grumbled, still trying to wake up.

'Half six, sleepy head.' He laughed, jokingly rubbing my bed head.

I sat up and began quickly pulling the covers off.

'Sorry, I'll be ready in a minute, and you can lock up.'

'Hey, hey.' He stood up, blocking me from leaving. 'Get back into bed. There's a spare key in the door. Just keep a hold of it till Monday, okay?'

'Are you sure? I could get a taxi,' I lied. I would not be able to afford it and would have had to walk for miles to get home and I had already carried out enough exercise this week with my shagging antics.

'I insist. Now, get back to sleep.' He leaned over one last time, and we kissed passionately. I could taste the minty scent of his toothpaste in my mouth.

'Now, look what you've done.' He stood up with a massive hard-on visible through his trousers.

'You could always come back to bed?' I whispered, hoping he would say yes.

'I wish I could. Okay, see you Monday.' With one last kiss, he left, leaving me to starfish on his super king-sized bed, falling asleep with the taste of my man lingering in my mouth.

I woke up just after ten to the noise of a baby crying from the park. I had almost forgotten Tom was gone, turning seductively round in bed to find an empty space. *Oh, that's right; he's left a key. Wait, I have a fucking key. Next stage, I'll be moving into this shag pad.*

Excitedly, I checked my phone—no new messages. *He is in a critical learning event, Zara, stop being so needy.*

I made my way to the bathroom, enjoying my morning pee before a thought crossed my mind. *I wonder if the earrings are still here?* I wiped myself down and opened the bathroom cupboard to find them sitting exactly where I had left them, with the pink bobble also there. *Okay, surely that's a good sign? No one has collected them.* And now I had a vital opportunity to examine them in more detail. The earrings were small—initially I'd thought they were studded, but now I realised they were pearls. Two light pink pearled earrings. *I mean, who the fuck wears pearls these days? Maybe they're his gran's?*

I continued through to the kitchen, searching for some left-over pizza for breakfast, and once it was heated, I sat at his breakfast bar, nibbling away and admiring his home. This place was fantastic. He had gadgets everywhere. The TV lifted from the kitchen worktop and you could turn the lights on and off with a voice command. I was scared to explore the fancier appliances in case I fucked something up and lost my key privilege. I smiled as I heard the kids play in the park down below. Maybe that would be my kids one day.

I finished off my pizza slice, wiped my fingers clean, and got dressed, ready to hit the subway. Before I left, I cleaned up last night's boxes and wiped down the worktops, taking the rubbish out with me.

As I sat on the noisy subway, I wondered when Tom would text. *Maybe I should text him first? I mean, just to let him know his house is empty. No, no, Zara, be strong; it's only been a few hours.* I put my phone in my bag and smiled at the businessman sitting across from me. God, the journey was incredibly dull, with no views or magazines to keep me distracted. My legs were bouncing. My fingers were twitching. *Okay, fuck it, one text.*

Hey, that's me locked up the house. Hope you're having fun and arrived safely. Going to miss you :- (x

Send.

Failed.

Send.

Network error.

What the fuck was going on with my phone? I started raising it in the air for a signal. *Come on—send!*

'The next stop is St Enoch's,' a voice called out over the tannoy. *Great. I've missed my fucking stop.* I'd been so engrossed in my phone I hadn't noticed. I stood up, making sure I didn't miss the next one, watching the businessman smile as I passed by. I held onto the pole for dear life, finding my balance just as the subway whooshed into the station with unexpected whiplash. Stepping out, I made my way to the ground level.

As soon as I hit the fresh air, my phone went into a frenzy.

Ping, ping, ping, ping. Message sent. Message sent.

Shit, what's going on? I clicked on my last message to Tom. Great, it did eventually send. *Twenty-five fucking times.*

I walked slowly up the hill, window-shopping as I passed by Frasers, and headed through the lively streets, past the buskers, and eventually up my stone steps. I sat on the bar stool with my phone on the kitchen worktop, patiently waiting for a reply. But nothing. Maybe I should text and explain about the signal issue. I grabbed my phone but then stopped myself. *What would Ashley say?* She'd tell me to put down the phone and find something else to do. Reluctantly, I did just that. I changed into my PJs and pulled out a surgical book and sat on top of my bed to read. I had to prepare for placement, and this was as good a time as any.

Still, I only took in half of what was in front of me, refreshing my phone every few minutes. Nothing. Message delivered. Not even read. Around six, I started raiding my cupboards, starving and depressed. Both those feelings could be solved by one thing: Super Noodles with a piece and butter at the side. A short while later my meal was dished, and I was somewhat impressed.

This looks fucking delicious.

Just as I was about to start munching, he finally replied.

Wow, 25 new messages. Thought someone had died. I got here safely, just finished a lovely meal, and heading for an early night after all that travelling. X

I blushed as he acknowledged the message fuck-up, but just as well someone hadn't died, Tom, because you would have been useless!

When a picture of a perfectly cooked steak, chips, peppercorn sauce, and vegetables came through, I looked down at my own bland meal and laughed.

I'm sorry, my phone had Tourette's earlier. Your dinner looks amazing. Going to bed so soon? :- (I was hoping for a cheekier picture first?

Read.

Oh Zara, do you want to see my steak? Send me some pictures of you then to get me hard x

I smiled. I had only to mention indecent images to get him texting a bit swifter. I left my meal, pulled my tea-stained PJ top off, and stood in front of my bedroom mirror, taking pictures of my tits shamelessly. *This is not working.* Standing up, I looked like a young man with midgie bites. I needed a better angle. I lay on my bed, and with the flash on every vein and nipple pube showed up. *Nope* . . . With a pang of sadness, I realised this was when I required Ashley's help. I pulled the bedcovers up over my stomach and pushed my tits together forcibly with my arms, making them look perky and full. *Now turn the flash off.* And click. *That will do,* I thought unconfidently.

Send.

Oh, la la. They look bigger. What about this, baby?

Tom sent a picture through of his dick, secretly peeping out of his expensive trousers at the fly. I zoomed in, examining the background—hmm, a nice hotel room. I wasn't overly impressed with his penis as I had seen it a million times before. I replied with love-heart eyes.

Show me more, Zara? I wanna see your tight little pussy.

Wow. Rarrrr . . . Okay, Thomas, now we're talking. How the hell do I angle this? I looked down at my sad little stubbly vagina. *Don't let me down, girl,* I thought and began her first ever photoshoot. *Oh God, no!* I was frantically tucking in my fanny lips, trying to avoid the overpacked jumbo ham sandwich look. *Jesus Christ, no.* It looked like roadkill. Every angle was worse than the next. *No wonder Tom doesn't want to lick this. I'm finding it challenging to take a fucking picture of it.* Flash on, flash off, nothing was improving the ghastly gash. Maybe I could edit it in one of those apps? But my arms were growing weaker as my confidence was growing smaller, and after fifteen minutes of staring at my axe wound I called an end to the photoshoot.

Tom, I'm sorry, I can't. It feels weird xxx
Send.

Ah, spoilsport. Night x

I slumped my phone down to the side of the bed disappointedly and sighed. The smell of my Super Noodles wafted in from the kitchen. Feeling sorry for myself, I eventually toddled through and ate the stone-cold noodles, wondering if all vaginas were as vile as my own.

My night of reading up on surgical emergencies continued, and my eagerness for Monday returned.

The following day I organised myself for placement—ironing my grey tunics and washing my hair, feeling anxious, scared, and excited to finish off my training. I didn't hear much from Tom beyond receiving the odd food picture. I understood he was busy, but I missed him. Things at the hospital would certainly be interesting.

That night, I lay in bed imagining scenarios of Tom and me meeting in the hospital corridor and sneaking into a store cupboard for a secret kiss or a cheeky grope. I wasn't sure how it would work, but I knew I would make it work, somehow.

Chapter Nineteen

I walked nervously up the hill facing the Glasgow Royal Infirmary. It was six-thirty on a very early Monday morning. I felt nothing but dread and nausea throughout my entire body.

The fantasies about Tom had fled my anxious shell, and instead the reality of meeting Anne again overcame me. *Maybe I should pretend I don't recognise her? Or maybe I should introduce myself straight away?* I had no idea.

Entering the building and walking down the hospital corridor felt surreal. I had always loved this hospital. The architecture, the long Victorian hallways and wards, the magnificent grounds and beautiful church all oozed with character. To me, the entrance looked more like a castle and walking sheepishly into Ward Seventy-six made me feel like I was about to be hung, drawn and quartered.

My heart raced at the sound of monitors and voices echoing down the corridor. I could smell that distinct hospital smell, a mixture of antiseptics and hand sanitiser trying to mask more unpleasant odours underneath. I carried on down the hallway, passing patients' rooms, smiling briefly to them, hoping they wouldn't ask the new nurse a question. A crowd of nurses, physios, doctors, and students were all chatting away to themselves around a large desk at the bottom of the ward. I looked around for a less occupied nurse and approached her.

'Hi, I'm Zara, the new student. It's my first day.'

'Hi, missus, nice to meet you. I'm Maggie, I'm just finished nights and about to handover. Grab a seat from that room over there and take a report. We'll be starting any minute.'

'Sure, thanks.'

I sat my bag down at the side of the corridor and returned with a chair, then managed to reach over the crowded desk and look at the report on each patient. It all looked like another language. I flicked through the pages, wondering what any of the jargon meant. Each ward seemed to accumulate different shorthand and I panicked looking at the page. I rustled about my bag for a pad and paper to jot down some things I could look up tonight.

'Okay, are we ready to start?' Maggie called out.

'QUIETTTT!' said a booming voice.

I glanced round to see Anne standing in a navy-blue tunic, looking as constipated as ever.

Silence fell, and Maggie began the report.

'Okay, bed one we have fifty-one-year-old Mr Tay. He was admitted on the first of the month with severe abdo pain. PMH of COPD, PVD, CABG in 2002, previous smoker. He had a laparotomy three days ago, and some tissue was sent. Last night he became pyrexial and started on IV antibiotics for an exit wound infection. He has IV fluids running, and NEWs score is a two.'

I was trying to keep up with both the report and my notes when Maggie stopped talking. I looked up to see Anne raising her hand.

'Sorry, Maggie, I've just noticed we have a new student. What's your name?' She was looking directly at me.

My heart started thumping out of my chest.

I had to clear a nervous saliva pocket from my throat and eventually said, 'It's Zara.' I looked at her, smiling, trying to jog her memory of meeting me. I couldn't tell if she knew exactly who I was or had forgotten completely.

'Zara, what are you doing with the writing?'

'Oh, emm . . .' I laughed a little to myself, feeling my hands begin to shake as everyone stared at me. 'I'm just taking some notes of the abbreviations I'm not familiar with.'

'Ah, okay. You seem to be writing a lot. It's very distracting. What stage of your training are you at—first?'

I cleared my throat, feeling embarrassed. 'No, this is my final placement.'

Anne looked shocked and held her chest dramatically. 'And you're still taking notes?'

'I guess so.' I shrugged nervously.

Anne nodded. 'Carry on, Margaret.'

I listened to the remainder of the report feeling self-conscious and stressed. My hand was soaked in sweat as I took notes, trying to scribble them quickly, away from Anne's vision. Eventually the report ended, and I followed the line to return my chair.

'Zara, do I know you?' Anne asked as she walked past me.

'Yeah. Well, we were out for dinner a few weeks ago with T—'

'Thomas. Yes. You're the Botox girl. I didn't recognise you with your clothes on, you see. Okay, you can team up with Jason while you're here.'

'Okay, thanks, Anne.'

'It's Sister on this floor, okay?' She stared at me frostily.

'Yes, I'm so sorry.'

'And, Zara, I expect strict professional boundaries when it comes to relationships in here. You're only here for a few weeks. Don't mess it up.'

'Yes, of course.'

Anne waltzed away with her phone ringing from her waistband, and I took a deep breath in. *Hopefully, that's as bad as today's going to get.* I scanned the rest of the ward for a male nurse, anyone who looked like a Jason, keen to find my mentor. I could hear a camp, high-pitched voice from one of the side rooms and chapped the door to find a handsome, impeccably well-groomed man chatting to an elderly patient who was tucked up in bed.

'Hello, are you Jason?' I asked, edging my face through the door.

'I am indeed. And this young lady is our Vera.'

I smiled at Vera, snug in her bed, as Jason adjusted her drip.

'And you're Zara. I'm not psychic, but my toes were curling for you at that handover. Ignore Sister. She can be so ruthless.'

'Yes, well she's teamed me up with you for the next few weeks.'

'Awww, great. I love a wee student. Mon then, I'll teach you everything you need tae know. Vera, keep that arm straight. You're warned, sweetheart, okay?'

I followed Jason out of the room as he left Vera laughing and happy.

'Let me give you a tour. We'll start at the top,' he said. I instantly warmed to Jason's fun, bubbly, caring personality and kindness towards me.

'Thank you, Jason.'

'Don't thank me yet. We've got a long six weeks together, Zara—thank me then.'

The morning flew by. I spent my time familiarising myself with the ward routine and getting to know my colleagues. In my three years of training I had learned to gauge people's reactions to students; most would be approachable if I had a silly question to ask, and others I learned to avoid. There were a few in this ward who acted like I was invisible, and I knew from day one who to stay clear of. I worked closely with Jason, who seemed to be trusting of my abilities. He allowed me to carry out observations and, in the afternoon, asked me to prepare some dressings for one of his patients. I collected my trolley, thoroughly wiping down the steel ridges, placed my sterile pack and dressings on top and made my way to the patient's bedside.

'Hello, sir, I'm Zara, I'm one of the student nurses. I'm here to clean your wound and put a clean dressing on it. Is that okay?'

The gentleman in the bed smiled up at me, reaching out for my hand.

'Of course you can, hen, it's nice to meet you, Zara. Call me Bill.'

I squeezed his cold hand gently before letting it go to wash my hands and pop an apron on. *I've missed this.* When my hands were scrubbed, I edged back behind Bill's curtain to find him lying with his pyjama top pulled up to his chest, the dressing had fallen off and was stuck to the side of his PJs.

'It's awful itchy now, Zara, so give it a good scrub when you're down there.'

I smirked briefly, concentrating on his large abdominal wound.

It was very red and had pus oozing from one side.

'Ouch, Bill, what did you have done?'

'They cut me open, hen, and removed a tumour from my bowel. I went in with a sore tummy, and I'll be coming out like Frankenstein.' He winked at me.

'And has your wound always been this red?'

'Eh. I don't think so, darling. I only got it done about three days ago. But I don't know.'

'That's okay. I'm going to get a wee swab before I clean it. I'll be back in a second.'

'Right you are, hen.'

I popped through the curtain and scanned the ward for Jason. He was chatting to another nurse, so I stood behind him, waiting to interrupt their conversation like an impatient child.

'You okay, Zara?' he asked, looking harassed.

'Yes, sorry to interrupt, I was doing Bill's dressing in bed seven, and it looks infected to me. It's just in case you want to see it? I was going to swab it too.'

'Oh okay, the swabs are in the cleanroom, second cupboard on the right, and just ask one of the docs, they'll cast an eye over it.'

My heart started to beat fast at the thought of wandering round to the doctors' room and seeing Tom. I hadn't had a minute to check my phone all day to see if he had even messaged.

'Oh, there's Harriette, ask her, she's lovely! Harriette!' Jason yelled and flagged over a beautiful doctor with golden-blonde hair and sallow skin.

'Hi, I'm so sorry, I'm Harriette! I haven't had a minute to introduce myself today. What can I do for you?' she asked.

'Oh no, that's okay. I'm Zara. It's just, I'm doing a dressing in Room Seven, Mr Grant, and it looks infected. It was just to cast an eye over it.'

'Yes, of course. Let's go.'

'I'll just get a swab, will I get you in there?'

She nodded politely, and I raced to the cleanroom, rustling around the cupboards, lifting boxes up and down, until I eventually found a swab. When I returned to the bed space, Harriette was crouching down, chatting to Bill.

'Yes, absolutely, Zara,' she said, turning to me, 'it's a small infection, but you've caught it early. I'll start him on some oral antibiotics. Good job. You're lucky you have this one looking after you, Bill.'

'You're all wonderful, Doctor. Every one of you,' he replied.

She stood up and rubbed my shoulder.

'I'll let you get on. If you need anything at all, I'll be in the doctors' room.'

'Thank you, Harriette, I appreciate it.'

I finished off Bill's wound care, sent his swab to the lab for analysis and returned to the ward to catch up with Jason. We were sitting at the desk, going through paperwork and wound assessments that I had never seen before, when I heard a familiar voice shout out.

'ZARAAAA!' I looked up to see Raj standing before me, dressed in a pristine suit.

I leapt off my chair. 'Raj, oh my God, this is a nice surprise.' I hugged my friend tightly, glad of a friendly face.

'I hope they're looking after you?'

Jason rolled his eyes at Raj jokingly. 'How do you two know one another then?' he asked.

'We work together. Well, I work at Raj's shop.'

'No, she runs my shop!' Raj said. 'Are you due a break?'

I looked around at Jason, who was still smirking.

'On you go, since you've done practically all of my work today. Take twenty.'

'Thanks, Jason. Do you want anything back from the canteen?'

He shook his head, picking up the phone as a call came in.

I was excited to see Raj. We made our way to the hospital café while he filled me in on client gossip. In the café, I stood anxiously beside him.

'I'll get this. You find a seat,' he said.

I scanned the packed seating area for any signs of Tom, but he wasn't there. I sat down at an empty spot in the middle of the bustle and took my phone out, eager to check my messages. But nothing.

Raj joined me at the table with two large lattes and a chocolate chip cookie.

'I got you your fav,' he said, laughing.

'Thank you. I'm so happy you came to visit me today; it's literally cheered me right up.'

'Of course. I would have come earlier, but I had clinics all morning. How was your first day?'

'Well, the Sister hates me for a start. She outed me in the report for taking notes because I didn't understand the abbreviations.'

Raj put a hand to his mouth, trying to keep his coffee down as he giggled.

'No, seriously, she's horrible,' I said.

'No, I know her, she really is. Just keep your head down. That nurse seems friendly enough to mentor you, and you'll be finished before you know it.'

'Thanks, Raj.' I began munching into my cookie, making funny faces as Raj watched me in disgust. He was always so healthy, only eating vegan meals and drinking protein shakes at work.

'Oh my God, is that you, Raj?' Harriette was towering over the table, and Raj's face lit up.

'I heard you were back in town,' he said. 'How are you? Oh, sorry, Harriette this is—'

'Zara, yes, we met in the ward. Wait. You're Zara from the clinic!'

I laughed at how enthusiastic she was getting while trying to scrub any cookie residue off my teeth.

'Tom has told me all about you, how much you do at the clinic.' She sat down, joining us at the small circular table.

Raj nodded. 'That's true, I can't disagree,' he said.

I couldn't help but feel awkward at the mention of Tom in front of Raj, but I felt flattered, too, and my face beamed with the compliments. *Was Tom talking about me with his work colleagues?*

'So, when did you move back up from London?' Raj asked Harriette.

'Just this weekend. I did a few shifts up here last month, but I officially moved my things up yesterday.'

'It's nice to have you back anyway. I mean that. Zara, Harriette is partnering with Tom at his clinic when it opens in a few weeks.'

The smile suddenly drained from my face.

'What? Oh, oh, oh, oh, so you're Dr Finn Finn?' My Gareth Gates stutter returned.

'That's right, Harriette Finn. So, you will never guess, Raj—on Saturday we popped into a product conference and guess who the rep was? Tim Peters from uni, do you remember him?'

While the pair laughed and caught up, I watched on, green with envy, sitting next to Britain's Next Top Model. *Tom was with her all weekend? The most beautiful, kind, clever woman in the hospital and he picks her to set up a business with.* I was in a daze as the conversation went on around me, feeling worried and threatened.

'I better head back to the ward, Jason will be looking for me. Thanks for the drink, Raj.'

'See you Thursday, Zara.'

Harriette waved politely to me, and I shuffled my way back to the ward. I returned to find Jason writing up notes, and I joined him at the chair.

'Sit, lady.'

I sat down and looked at him curiously.

'Well? Is he single?' Jason asked.

'Who, Raj?' I shook my head. 'Married.'

'Damn, he's bloody gorgeous.'

I laughed. I'd never even thought of Raj being anything more than my friend.

Anne appeared from round the corner like Miss Trunchbull, and the ward fell quiet.

'What's all the giggling about, people? Jason?'

'We were just giggling because it's Zara's first day and a lovely surgeon called Raj bought her a coffee, that's all.'

Anne smirked but it wasn't friendly. 'Did you not realise? Zara has lots of surgeon friends. Don't you, Zara?'

I met her eyes briefly, then put my head down until she walked away.

'Come on. We'll find a quieter corner to skive and stop her earywigging,' Jason said.

The rest of the shift went in quickly. I helped with meals and paperwork as well as blood pressures and basic monitoring. Jason let me finish up half an hour early, and I stumbled out of the ward at 7.30pm, exhausted and drained. As I checked my phone, I saw Tom had messaged me ten minutes before.

Good day?x

I was relieved he had messaged but I couldn't help but want more. *Why didn't he wish me luck? Why didn't he mention his business partner looked like Kate fucking Moss? Why didn't he come to visit me?* I was tired and upset. I slipped my phone back into my bag and walked the cool, dark route home for a long bath and an early night, apprehensive to do it all again tomorrow.

Chapter Twenty

I survived the handover the following day without any embarrassing interruptions from Anne. Jason was incredibly bright for first thing in the morning, and before we got started, we spent five minutes chatting about the jam-packed day ahead of dressings, blood transfusions and drug rounds.

At times I wondered if I'd ever be able to carry out the tasks he did so competently by myself. I admired his work ethic, his thoroughness, and his compassion towards the patients. Even though we had only worked one full shift together, I felt like I knew him. Between patients, he'd disclosed his entire life story, from boyfriends and breakups to beloved pets and previous employments. He definitely overshared, but he was kind to me, and I enjoyed working with him. I began to understand the ward a wee bit more on that second day, where things were, who I could ask silly questions too and the routine in general. I felt like I had a purpose there. I knew the patients from the previous day, and it felt less daunting having the same people to care for again.

Mr Grant wasn't feeling himself and spiked a temperature overnight despite getting started on his oral antibiotics the previous shift. Jason assigned him to me that day, allowing me to get the management experience of caring for a deteriorating patient. I was in and out of his room, cooling him down and monitoring his vitals. Just after lunch I approached the nurse's desk, Mr Grant's heart rate had crept up throughout the morning, and his blood pressure was slowly declining.

'Jason, I think you should have a look at Bill, his vitals have deteriorated again.'

'Just ask the junior doctor, they'll come up with a plan. That's exactly what I would do, Zara.'

I looked around the noisy ward. Everybody seemed incredibly busy and I was still learning their names. I was trying to decide who seemed most approachable to ask for help when I suddenly felt a tap on the shoulder. I turned around feeling harassed and flustered, and found Tom standing there with his arms crossed at his chest.

'Hello.' He smiled. He was wearing his scrubs with a little scrub cap placed neatly over his hair, his stubble was heavy after a long weekend away but he looked as handsome as ever. I felt instant relief when I saw him.

'Hi—oh my God, it's so good to see you,' I gushed, automatically placing my hand on his arm.

'You okay?' He was looking around the ward, distracted in case anyone spotted us together.

'Not really. I need a doctor and I don't know which one to ask.' I stood still, examining the congested floor, hoping one of the junior doctors would make eye contact with me.

Tom took a handover report out of his top pocket and observed it. 'Who's the patient?'

'Mr Grant, Room Seven.'

I watched him read the report, his brow slightly furrowed in concentration as he took in the information. I knew this was literally his job, and I'd be worried if he didn't know what he was doing, but still, I was so impressed by his knowledge.

'Mr Stewart did his operation. He's off today.' He looked at his expensive watch. 'I can have a quick look at him before I have to go—what's up?'

As we walked to Mr Grant's bedside, I explained how I had swabbed his wound yesterday and a junior doctor had reviewed him. Before we entered the room, we reached for some gloves, and Tom took the opportunity to speak quietly.

'You didn't return my text last night,' he said.

'I know, I'm sorry. I was exhausted and I had a horrible day.'

'Okay. Just checking you were okay.'

'I'm good. I'm happy now I've seen you. I've missed you the past couple of days.'

'Yes, me too. I'll pop round to yours tonight then?'

Mine? *Shit*, my house was a midden! It resembled Marvin and Dayna's gaff from the scheme more than an expensive city flat.

'Emm . . . yeah. I don't get finished till eight and by the time I get a bath it'll be after nine, though—is that okay?'

'Okay, that's fine. Right, come on, after you.' He opened the door for me like he had done so many times before and we went into the room.

As I watched him shake Mr Grant's hand and examine him, I felt so lucky that this handsome, intellectual, talented surgeon would even be interested in me. Watching him at work made my heart race. He was caring, gentle and kind, not to mention his physical attributes; his model-like face, his sculpted jaw, his muscular arms . . .

'Zara?'

Shit, I was daydreaming.

'Oh, sorry, yes?'

'He needs an abdo X-ray. I'll escalate his antibiotics, but he may need to go back to theatre this evening. I'll page whoever's on call tonight to deal with it. Good work on his vitals though, nurse.'

I smirked as he glanced down at me.

'I'll let myself out. Bill, it was a pleasure to meet you, sir. We'll get you feeling a bit better soon.'

He walked past me, giving a quick wink as he left.

As soon as he was gone, my heart burst with warmth again. Why had I spent a full night doubting him? He'd been thinking about me just as much as I had him—well, probably not that much but even so, he'd missed me!

I looked forward to the night ahead with a little glow inside. We could watch a movie, cuddle all night and leave for work together the next morning. Maybe I could ask him about Harriette too.

I adjusted Bill's pillows and recorded his new plan in his notes.

'He was a nice doctor him, hen, ' Bill said.

'Yes, Dr Adams is very nice, isn't he. Hopefully we will get you feeling better with his new approach, eh?'

'I think it's a wooden box I'm needing! But aye, hen, a nice fella him. Maybe he's got a handsome son about your age too, Zara. You never know.' I looked up from the paperwork to find Bill winking across the room. I giggled back, shaking my head, and walked out the room to update Jason with the new care plan.

'Okay, good work, Zara,' he said. 'Now, if a patient is potentially going to theatre, what do you need to do?'

'Erm . . . put them in a gown?'

'Before that.'

'Consent them?'

'Yes, well, the medics will do that, but before all of this.' He was moving his hand around, encouraging me to think quicker.

'Oh, fast them!' I exclaimed.

'Yes! Get a 'nil by mouth' sign on his door and hide his munchies.'

I did just that and continued the shift that day enjoying the chaos of the ward. I had a long way to go before I knew how to be a perfect nurse, but my second day was certainly less dramatic than the first. Around seven Jason and I handed over and I jogged happily down the hospital corridor, eager to get home and declutter for my late-night session with Tom.

Outside, I felt the rain spit lightly on my hair. Shit. I had no hood or umbrella so I skimmed over my pockets hoping to have enough money for a taxi. *Nope!* Not fancying my chances with the Glasgow bus service, I rushed down the hill, checking my phone for the time every block or so until I eventually reached my flat, soaking wet.

I pelted up the stairwell, into the flat and began kicking the pile of clothes that were accumulating on the living room floor into one sizeable heap. Then I lifted the dirty laundry mountain, almost breaking my back, to conceal it in my wardrobe for a much later date. In the kitchen, I gathered the crusty dishes in disgust, then ran warm, soapy water in the sink to steep them while I cleaned myself. I jumped into a steamy shower, washing the hospital smell from my hair and exfoliating my body till it gleamed.

It was 8pm when I got out and immediately began scrubbing my worktops, hoovering my floors and lighting my favourite Yankee candle to mask any unfavourable odours. As I put the last dish to dry on the draining board, the smell of clean cotton had radiated throughout the flat, and my work was finally done. I was exhausted. I had just worked two twelve-hour shifts with another scheduled for the next day. My legs ached, and my eyes felt dry. But there was no level of exhaustion that would stop me from seeing Tom. I had missed him more than anything.

I sat at the front living room window, overlooking the busy street, waiting patiently for any sighting of him.

I watched cars passing outside and felt butterflies in my belly each time one slowed down in case it was him. I had literally taken part in a sixty-minute makeover, and my place was gleaming. I looked around the flat, imagining welcoming him into it, and felt impressed.

But Tom was taking his time. It was approaching nine twenty before I decided to text.

Hey, where are you? I'm excited to see you x

Send.

I sat for a further ten minutes before pacing around the living room. No reply yet. I went out to the hallway and lifted the handset of the buzzer system, making sure it hadn't broken.

'Testing, testing.'

I could hear the laughs of passers-by wondering where the voice was coming from. It definitely worked. *Where the fuck is he?* He always said he was a stickler for time. He hadn't even read my message yet. My heart began beating faster and harder. I felt my face get warmer with hurt and anger. It felt like Mark all over again.

Maybe I should call him?

I tried, but it went straight to voicemail. I felt nauseous. What if he was with someone else?

It had just passed ten, and after stewing for over an hour, I finally accepted he wasn't going to come. Still, I lay on top of my bed, fully dressed with my face plastered in makeup, just on the off chance he was running late. My pillow was growing damper with tears as I lay there exhausted, drained, and feeling pathetic once more.

The next morning, I woke to my alarm ringing and jumped up to check my phone. He hadn't replied to my text, but he'd read it at 1am. *What the fuck?* He'd never left me without a reply for so long, and definitely not when we had plans. I couldn't help but feel an almighty pit at the bottom of my stomach, full of anxiety and my last ounce of self-respect.

As I got ready for the long day ahead, I wondered nervously about how to act if I saw Tom. Should I ask him why he didn't show? Or pretend like I didn't care? Maybe I should give him the silent treatment and avoid him the entire day. I didn't have a clue, and with Ashley still not speaking to me, I had no one to offer crucial advice. I walked up the hill that morning, rehearsing possible scenarios repeatedly in my head, thinking up witty answers to ensure I was prepared for anything.

Throughout the morning, I heard Tom's name bandied about the ward, but I hadn't seen him. *Thank fuck.* I carried on with my work but felt distracted and less motivated than on my previous shifts. I continued to nurse Mr Grant myself, who was doing a lot better since his antibiotics changed. Although everyone was being friendly to me and I adored Jason, I missed Ashley more than anything. Especially now when I was feeling like shit. I fought desperately that morning not to text her, fearing that she still might not want to patch things up. I don't think I could have taken that blow on top of everything else.

At lunchtime I wandered down to the canteen cautiously by myself, hoping I'd bump into Raj for a friendly chat and a bit of advice about Ash. It was his day in the hospital and I was eager to see a familiar face that might distract me from Tom. But he was nowhere to be seen, so I squeezed into a small table by the window and took out my lunch box to eat alone. I sat sheepishly unravelling my squashed-up Nutella sandwiches from the tinfoil, praying no one around me had a nut allergy, as it was the only condiment I had left in the house.

'Zara?'

I looked up to Tom standing over me holding a salad bowl from the café. He sat down across from me. I angled my sandwich away to avoid him sighting the filling.

'How's Mr Grant today?' he asked.

I froze, staring at my banned sandwich trying to resight my earlier responses I had prepared for this moment.

'Zara? Mr Grant?' He glanced at his phone in his hand not looking interested.

'Erm . . . much better, he's just a little tired.'

'Are his infection markers improving?'

'Apparently. Students don't have lab access though. You should maybe ask Jason these questions.' I shrugged.

Tom looked up from his phone. There was awkwardness in the air, and I wasn't sure if I should mention it first.

'Is there something wrong?' he asked.

'No. Well, yes actually. It's just that I waited ages for you last night and you never came over.'

'Zara, I'm sorry, I had theatre.' He sighed disappointedly, as if to say I shouldn't have brought it up.

'Okay, but I'm not a mind reader, Tom, I didn't know. You could have texted me and I wouldn't have sat around all night wondering.'

'Just calm down a bit, Zara. God.' His voice was slightly raised, and he moved his chair out frustratedly.

For a few seconds, there was silence.

'Fuck, I don't mean calm down, I apologise. I'm just so stressed. I have this fucking clinic opening, working in here, fucking Raj in my head all the time. I haven't slept all weekend because I was away and I'm working till eight tonight. I'm seriously fucked.'

'I know. I'm sorry, too. I forget how busy you are. I just missed you.'

'And I missed you.' He smiled briefly, his perfectly straight teeth grazed his bottom lip while he was thinking. 'Let me finish all this shit tonight, and I'll come round to yours tomorrow for a bottle of wine?'

'Mine? Okay.' My mood lifted instantly. I grinned back, reining it in quickly hoping I didn't have Nutella teeth.

'Yes, yours. I don't remember you ever inviting me up! And I've been feeling extra horny from seeing you in that little uniform this week.'

I began to chuckle as I looked down at my grey, washed-out, crumpled tunic.

'I could wear this tomorrow night . . .' I raised my eyebrows jokingly.

'If there weren't a high chance of getting MRSA on my dick, I'd maybe take you up on it. If I wasn't so tired, I'd tell you to come tonight, but honestly, I'd be rubbish in bed and force you to do all the work. I know you wouldn't want that now, would you?'

I made a disgusted face and shook my head.

'Let's leave it till tomorrow when you've recharged your batteries,' I said. 'I'm tired too.'

'Yes, let's! Right, I've got to go, I have umpteen patients still to see, will need to eat this in the office. I'll text you.'

As he walked away from the table, I noticed people around us in the canteen watching curiously. Probably wondering why the hottest surgeon in the hospital was talking to me. I finished off my sandwich and returned to the ward with high sugar levels and a lifted spirit.

'You seem chirpier!' Jason said, smiling.

'I am. I was being crabbit with my boyfriend and felt crappy. But we're fine now.'

'Oh, spill. I love some juicy gossip.'

'He's a surgeon, he was in theatre last night, and I was annoyed because he didn't come to see me.' I giggled as I realised how pathetic I sounded. He was delivering lifesaving fucking treatment and you were behaving like a desperate nymphomaniac.

'Zara, you are savage!' Jason was laughing, holding a hand over his mouth as he did.

'So, is he working tonight?'

'He's working till eight, and obviously so am I. So, I'll see him tomorrow night now.'

'Why don't you make it up to him? Go home, wear some sexy underwear and rock up to his door!'

He was getting excited about planning my night out in his head.

'I don't know. We've only been together a few weeks. He'd maybe think that's a bit much.'

'Trust me. I'm a guy. Harassing him about a date night when he's saving someone's life is a bit much—turning up half-naked after a hard week's work is perfect.'

'Okay. Maybe, I will.'

'Go for it. When Anne leaves, you can go too.'

'Are you sure? That's so kind, Jason.'

'Shut up! I'm just jealous you're getting some—I wish it was me! What's he like? Are you guys serious?'

'Well, he's gorgeous, I've fancied him for years and yes, I suppose we are serious. Without a doubt the most serious relationship I've been in actually. We just work I suppose.'

'Ohhh, Zara. Do you love him?' Jason's eyes were lighting up with romance.

'God yes, I do. But I think I loved him before we even kissed. Is that mad? We've never had the full convo about the L word, but he is older, and I don't want to sound immature saying it like it's a big deal. God I'm blushing even talking about it now.' I lifted my hands to my face and could feel my cheeks get warm in an instant.

'Oh, Zara. No, tell him, though. You seem to have the world on your shoulders all the time. You question everything. If you feel something then tell him. Life's too short.'

Jason was right. I did love Tom. I loved every inch of his perfectly sculpted body. His chiselled jaw, his white smile, his warm hairy chest . . . But also, his manners, how he forever opens doors for me and holds my lower back when I walk. His devilish humour and witty remarks, how he makes me laugh in the most serious situations. His overall intelligence and having such a compassionate job in general, he was undoubtedly perfect, and I was unbelievably lucky he even gave me a second look. Yes, I was completely and utterly in love, and that night, I planned to tell him.

Chapter Twenty-One

Jason stuck to his word, and at six-thirty, I left the ward, completing week one of my final placement. I was off for four days now, and I planned to fill them with sex, sixty-niners and more sex.

I headed home and began the plucking process for tonight's rendezvous. After a hot shower, I styled my hair in a loose wave and sprayed some black hairspray to cover my grey roots. I scrubbed, exfoliated, and tanned my skin. My body looked as smooth as silk, gold like caramel, and although I'd been working such long hours, I was prancing about my flat excited for some unexpected fun.

Then I remembered.

I yanked open my dildo drawer and began rummaging through the back till I found an old Secret Santa gift from many years before: an edible candy string bra and thong set from Anne Summers. Ash bought it for me thinking it would be fun and I'd completely forgot about it until now, or I'm sure it would have ended up eaten when I was mid-month and completely starving. I took the set carefully out of the box and inspected. They still smelt vaguely sweet and there were no signs of decay, even though they were a couple of years past their sell-by date. Surely sweeties didn't go out of date, did they? I popped the set on over my smooth skin.

I walked around the flat in the bra and thong, practising what I could say in a sexy voice. *Dinner is served, Sugar Daddy.* No, too cringe. *In here, Thomas, I hope you're hungry.* Too dominating.

I still had Tom's key and thought even if he wasn't home I could go and sprawl out on top of his bed, covered only in these little sweets. It was approaching eight and the rain was pelting down outside, so I emptied the last of my emergency money tin to get a taxi to Kelvingrove. I put on my short black raincoat and slipped my feet into a pair of red stilettos. I felt super sexy. Opening the coat, I looked in the mirror at the semi-naked figure and couldn't believe how brave I was being. The pastel-coloured beads covered my nipples but not much more. The thong was low and dug into my hips. *What fucking size did Ash get me?* They were cutting into my love handles and would undoubtedly leave a mark, but I hoped they wouldn't be on for very long. I imagined Tom biting off each sweetie and hopefully nibbling me for making such an effort.

Outside, my taxi beeped its horn. I grabbed my phone and my bag and on the way out of the flat, skooshed the last of my Jo Malone down my neck and chest. *Perfect!*

Sitting in the taxi, I couldn't help but think the driver was judging me by his surprised look and dry manner. Scotland's short-lived summer was currently non-existent as the rain fell hard on the streets, yet here I was dressed in only a short raincoat and stilettos, looking and feeling like a prostitute. I smiled to myself as I caught a glimpse of my reflection in the car window. This was the most daring thing I had ever done. I was fidgety with excitement and nerves, and every time I moved I felt the candy beads turn and twist. I forced myself to remain as still as possible in case one of the strings popped and I made a crumbling mess on the floor. I put my hand in my pocket to make sure the key was there, and felt my hand grow sweaty around it.

The taxi pulled up outside Tom's flat and I paid the judgemental taxi driver with a handful of fifty pence coins before heading up the outer steps. Taking a deep breath, I put his key in the lock and let myself in the bottom door. It was just past eight, and he never seemed to get away from the hospital early, so I doubted he would be in yet, which gave me time to light some candles and pour some alcohol for added confidence. I walked up the flights of stairs towards the top floor and approached his door when I heard a noise from inside.

It sounded like the TV. *Shit, he's home—plan B.* I opened my short coat up, exposing my entire body, covered with the tiny edible underwear. *Be confident, Zara. He will love it!* The stairwell was freezing, and I could see my nipples pop out between the beaded rows. My heart was racing. I took another deep breath to calm my nerves and chapped the door.

'Oh, Tom, shall I get the door?' said a voice from inside, and my body went stiff.

Who the fuck is that? There was something familiar about the tone.

I was still standing trying to figure it out with my coat wide open when I heard the key turning from the other side of the door. I quickly shut the coat over myself and tied the belt again as the door was pulled open. Standing there holding a wine glass and looking incredibly cosy in her pyjamas and slippers was Harriette.

'Ohhh, it's Zara! What a lovely surprise. Tom, it's Zara,' she said, calling back over her shoulder.

I froze, unable to move or stop staring at the beautiful woman in front of me.

'Are you coming in? You look lovely!' she added.

Footsteps rushed to the door behind her and suddenly Tom was there.

'Zara! Oh God, I forgot you were returning my key tonight.' He turned to Harriette and placed his hand on her shoulder. 'I left it at Raj's clinic.'

My eyes were watching this unfold, but I was dazed, as though it wasn't really happening, as though my brain couldn't take any of it in.

'Zara?' Tom said, and put out his hand. His eyes opened widely while he stared at me. 'The key?'

'Yes, sorry, your key. Here you go.' I rustled around my pocket carefully, trying not to expose myself, and handed it to Tom.

'I better go. I was . . . heading out. Have a good night.'

I turned to the stairwell, and my bottom lip began to tremble. *What the fuck is happening?* Why didn't I have any courage to ask Tom what was going on? I carried on down the stairs, my stilettos shaking with each step.

'Zara, wait. I'll walk you out. I'll be back in a minute, Harri,' Tom's voice called out from above, and I heard the door shut over. 'Zara. Wait.'

I couldn't wait; I ignored his calls. I didn't want him to see how upset I was. I tried to pick up the pace, but as I did I felt candy beads plunge from my body and sprinkle all over the ground. The strings clearly weren't robust enough to deal with this amount of action. I was leaving a trail of candy down his staircase, and I could hear it crunch under his feet as he rushed after me. When I reached the bottom hallway, I felt Tom grab my arm.

'I'm sorry,' he whispered, pulling me around to face him.

'Are you together?' I asked, praying for a misunderstanding.

He nodded and put his head down. My eyes streamed.

'We went to uni together. She lived in London, it was long distance, but she's moved back for the clinic. I'm sorry I hurt you. It was all just a bit of fun.'

'I can't believe this. I was coming to tell you that I—' I paused as the tears perished from my eyes. 'All this time, I was just a bit on the fucking side? I'm sorry, I feel sick. I can't do this. I need to leave.'

I reached for the door to open it but he put his hand against it, holding it shut.

'Wait. It's raining. I'll give you a lift home.'

I whirled around angrily. 'No, fucking leave me.'

I pulled the heavy door open and began walking in the rain down his street.

'Zara!' he shouted and continued to follow behind me.

'Leave me alone, Tom.'

I pulled off my high heels and started to run. My coat opened up with the late-night breeze, exposing what was left of the rapidly disintegrating candy string set, while I sobbed, desperately trying to cover myself up. I could feel the splash of wet puddles bounce up my tanned legs, and the bitter coldness of the rain glued my soaking wet hair to my face, but I didn't care about any of it. I had to keep going. I wanted to run away from all this heartache.

I wasn't sure when he stopped following me, but I continued, not wanting to look back at the man I had lost. My heart was broken, and I had no one.

My head was pounding. *How could he do this to me?* I was so embarrassed. I wanted to shut my eyes and for all of this to go away. *I didn't want to be alone, but how can I tell anyone what he has done?* I ran and ran, feeling my bare feet hit the ground hard, soaking up the dirt and stones pushing into my skin. I couldn't turn up at my sister's dressed only in a couple of mix-ups. My mother lived too far away, and Raj's wife would never forgive him if she thought he hired a prostitute for reception. My legs continued as my mind churned faster, remembering all the clues I'd ignored the past few weeks. *How could I be so fucking stupid?* The earrings, the weekend away, his attitude when I told him I was going to do my placement in the same hospital as him. *Why would someone like him ever fall for someone like me?* I must have been crazy to ever believe this could work out.

After fifteen minutes of continuous movement I stopped, panting for breath and limping from the pain in my feet. I was outside Ashley's flat. She was the only person in the world who could help me, but I wasn't sure she'd even let me in. I stood outside her ground floor flat, opposite Charing Cross Station, barefoot and sobbing. People passed and nudged their friends at the state of me looking like I had just fled an asylum. Ashley's lights were on, and I could hear her TV from inside. I wanted to go in, but I was apprehensive. *What if she turns me away too?*

Before I could talk myself out of it, I chapped her door. I heard footsteps approaching and felt sick. The door opened and Ashley looked at me.

'Zara? Are you okay?' she gasped.

I burst into tears, shaking my head. As soon as I saw my best friend, though, I knew I had come to the right place.

'Come here, come in.' She pulled my arm into her warm home and hugged me tightly.

'Tell me what's up. Here, you're okay now.'

'I'm so sorry about what happened between us, Ashley.' I cried into her shoulder, smelling that sweet perfumed smell I missed. 'You're the only person I can talk to.'

'No, I'm sorry. I was the one who acted like a proper bitch, Zara. Forget about it. Tell me what's wrong.'

I glanced up at my best friend and saw tears in her eyes. She was feeling my pain with me.

I knew at that moment, no matter what happened to me, I had my someone.

Chapter Twenty-Two

Ashley and I stood there in her hallway holding one another for a few minutes in silence. I could smell her Chanel Chance perfume and her body heat felt nice against my skin as she slowly warmed me up.

'Are you ready to talk?' she asked.

I nodded, and she walked me through to her living room. Her flat was modern and trendy, with grey interiors and glass ornaments scattered throughout. She had candles burning and I took a deep breath, inhaling the pomegranate smell before sitting down on her sofa.

'Tom and I are over,' I said.

I looked up to see Ashley nodding for more information.

'He's been cheating on me with the most beautiful doctor. She's blonde, kind and absolutely gorgeous. She looks fucking Scandinavian or something. Too tall and healthy to be British.' I sobbed.

'Oh, Zara. Come here.' She pulled me over to embrace me once more and I could feel a crunch from my underwear.

'Ouch.'

'What was that?'

Ashley looked at me, puzzled, while I stood up and opened my coat. My string bra was still intact, but the thong was missing candy beads all over.

'Is that your Secret Santa gift from . . .'

I nodded. 'Yep, thought I would surprise him.' I shrugged shamelessly.

'God, that's like ten years old—you would have probably killed him.'

'If only.' Ashley giggled warmly while I struggled to see the funny side of it and looked down at my disgraceful body. My legs were covered in goosebumps and my feet were black, engrained with dirt. I had splash marks from muck and puddles up to my thighs.

'I'll run you a bath. You can stay here tonight, and we can talk.'

'What about Dave? I don't want to put him out.'

'Are you kidding? He's at his mate's now, he's desperate for a night off. I'll text him and tell him to go back to his mum's tonight.' Ashley smiled, stood up and briefly ran her fingers through my matted hair. 'I'll run the bath now or you'll end up sticking to the couch when your sweeties dry.'

She left the room and I took my phone out of my pocket. One missed call and one text message from Tom reading simply: *Can we talk?*

I slouched into Ashley's couch, questioning why I was in such a state. *People get cheated on every day and I've been seeing Tom for six weeks and I'm absolutely distraught. Am I overreacting? Maybe, we weren't officially exclusive. In which case, has he even done anything wrong?*

Ashley came back into the room.

'That's your bath ready. C'mon, I'll sit with you.'

I followed her into the bathroom. Steam from the bath billowed up and warmed the room. I took off my drenched coat, carefully peeled away the remaining underwear set and stepped into the bath. It smelt fresh, like Radox and lavender. I flinched as pins and needles travelled up my legs until they became used to the heat. Ashley sat with her legs crossed on top of the toilet seat.

'So, what happened tonight?' she asked, looking concerned.

'Basically, he was supposed to see me last night and didn't show up. Then, I saw him in the ward and asked why he didn't come over. He got pissed and said he was operating. I felt so selfish that I was annoyed at him. My mentor Jason said I should surprise him. So, I went round to his house tonight dressed like Katy fucking Perry, and that beautiful doctor who also works in the ward answered the fucking door. He pretended to her I was dropping something off to him. Like I was nothing. And I just walked away.'

'What the fuck?' Ashley's mouth was open in shock.

'I'm so embarrassed. I can't believe I was so stupid to ever think this could be something. I love him so much, Ash.' My tears started plopping into the bathtub. I sat upright and rinsed my face in an effort to stop.

'This isn't on you, Zara. There's a reason men like him are single at his age. I mean look at the way he treated Raj, that's his best friend. I'm fucking raging! So, wait, your placement is in his ward?'

I'd forgotten how much she had to catch up on. Had it really been this long since we'd properly spoken? 'Yes. Oh my God, I can't go back there, Ashley, I can't.' I was in a panic. 'How could I face them every day for the next five weeks feeling like this?'

'Hey, calm down. Just get tonight by and we'll sort your placement out,' she said reassuringly.

'He texted me ten minutes ago, wanting to chat. What should I say?'

'There's nothing he can say or do to make this situation better, Zara. Don't reply.'

I knew she was right, but my heart pined for him. *Maybe he'll choose me?* If I lost some weight, started a regular skincare regime, made regular appointments with the hairdresser's instead of buying root spray—maybe if I did all that, he would realise how good we were together. How much we worked. How much I loved him.

Ashley and I sat in silence, completely overwhelmed for five minutes.

'Do you want to come out now? I can see your mind overthinking again,' Ashley said, breaking through my thoughts.

I smiled at how well she knew me. 'Yeah, I'm ready.'

I stood over the bath and my friend wrapped a towel around my shoulders. When I'd dried myself off Ash handed me a pair of pink fleecy PJs and socks.

'Will we watch a movie? I can make you a gin?' Ashley offered.

'Do you mind if I go to bed? I just want this day to be over.' My bottom lip trembled as I said the words and I let out a large sigh.

'Of course not, I get it.' She hugged me tightly. 'I'll come in soon, I'm going to let Emily know you're here.'

I nodded and walked through to her bedroom.

Ashley's blinds were still open and I could hear people chat as they passed by her window, but I had no energy to get up and close them. Instead, I lay on top of her silky sheets, feeling sad and alone. I glanced at my phone. Nothing. He didn't even fight for me. He didn't care. Just like that, we were over.

My eyes were heavy and painful from all the tears, and my heart just felt empty. I could hear Ashley fighting my case to my sister on the phone, telling her all about my night from hell and I was mortified. I'd put everything into this relationship with Tom, boasted about 'my boyfriend the surgeon', I fell out with my only friend trying to protect him, hoping he was the one, praying that he felt the same, but instead I was humiliated. I shut my eyes and cried, trying to be as quiet as I could so as not to disturb Ashley. Eventually, exhausted from everything, I must have fallen over.

Chapter Twenty-Three

The next morning, I woke to Ashley rummaging through her drawers to get ready for work. I shut my eyes tightly, pretending to still be asleep, hoping to avoid another chat about Tom.

She shut the door and immediately reopened it. I felt the glare of the light peering in from the hall, I then felt her bounce on the bed towards me, kiss my forehead and leave once more. I heard the outside door shut and tossed around the mattress a little more. I felt so fragile. So alone. I closed my eyes again, hoping to sleep through the pain.

I woke around lunchtime with a light illuminating Ashley's bedroom. My phone had fallen on the ground, and I leaned over, following the glare. Six missed calls from Ashley, two from Emily and half a dozen WhatsApp messages. Nothing from Tom. I sank back into the bed, prepared to sleep some more of the day away.

There was a loud chap at Ashley's door. I jumped up and immediately lay back down, *they will go away*. The knocking continued and I could hear shouting from outside the door. *What the fuck?* I eventually stumbled into the hall, my puffy face still red and tender from tears.

'Fuck sake, Zara. I was worried sick,' Emily yelled when I opened the door.

'I was sleeping, for God's sake.' It was the first thing I'd said since last night and my throat was croaky.

I held the door open as she marched in.

'I've just had to drop the kids at Mum's because I was in such a panic. Ashley said you were in some state last night.'

I followed her into the living room.

'That was nice of her,' I replied sarcastically.

'She told me what happened, Zara. What a fucking dickhead.'

I nodded in agreement.

'So, who is she? Did you have no idea?'

'I honestly don't want to talk about it, Emily.' I lifted my legs into a ball and lay on Ashley's sofa.

'Okay, I get it. When are you back at work? Do you want some tea or breakfast? I'm going to put the kettle on.' Emily walked through the living room into the kitchen. I heard her click the kettle down and open the fridge door.

'I'm supposed to be in the clinic tomorrow, but I'll text Raj. I don't want anything, Em. I'm not hungry.' I lay there with my eyes shut, hoping she'd leave.

'You can't let Raj down, Zara. What about place-ment?' She came back into the room towards me.

'I'm not going back. I don't care. I don't want to see or speak to anyone right now.' I sat up angrily and burst into tears.

Emily came over and put her arm around me. 'You'll

be okay, Zara. I know it's tough, but you will be.' I nodded back, trying my best to stop crying.

'But you need to go to placement. It's your last bloody placement, Zara.'

I slammed my hands off my legs and stared at my sister. 'I just want to be left alone,' I snapped.

There was silence in the room. I closed my eyes briefly and took a deep breath.

'I'm sorry. I know you're trying to help. I feel so shit. I want to phone him, but I know I shouldn't. I have a million questions to ask, but I don't know if I want to hear the answers. I feel so sick he done this, Emily. Like I could genuinely vomit.'

'Come here.' She hugged me, running her arm up and down my back. 'If you have questions, then ask them. But I don't know if they'll do your mental health any good. You're torturing yourself.'

She was right. Mentally I wasn't prepared for anything. The thought of even getting dressed to return to my flat was beyond reasoning right now.

'Wait a few days even. Then text or call him. You might see things differently in a few days but let him shit himself in the meantime. Don't contact him—honestly.'

'Okay.' I attempted a smile at my sister.

'Are you staying here? I could drop you off home?'

'I suppose I should get ready and go. I have no money to get home, and the thought of walking is too much. I can't be bothered getting ready though. In fact—' I put my face in my hands, remembering the clothes I had on last night.

'I'll just go home in these.' I looked down at Ashley's fleecy PJ set.

'Grab your things then. I can stop into the shop on the way home if you need food.'

'No, it's fine. I don't feel like eating.'

'Zara, stop being so dramatic.'

'If you saw how thin my boyfriend's new girlfriend is, you would stop eating too. Trust me!'

Emily laughed as I stood up and headed back to the bedroom to find my phone and bag from last night.

I sighed. 'Ready.'

'Let's go. I'll drop Ashley's keys off to her on the way back from yours.'

'Tell Raj I'm not well. Please. I'll text him later too.'

Emily looked at me uncomfortably.

'I hate lying to people, Zara,' she mumbled.

'It's not exactly lying, is it. I'm a fucking mess. Oh, Emily, one more favour, can we drive past Kelvingrove on the way home. I want to see if Tom's car's there.'

'Zara, no. C'mon, the kids are at Mum's. I don't have time for this.'

'Emily! Please. I promise I need to go by, just this one time.'

'Oh, for fuck's sake. Hurry up then.'

Emily locked up Ashley's flat behind me, and I hurried into her car in broad daylight with the pink PJs and fluffy socks on. As we drove towards Tom's house, I could feel anxiety pains shoot from my stomach to my heart. I had flashbacks of me running the same route last night. We were getting closer, and I lowered my body in the passenger seat in case we drove past him.

'Slow down, slow down,' I demanded. 'It's the next block.'

Emily drove slowly past Tom's house. No sign of his car.

'I wish his floor wasn't so high up and we could peek in the windows,' I grumbled.

'Do you realise how crazy you sound?' Emily giggled.

'Yip.' I shrugged. 'Can we drive past his new clinic? He could be there,' I suggested.

'No, absolutely not. Let's get you home before I'm arrested.'

On the drive to my flat, Emily tried to distract me by nattering about her new gym classes and fitness instructor who specialised in women who had children. I nodded in a daze preoccupied with my own childless barren woman thoughts.

'What are you going to do now?' she asked, pulling up outside my close.

'Cry myself to sleep again probs.' I chuckled at my accuracy, then dragged my legs round to the side of the car door.

'I know it doesn't seem like it now, but you will feel better. I promise, sis.'

Emily peeped the horn as she drove off, drawing even more attention to my sleepwear.

I let myself into the flat. It was spotless from the night I thought Tom was coming round. No letters. No voicemails. Nothing was here. Just me, alone, once again.

I went into my room, lay down on my bed, and re-read every message Tom ever sent to me. I smiled at the cute, funny texts, ones from the first few weeks of dating when everything was so exciting and new. He must have liked me at some point? I'd left in such a rush last night—maybe I should call him? Without a second thought, I replied to his last message.

I can talk now if you're free?

Send.

He was online immediately, and the blue ticks appeared, indicating he'd read my message.

My phone began ringing. *Tom.*

My heart was thumping, and my breathing turned shallow. I didn't even know how to act. Annoyed? Angry? Pissed? Upset? Should I beg? I had no idea.

'Hello,' I answered, pretending I didn't know who was calling.

'Hi, Zara, how are you?'

I laughed a little at his formalities. 'Been better.'

'Me too. So, I suppose I should start. Firstly, I want to apologise for last night. We've been friends for a lot of years, and one day I hope to get that friendship back.'

'To be honest, Tom, I still have no idea what's been going on. Are you and Harriette a couple?'

The phone went silent for a few seconds.

'Yes,' he said eventually.

I could feel myself breathing more deliberately and deeply in an attempt to stop myself from crying.

'So, what was I then?'

'Oh, Zara. Come on. Please don't make me feel worse than I already do. We would never have worked out. Fucking hell, you're years younger for a start, and you're a bloody student.'

'Ahh, right. Well, I wish I knew that's how you felt at the time, Tom.'

'I'm sorry if I led you on, Zara. We had a lot of chemistry, there's no denying that. Look on the bright side, we don't have to work together at the clinic now, and you only have a few more weeks left at the hospital, and I'll be out of your hair for good.'

'Oh, I'm contacting the uni. I'm not going back to that ward, Tom.'

'Yeah, perhaps that would be for the best—for everyone involved.'

Silent tears were coursing down my cheeks as he spoke. He had tossed me to the side so quickly. Like I was nothing.

'Does Harriette know about me?' I asked.

'Of course she doesn't. I mean, I have no idea what she got up to in London for all those months either. But no, she doesn't.'

'Okay,' There was a beat of silence.

'Listen,' he said, 'I'm rushed off my feet with the clinic, all the decorating's being done today. I'll give you a text later on, okay?'

'Okay.' I got off the phone and let out a loud cry.

Every emotion that I held back on the call came out of me now. *How can he do this to me? Why am I not enough for him?* I rocked myself back and forth, praying he would phone back and change his mind. The thought of never seeing Tom again made me feel sick, but he wanted me to leave the ward, he didn't even want to see me again. I'd thought when I mentioned placement, he would encourage me to stay, but no.

How could twenty-four hours change so much?

I scrolled through the university's app and completed a change of placement request form, citing personal circumstances. I couldn't go back there. There was no way. How could I watch the man I loved with someone else right in front of me?

I waited for a text back from him, but it never came.

Eventually the tears dried up, but I continued to lay on my bed where I remained for the next few days.

Chapter Twenty-Four

I spent three days in bed, unwashed and only eating hardened Doritos and a tin of spaghetti hoops I had in the cupboard.

When I wasn't asleep, I stalked Tom and Harriette's social media. I had even begun following her Depop page, idolising her expensive dress sense and size six clothing. Ashley, Emily and Raj had all checked in with concerned messages, and I was waiting on my personal lecturer getting back to me about switching wards. Right now, my degree meant nothing. I was broken. I felt empty without Tom. I didn't care about my career or my health. I just lay around my bedroom sobbing, then occasionally walked through to the bathroom with my duvet attached to me. I spent hours scrolling through WhatsApp, watching Tom go online, then count how long he was active for, wondering who he was messaging. I must have changed my own WhatsApp profile picture at least sixteen times hoping he'd notice, but he didn't call or text. I was going crazy and fully aware of it.

On Sunday morning, I heard a buzz from the intercom. I sat up in bed, feeling a little dizzy as I hadn't moved for such a long time, but stumbled through to the living room to answer it.

'Hello?'

'It's Ash. Let me up.'

'Okay,' I sighed, disappointed it wasn't a florist bringing *forgive me* flowers. I opened the door and lifted a hefty pile of mail I had been ignoring, then made my way to the living room sofa, waiting on Ashley's arrival.

'Jesus, Zara, you look terrible,' she blurted when she came in.

'Thanks,' I replied, looking down at my four-day-old PJs.

She popped her gym bag at the side of the sofa while taking a seat herself. 'Have you even washed since Wednesday?'

'Only with my own tears,' I answered dramatically.

She began laughing.

'Stop! Right, get dressed. We're going to a gym class, let's get you motivated and moving. I'm literally not taking no for an answer.'

'Ash, seriously, I can't. Look at me.'

She stood up, grabbed my wrist and started pulling my smelly overweight body off the sofa.

'Move!' she yelled and pushed me.

'I can't go, I fucking stink.' I stopped and folded my arms in protest.

'You can get washed after a workout, silly. Come on. You get ready, and I'll tidy up a bit.'

I knew there was no way she'd leave me alone, so I let out a childish scream before reluctantly heading to my wardrobe and sifting through the mound of clothes to find gym attire. I chose my black Adidas leggings and a white T-shirt. My hair was thick with grease, so I pulled it back into a tight ponytail. I looked a fucking mess. My skin was pale, and my cheeks were puffy.

'Is that you then?' Ashley called out.

'I look too fat and ugly to go anywhere, Ash.'

'A few more gym classes and you will be a skinny minnie! And Zara, trust me, you're certainly not ugly, I wouldn't hang about with a munter!'

I attempted a smile as we left my flat and walked down the hill towards Pure Gym on Hope Street.

'What class we doing then?'

'Hot yoga! It's my new fave.'

'I can't do cold yoga never mind fucking hot yoga, Ash.'

'Shut up. Stop being negative. Today is about getting you out the bloody house and starting to feel good again.' She smiled over, showing me her entirely white veneers, reminding me I hadn't even brushed my teeth since the incident. I couldn't help but feel grateful towards my friend. No matter how much I didn't want to go to this class, I knew her intentions were good.

'So, have you heard from Arsehole Head?' she asked.

'Nope. I don't think I will either. He's totally over it.'

'Yeah, because he has a new fucking girlfriend instantly to occupy his ego.'

I shrugged, still feeling a stabbing pain in my stomach even thinking about him.

'You know his clinic launch is on Friday. Raj thinks we should all go,' Ash said.

My head turned slowly to face her.

'She'd be there too.'

'No shit, Sherlock. But you could get dolled up. Call Sarah at the salon, I'm sure she'd fit you in, and we'll get you a beautiful dress. Make him jealous Zara, fuck it.'

'I don't think I'm ready for that.'

Ashley shrugged as we walked through the doors of the gym. The music was loud, and I instantly felt self-conscious at the number of young girls in belly tops and hot topless men parading in and out of the lobby. My eyes expanded with lust at the smell of sweat and masculinity as we approached the desk.

'Two for the hot yoga please, Dale.' Ashley popped her card on the counter while I examined the facility.

'Sure. And your friend's name, Ash?'

I turned to greet Dale with a yellow, gritty smile.

'Zara, this is Zara.'

'Nice to meet you, Zara. It's in Studio One today, ladies.'

'Thank you.' I smiled at how young, fresh and pre-pubescent Dale looked. He didn't look old enough to go to the gym, never mind work in it.

'You're welcome. Aw nice, did you have a swim before class too? She's keen, Ashley. We should get her signed up.'

He was pointing towards my head. I nodded politely back at him, but inside was thinking, *No chance I'm signing up to anything, Dale. Nice try!*

Ashley laughed loudly as we turned the corner, taking my arm while ushering me towards the studio.

'What's he talking about?' I whispered.

'Your fucking hair. You could fry a pan of chips on your head, Zara. Poor Dale thought it was wet from a swim,' she giggled, walking up the corridor while I chuckled, slightly offended.

'Cheeky bastard!' I said, trying to brush through my greasy locks with my fingers.

We entered the class, and I was immediately taken aback by the heat. It felt like I had just walked off a flight to Florida.

'Fucking hell, Ash.' I was panting before the class began.

'Shhh, go get a mat.'

I proceeded to collect a mat from the corner and sat my belongings to the side. I joined Ashley and copied her, putting my legs in a basket, waiting for the class to begin. The instructor was called Tony. He had long blonde hair wrapped into a man bun, and wore Aztec trousers and a tie-dye vest. I smiled at how stereotypically hippy he looked.

'Let's begin,' he called out and began chanting.

I shut my eyes to avoid immaturely sniggering to my friend and ruining everyone else's workout.

I was moving from pose to pose, fixated on Tony. He was incredibly flexible, and within ten minutes, I was mastering downward dog, into the dolphin to bridges. This was quite fun. The more the class was going on, the more I began to wonder if Tony was giving me the eye. His muscular arms, his sweat, his flexibility, I couldn't help but think he would be some shagger-capable of many positions, but it was too soon to move on Tony. I'd have to let him down gently if he asked. I was changing poses in my best attempt to be seductive, after all a little flirt didn't kill anyone, I felt like J-Lo, until I caught a glimpse of myself looking like Mandy Dingle in the mirror. Shit, maybe not. I was a riot. I was stretching frantically, but my legs and back finally gave in. It was too much. After half an hour, the class ended, and I was fucked.

'Namaste,' Tony said to the class, before walking over to me.

'Zara, lovely to have you here today.' I blushed still feeling the sweat fall from my face. *I bloody knew it, he fancies me!* I smiled back politely, trying to catch my breath.

'But perhaps the Monday morning beginners' class would be best suited. Start from the basics. I think you were struggling today. Namaste.'

'Aye, Namaste,' I replied shocked.

My face fell as he walked off and I took in his insult. *What a cheeky bastard.* Ashley erupted into laughter and I joined in briefly, feeling offended.

I waited until he was out of sight. 'What a prick! I think I did better than half the fuckers in here, Ash.' She was still laughing, trying to control herself.

'Oh, Zara, you did well I thought.' Ashley sipped her water, letting out a giggle mid-drink and spurting it out everywhere.

'I thought he was coming over to ask me out, he can shove his beginners' class up his arse,' I grunted offendedly.

I lifted my steamy phone to find a new email from uni.

Placement request denied. Please contact ward manager tomorrow at 9am.

Shit. My heart began pounding.

'What is it?' Ash asked, seeing my face.

'I have to contact Anne now and explain why I want to leave. She hates me enough as it is.' I was panicking.

'It will be a formality. Go into the ward, sit down and chat to her, she can't be that bad.'

I huffed. 'I can't. Why are things never easy for me?'

Ashley and I headed back to my flat with aching legs, pleased to get some cold fresh air on our way.

'Do you want to get drunk tonight?' I asked.

She rolled her eyes. 'No. I'm working tomorrow afternoon, and you have that meeting. Zara, come on!' She seemed pissed that I couldn't get out of my slump.

'Okay, okay.'

As soon as we got into the flat, I made a beeline to get washed. I stood under the warm water, questioning how I'd let my life get so out of control. I had no money, no job, no boyfriend, no kids. I lived in my mum's flat because I couldn't afford my own. I was almost thirty and had fuck all to show for it. I hadn't eaten a proper meal or washed myself in over three days and was only doing it now because my friend persuaded me to. I sobbed under the water for the strength to get over this.

When I came out, Ashley was on the sofa, flicking through Netflix. She turned as she heard my squelching steps.

'Come sit and watch this with me.' She patted the sofa next to her, encouraging me to sit. I walked over, wrapped in my damp towel with hairy legs and dripping wet hair.

'What is it?' I asked.

'Have you heard of that Tony Robbins? Or *The Secret* or the Law of Attraction even or any sort of motivational shit like that?' She sat up excitedly, ready to explain.

'I've heard of them,' I said and rolled my eyes, preparing for another life lesson.

'Okay, so that's totally what you need right now. Some guidance. Like, the Law of Attraction is basically when you create your own luck. You look for signs or opportunities and grab them. Take risks!'

'But how do I know what's a good sign and what's a bad sign?'

'You *know*. Your gut tells you. And then you have your breakthrough!'

I started to laugh. 'My what?'

'When a moment happens, and you suddenly have an idea or realisation. It just comes to you, and you know exactly what to do at that exact moment to change your life. Everything all of a sudden makes sense. For instance, people want to get a job but they don't know what to do, so they search for signs. The following week they could be walking down the street and an old lady falls over, they might help and sit with her

232

until a paramedic arrives and the old lady says, 'You would make an excellent nurse,' and boom—there's the sign. It's like a light bulb going on in your head.'

'I think it's Tom who's needing one of them breakthroughs, not me,' I said.

'Seriously, Zara, it's about self-love and being grateful for what you have too. Will you watch this film with me?'

I turned to my friend, who was sticking out her bottom lip.

'It's not as if I'm doing anything else anyway, is it!' I laughed and pulled a blanket over to cover my spiky legs.

We lay together, laughing and crying at *The Secret, Dare to Dream*, part of me thinking it was a load of bullshit, part of me praying I would one day get a breakthrough myself. I had missed Ashley, her company, her compassion, her optimism—and for a few moments that night, I felt like me again.

Chapter Twenty-Five

I woke the next morning to Ashley hovering over me with a hot cup of tea and some toast.

'Morning, sleeping beauty,' she whispered.

I managed a grumble in response.

'I've got breakfast here. You need to wake up,' she said.

'Time is it?' I mumbled, attempting to resume my perfected foetal position.

'It's seven, but you have a meeting with Anne.'

I opened my eyes and immediately felt a stabbing pain of anxiety in my heart.

'I don't think I can go.' I sat up, shaking my head.

'Stop. Yes, you can. I'll come with you. This is your career, Zara, you can't just leave it because of a fuckin' arsehole man.'

I knew she was right, but the thought of any confrontation made me want to crawl back under my covers.

'Here.' She passed me my black tea and toast caked in Lurpak and mashed banana.

I smiled at her gratefully and sipped my tea.

'What am I going to fucking say, Ash?'

'Be honest? That's all you can do. Ask to get moved for personal reasons. I don't think anyone can argue with that.'

'Yeah, I suppose. I actually ended up loving that ward too. I hate how I have to move. When I started, Anne said she wanted strict professional boundaries while I'm there. Shit.'

'Well, it's him that goes out of bounds, Zara. She knew about both of you before and it's not as if you met on shift.'

'I suppose.'

'Come on, finish that, and I'll do your hair and makeup.' She knelt up on the bed, clapping her hands. 'I think glamourous curls, plain but pristine makeup with a dramatic flick liner and some lashes. That way if Tom sees you, he'll be like 'goddamn'.'

'I doubt he'd even bat an eyelid when he's next to Daenerys Targaryen,' I said. Ashley pretended to laugh, having never watched an episode of *Game of Thrones* in her life. 'But thanks, Ash, that all sounds good.'

I reluctantly prised myself from the bed and sat in front of the mirror while Ash curled my hair. We sat silently as I went over and over Wednesday night for the millionth time. *Maybe I shouldn't have surprised him, and right now I'd be none the wiser. Happy and still in love.*

When my hair was done, Ashley turned me around and told me to close my eyes, allowing her to do my makeup. I could feel the plod of beauty blenders and brushes bouncing off my skin but didn't know or care what the finished result would be. Ash continued for half an hour, concentrating intensely, while I looked up to the side, stayed still and followed her instructions.

'Okay, now look,' she said, finally finished.

When I faced the mirror I was gobsmacked. I looked amazing. My skin was flawless, and my lifeless hair was bouncing as I turned my head this way and that, admiring it.

'WOW. Ash, I love it. Do you think I look OTT for a meeting though?'

'Fuck no. You can never be overdressed, Zara. Tell them you're going out after or something. In fact, it's none of their business.'

'Yeah, that would be funny. I can just imagine Anne's face.'

I continued to look in the mirror, admiring my new look.

'What about clothes?' I asked.

'I think a sleek black dress and tights. Yes. Tights are sexy and professional. Plus you have definitely lost weight in your depression.'

'Okay.' I took a deep breath. 'Let's do this.'

I slipped silky black tights over my razor-sharp stubbly legs and wore a black midi wrap dress over the top. I looked out a pair of kitten-heeled black pointy shoes, thinking they would make me look more professional.

Ashley shoved her hair in a large bun, borrowed my skinny black jeans and a plain grey top, and paired them with her gym trainers from the day before. We stood outside my flat, waiting for a taxi to arrive. The weather seemed dark and gloomy, dry but like it could rain at any second, so we waited at the door until we saw the car arriving. I didn't want to take any chances with Ashley's amazing work on my hair.

'How are you feeling?' she asked once we were in the taxi.

I felt my cold hands tremble and showed her. 'Terrified.'

'Don't be. You're asking for a change of placement, not a fucking kidney, okay?'

I nodded, staring out the window, hoping I didn't see Tom or Harriette walking into the busy hospital together.

We arrived at the Royal, and Ashley paid the fare.

'I've texted Raj. I'm going to meet him in the café. You can come get us when you're finished, okay?'

My mouth was too dry from nerves to speak, so I just nodded.

We strolled through the corridor together and I directed Ashley to the café. It was ten to nine, and I had ten minutes before the dreaded meeting with Anne. My heart was pounding, and my breathing had turned shallow. Ashley was trying to calm me down.

'Zara?' a voice said.

I turned around to find Tom standing with a bunch of medical students quick on his step. He was wearing a black suit with a black shirt.

'Are you serious right now?' Ashley snapped at him. He looked surprised to see her.

'Ash, don't make a scene,' I said. 'It's fine. What's up, Tom?' I was trying my best to appear confident. I could smell his fanny-tingling aftershave, and all I wanted to do was wrap my arms around his broad shoulders.

He looked down at the shiny hospital rubber floor. 'Can we speak?'

'It'll have to be quick. I have a meeting at nine.'

He turned to the students waiting expectantly behind him. 'Guys, you carry on, and I'll meet you outside Theatre One in five.' When they were gone, he turned to me and jerked his head to the side, suggesting that I should follow him.

Ashley stood, arms folded, giving him the death stare. 'Do you want me to come?' she asked.

'No, honestly. See you soon. I'll meet you here, Ash.'

I waited till Ashley had gone and then followed Tom a few steps to the side of the corridor.

'Firstly, I want to apologise for last week, Zara. I didn't want you to find out like that.' He began with his hands in his pockets and watching the corridor behind me pass by.

'It's fine. These things happen.' I shrugged avoiding eye contact.

'Okay, I'm glad you're being so understanding, I don't think I would have been.'

I gave a brief tut, nodding my head.

'Did you get your placement swapped?' he asked.

'That's where I'm going just now. I have a meeting with Anne.'

'Oh, that's good. Phew, eh.' He let out a sigh of relief.

'Is it good? I was really enjoying my placement. I'm a bit gutted, to be honest.'

'I mean, I suppose it's good for me not having any awkwardness in front of Harriette, but I understand you're disappointed.'

'Yes, disappointed but glad not to be in more situations like this. I need to go.'

'Yes, of course.'

I began walking away towards the ward.

'Zara, thank you,' Tom shouted behind me, walking off in the other direction.

He didn't care how I felt at all. He only wanted to protect his relationship with Harriette and his reputation at the hospital. I could feel my eyes fill with tears even as I fought against them. The last thing I needed was to start crying and walk into the meeting with Anne looking like a fucking drowned raccoon. I marched into the ward, getting angrier with each step and ready to demand a change of placement.

I stormed past a bunch of nurses, physios and students, making my way to Anne's office, and chapped her door loudly. Through the glass, I could see her engrossed in her laptop. When she heard my thumps, she slowly turned her head and took her time taking her glasses off before opening the office door.

'Good morning, Zara,' she said. There was a hint of sarcasm in her voice.

'Good morning, Sister,' I replied in the same tone, feeling brave with the adrenaline from my confrontation with Tom pumping through my veins.

'Come on in and have a seat.' She gestured to a seat in front of her desk and sat down in her more comfortable leather chair.

'I was surprised to receive the email from the uni stating you want to move placement, and before I accepted it I wanted a chat.'

'Okay.' The room fell silent for a few moments.

'Well?' She placed both hands flat on the desk and stared at me.

'I just don't think this is working for me, Sister.'

'Was it because I questioned your knowledge of the handover? Because we all have to take criticism now and again.'

'No, no, it's not that. I just didn't feel like it was working for me.' I shut my eyes tightly, not wanting to explain the reason. Tom and Anne were old friends, and I didn't want to come across as unprofessional. I sat back holding in my emotions.

'Zara, is this about Thomas?'

I opened my eyes, tasting the tears running down my face. I couldn't hold them any longer.

'I'm sorry. God, what is wrong with me.'

She pushed a box of tissues across the desk to me.

'You don't have to say one word. But all I will say is no one should make you feel like this. I can only guess what this is really about and, trust me, Tom was part of my family for many years—I can read him like a book. You're a good nurse, Zara—potentially a great one. Don't run away from somewhere you will excel because of a fucking man who can't keep it in his pants. Be brave, be strong and get the job done.'

I looked up unexpectedly at Anne's sympathetic face. Was she being nice to me? I was completely surprised and continued bubbling behind the desk into my tissue.

'I just don't think I can face them every day together and he wants me to leave.'

She let out a wild laugh.

'All the more reason to stay. This is my ward, Zara. I decide who I want here. We need strong women to help run it, and the day you stepped onto this ward with your little pad taking notes, I realised you were a strong woman. I was hard on you because I can see real potential, but it's up to you if you can see it too.'

'Thank you, Anne.'

'What do you think?'

'I'd love to stay, but . . .'

'There are no buts. Take this week off. You can make up the days. Get yourself together because when you come back, we will be making a real nurse out of you.'

I looked up, grateful and astonished. I felt lost for words. Going into the meeting I had my back up ready to declare World War Three but in fact she got it.

'Thank you.' Was all I could manage back.

'You're welcome. Now, I won't mention this wobble to the uni. Have this week to sort yourself out, and I'll see you next Monday.'

I nodded, feeling like there was a glimmer of hope in sight. I couldn't help but wonder why she was being so understanding.

'We don't need to talk about this again, Zara. Now off you go, I have a bed meeting in five.'

I patted my damp eyes down carefully with the tissue and smiled over to Anne. I wanted to come back, and with one person believing in me, maybe I could.

'See you next week, Anne. And thank you again.'

She gave me a wink and turned her swivel chair back towards her laptop. I walked back down the ward feeling lighter, with a purpose again. When I entered the cafeteria, I heard Raj and Ashley laughing from across the room. I went over to the table, and both of them glanced up.

'Oh la la, you look nice, Zara. You feeling better?' Raj asked.

'So much better, thanks.'

'Did you get it sorted?' Ashley wondered.

'I got it sorted but not in the way I thought it would happen. I'm coming back next week.'

'Whattttt?' Ashley looked confused.

'I'll explain everything in a bit, but first I feel like I owe you an explanation, Raj. You're one of my best friends, and I feel like I haven't been honest with you.'

'Zara, let me interrupt you,' Raj said. 'I know about you and Tom. He was my best mate, remember. I saw both of you together before he finished up and had an idea of what was going on. Ashley's filled me in since about Harri.' His big brown eyes looked at me sympathetically.

'Thank God. I was so nervous to tell you, Raj. You never said anything!' I hit his arm jokingly as I took the seat next to him.

'I knew you would tell me when you were ready.' He popped his head gently on my shoulder, and I felt so grateful to have a friend like him.

'So, guys. What are we doing about Tom's opening party?' Ashley interrupted our kind moment.

'I think we have to go. It would look bad on Individualise if we didn't. This way he can't talk shit behind our backs,' Raj said.

I lifted both hands up and, with a thump, crashed my head between them.

'You don't have to, Zara, but me and Ash should,' he went on.

'Too right I'm going to get a deck at this posh bitch,' Ash said. 'We should colour coordinate guys, make it obvious we're from another clinic.'

'I'm up for that.' Raj was nodding his head, liking the idea.

'If you are going, I am too,' I said, lifting my head. 'I might have to get drunk beforehand, but I'm in.' Ashley squealed with excitement.

We sat in the busy hospital canteen for another half-hour planning, coordinating and plotting for Tom's opening night.

I had a full week off to get my emotions, my roots and my weight under control, and I planned to make myself as irresistible as I could. Maybe then he would see sense and realise that he should have picked me.

Chapter Twenty-Six

The rest of the week, my emotions were all over the place. Sometimes I felt motivated, career determined and willing to return to the gym, but mostly I was unable to prise myself from my Pringle-stained couch. At times I contemplated pissing in a cup rather than taking my fat arse to the bathroom, with no energy levels to accomplish the smallest tasks. I continued to stalk Tom's LinkedIn account as well as Harriette's multiple social media platforms. I had even favourited his clinic's Insta page and carefully analysed each female who frequently liked his posts. I had half of fucking Glasgow to contend with.

On Wednesday, I woke up feeling sticky and bloated. I glanced under the duvet to a blood-stained butchering. *Well, that makes sense, fucking Shark Week back with a vengeance.* Just in time for the only night out I had planned for months, the night I was supposed to make my handsome ex mine again and my body was giving me a Code Red situation.

Perhaps this is a sign, Zara? I felt a sense of relief as I realised that the more extensive psychotic thoughts I was having could be blamed solely on this. Suddenly, daydreaming of keying Tom's car or drafting an unsigned letter of adultery to Harriette made sense. It wasn't me acting crazy after all, it was my menstrual bitch cycle returning and not taking being dumped lightly.

My hair appointment was at twelve that day, and I travelled through to Motherwell on the train, arriving at the luxury Bombshell Salon a few minutes early. One of the younger assistants sat me down in the waiting section with a hot latte for company. I flicked through my phone, searching for a perfect dress for Friday night's opening.

'Oh my God, Zara, you look so skinny!' my hairdresser, Sarah, declared, bursting loudly onto the shop floor.

'Thank you! And you're so glam as always,' I replied enviously. Sarah was wearing a leopard print midi dress and chunky trainers, with her hair sitting perfectly above her shoulders.

'No, seriously, are you working out? Or Slimming World?' She stood over me, analysing my body, looking pretty impressed.

'Break-up diet, I think.'

'Aw fuck, sorry to hear that. But you do look amazing,' she said sincerely and rubbed my shoulders.

Sarah had been transforming my and Ashley's hair for years. She also visited Raj's clinic regularly for treatments, and I considered her more of a friend than anything else. Her salon was now the go-to place for hair in the city—having no walk-in appointments or availability for new clients, I was grateful she'd squeezed me in.

'What are you thinking, doll?' she asked, pulling my hair tightly and examining the colour.

'A *big* change. I'm so fed up with everything right now, Sarah.'

'Okay, let's do it. Nothing like the break-up hairdo, hen! New hair, new man!'

Sarah and her team worked for hours on my hair, colouring, tinting and chopping. The bustle of the place was a great way to take my mind off Tom. I loved the warm aroma of the shop and the chat and stories from the girls. They were eager listeners, so I was happy to fill them in on my latest drama, and after three hours, I finally had my new look. My black hair was transformed into a warm, caramel balayage. The long, black, straggly ends were cut stylishly and bluntly to rest on my shoulders.

'What do you think?' Sarah stood back, admiring her masterpiece.

'I honestly love it. So stylish and trendy.' I couldn't keep the smile off my face.

'I love it too. It suits you so much better.'

'Thanks, Sarah.' I couldn't keep my eyes off the mirrors as I walked over to the counter to pay.

'Tag us in your selfies! I can't wait to see your pictures on Friday, and Zara, good luck!' Sarah beamed.

I left the shop and strutted back to the train station, feeling much more confident than on the journey in.

Ping. Ashley.

I have an idea of outfits for Friday x

I was about to reply when an abundance of photos came buzzing through my phone.

I want a red trouser suit. I think you should go for a red silk dress and Raj will have a black suit, black shirt and red tie with matching handkerchief. What you think???

I carefully examined the images. I loved them. They all looked amazing, and I had a sudden burst of excitement on the train as I imagined us glammed up together. Was I really going to do this?

LOVE them. Just had my hair done too. Kinda excited to gate crash now. Where will I get the dress from? xxx

Send.

Ping.

OMG send me pics of the hair now!!! From my wardrobe. You will be able to fit into it now, skinny. Just stay aff the Just Eats! x

I chuckled at her cheeky reply, knowing there was no chance I'd be able to pay for takeaway food after the trip to the salon.

Back at the flat, I skimmed through my underwear drawer to find a silky black push-up bra that was way too small. I stretched it on and stared at my reflection in my dirty spot-popping mirror. *This could work, I think.* Even though the upper half of my right nipple had popped right out of the bra, hopefully when the dress was on no one would notice. Plus, it gave an excellent lift to my breasts.

Next, I rummaged around my miscellaneous drawers, gathering old bottles of fake tan and carefully weighing them in each hand to establish which had the largest volume of product left. Then, with my old fluffy sock to hand, I began mixing and distributing the various brands of tan all over my body, smothering them thickly over my pale porcelain skin. I was concentrating incredibly hard, feeling like I was re-enacting a scene from *Breaking Bad*. Except it wasn't crystal meth, it was tan, and Tom was my addiction.

Once I was sufficiently covered, I stood with my legs wide apart, smirking at my little tampon string dangling between them. I stayed there for a while, allowing the tan to soak into my pores evenly as I endured the damp dog stench. *Hopefully the fucking smell washes off*, I thought. Mixing the various brands seemed to have made the odour worse. When I was almost dry, I slipped on some satin shorts and lay on my bed, painting my nails. This was the first day of self-care I had participated in for a long time, and it felt good. I looked healthy, and despite the circumstances, I was keen for Tom to see my new look.

Before bed, I closed my eyes and took the time to reflect on the past few weeks. Whenever I slowed down and my mind processed it all, I felt sick. *Why did he have to ruin this?* I felt like I was in mourning, like I had lost a part of myself. Like I had lost him completely. My eyes streamed as the doubt crept in again, that perhaps I just wasn't enough for him and never would be.

I took small gentle breaths, carefully patting the old brown sock against my mahogany cheek. I had to keep it together for a little bit longer. I wasn't prepared to ruin my tan.

Chapter Twenty-Seven

It was Friday. The day of the grand opening. I laughed as I saw the grey clouds descend on a cold, drizzly afternoon in Glasgow. *Perfect weather for his big night,* I thought.

I was getting ready at Ashley's house; Raj would pick us up in a taxi around seven, and the three of us would arrive together. My tan looked surprisingly even, my body was the skinniest it had been since puberty, and my hair was chic and seductive. If the circumstances were altered slightly, I would be geared up for a wild night out with my friends. However, the only thing on my depressive mind was to simply show Tom what he was missing. What could go wrong?

Ashley and I began getting ready around five; she styled my hair loosely and slid it into a side parting, then carefully contoured my skin, packed my large brown eyes with a mixture of golden-brown eyeshadow for a dramatic smoky effect and topped it off with a severe Russian-red lipstick. With a careful rub of my overdrawn lips, I was ready. It was the best I had ever looked. I felt sensational and couldn't take my eyes off the mirror.

'I feel so pretty, Ash.' I beamed at her as I paraded myself in front of her double-mirrored wardrobes with her fluffy dressing gown wrapped around me.

'You look it! This is the best you've ever looked. Tom is going to fucking *die* when he sees us all, especially you like that.' She was shaking her head in disbelief at her own makeover talents. 'Right, it's my turn now, Zara. Go get some wine from the fridge and try the dress on.'

'Yes, okay!'

I hurried out of the room and poured myself an extensive rosé while dancing around to TLC's 'No Scrubs' blaring from the Alexa. I was hitting the rap section when I felt a warm dribble run down my leg. *Shit.* Blood, I forgot my tampons too.

I grabbed some kitchen roll and rubbed my leg, then held the wad firmly at my vagina.

'Ash, where are your tampons?'

I hobbled into the bedroom like Quasimodo, using my shoulder to open the doors, refusing to let go of my wine with one hand and vagina with the other.

'Fuck sake. Top drawer in the wardrobe.'

I continued my limp towards it, balancing my wine carefully on top of the unit while I rummaged through the drawer.

'I don't see any, it's just pads,' I called out over the music.

Ash shrugged at me. 'Yeah, that's all I wear. I hate tampons.'

'These pads are like a bit of Warburton's flatbread, they'll never last me the entire night!' I exclaimed.

Ashley started laughing. 'They are very absorbent. Take a couple and change when you're there. You'll be surprised how much they hold, honestly.'

I was petrified at the thought of any mishaps or leakages but they were my only option unless I wanted to take Ashley's kitchen roll with me.

'Where will I put them when I've finished with them?'

'Oh, for fuck's sake, Zara. In the sanny bin, or shove it in your bag. Each pad has a wee wrapper that you put the used sanny in when you've finished with it, then you can dispose of it discreetly.'

I examined the pads and plastic cover. *I don't think I've used these since I was twelve!*

They'll have to do. I popped two more pads in my handbag just in case and stuck a fresh one neatly to my underwear. I wasn't going to let a little blood ruin my night!

Ashley had finished curling her hair by now, and I watched as she sprayed hairspray onto each section. It was vibrant and bouncing, and she ran her fingers through it, loosening the curls into big, bold blonde waves.

'Wow. I *love* it,' I said, admiring my friend.

'Me too, I feel like Beyoncé,' she said, turning from her reflection to find me standing there with just my pants on, large wings hanging out the sides.

'Will you hurry up and get ready?' she giggled.

'Yes. Yes. I'm going.'

I unhooked the silky red dress from the hanger and brought it through to the living room. *Please let this fit*. I slipped the thin straps over my head and watched it fall to my knees, sucking my stomach in slightly as I pulled up the side zip. Looking down, I could only see my tits, pushed up by the silky black bra, but I felt pretty.

I walked nervously back into the bedroom, waiting on Ashley's seal of approval.

'Oh my God. Amazing! You look amazing!' she gasped and moved towards me.

I caught a full-length view of myself in the mirror behind her. *Wow, I do look amazing*.

'Like, literally, Tom is going to die!'

I blushed, hoping Ashley was right.

While she finished getting ready, I sat in the living room—adjusted the strap to my gold shoes and sipped away at my glass of wine. It was almost a quarter to seven before Ashley was finally organised, and she looked unbelievable in her all-red trouser suit. She buttoned the suit jacket so that a black lacy bra underneath peeped through as she moved, and she had a large clip with 'Girl Boss' embellished onto the front of her curly hair.

'Let's do this.' Ashley lifted her glass, swallowed the rest of her wine, and headed to the front door.

I stood up behind her. 'Now?'

'Raj has been outside for ten minutes.'

I followed her out, suddenly feeling an overwhelming amount of nerves and anxiety. But there was no time to stop. I just carried on behind her, hurrying as the rain fell on the damp, gleaming street.

'Ladies, you look incredible!' Raj gushed as we squeezed into the cab, squealing at the rain.

He was dressed immaculately, just as Ashley had planned in a black tailored suit with a red tie.

'Next stop please, driver.'

The car began moving as we all adjusted ourselves.

'Are any of you thinking we will look a little too extra tonight? I'm a bit scared now.' I giggled, feeling nervous at how committed we all were, completely dressed for the occasion.

'Fuck yes, we're extra, and that's how we want clients to remember us, Zara,' Raj said, wrapping his arms around Ashley and me, hugging us tightly.

'I'm lucky to have you girls. I know that. Especially the past few weeks. And Zara, please tell me you're in tomorrow. I seriously need you, we're mobbed!'

'I'll be there. Sorry, Raj, I needed a few days,' I said, feeling guilty.

'No, no, I get it. A few days without you makes me wonder how on earth I'm going to cope when you're qualified and leave us. I'll seriously miss all your help!'

'Enough of that sob story, Raj. Pay for the taxi. We're here,' Ashley said, but she was smirking.

I gazed out the window surprised to see the stone steps of Tom's clinic now sporting a red carpet down the centre. There were black and gold balloons at either side of the grand entrance, and I glanced up to see the 'Ageless' sign, boldly lighting up the street from above the door. It looked elegant and sophisticated. *I'll give him that.*

Raj nudged me as my dark eyes fixated on the building. 'C'mon, wee yin, let's go.'

'Raj, you walk in the middle. Zara, you're over that side.' Ashley positioned us just so, and we walked up the steps together, heading through the doorway into the newly refurbished, bright building. The rooms were full, but between the chatter I could hear the soothing sound of classical music.

'Champagne?' a polite waitress greeted us, and as Ashley and I took a glass, Raj opted for the orange juice.

'It is a nice clinic.' Raj nodded.

The hallway was occupied with lots of pretentious upper-class people, and I was finding it difficult to concentrate on my friends' chat from jerking my neck any time I heard the name 'Tom' mentioned. My stomach was in knots. *Where is he?*

We wandered around the clinic as I showed the other two a layout of the rooms. We walked through a familiar set of double doors, and I smiled as I remembered the picnic blanket that he lay there for me once. Now, the floor was filled with an expensive buffet table and lots of high heels. I could smell a mixture of fresh paint and champagne as I studied the rooms.

'Ah, I'm glad you all could make it.'

I turned to that familiar English accent to find Tom standing in a navy suit.

'Ashley.' He kissed her cheek. 'Raj.' He shook his hand. 'Zara.' He leaned towards me, kissing my cheek too. I closed my eyes as he brushed by me. I could smell his scent of spicy masculinity, and my heart pounded.

'You all look fantastic,' he said.

He didn't seem to notice my new look. Nothing about me. He gazed through me as if I was invisible.

Ashley and I glanced at one another, not knowing how to reply.

'Thanks, yes. Our stylist here demanded we made an effort,' Raj replied, gesturing towards Ashley, who nodded back. There was tension between the two friends as Raj's eyes were scanning the room, appearing uninterested in Tom's conversation.

'Do you like the décor, Zara?' Tom looked at me with a grin on his perfect face. I looked around the room pleasingly. It was the wallpaper I had picked on that first date.

'Yes, I do. Whoever picked it must have exquisite taste, Tom,' I replied, feeling my face go warm. My heart pined as we faced one another. The room of chatty guests went silent as I glared at the man I loved.

'Raj! I'm so glad you came.'

My moment was interrupted by a perfect blonde bombshell, Harriette. Tom suddenly turned stiff and looked down at the floor.

'Well, what do you think of the place?' she asked, bursting with excitement.

'Very nice, very nice indeed. It's very chic,' Raj said politely.

I was looking at Ashley, who was tapping her black designer stilettoed foot off the wooden floor.

'We love it! Don't we, darling?' Harriette made her way back to him, putting her long thin arms over his muscular shoulders. He nodded at her excited face.

'Excuse me, guys,' I said. 'I'm going to nip to the loo.'

'Oh, it's just through the doors and—'

'It's fine, Harriette. I know where I'm going, thanks,' I snapped before I could think, and walked off through the crowd.

This was a bad idea. How could I ever think he'd pick me when he had her—a beautiful, tall, intelligent doctor. I burst into the bathroom and let out a sigh. The emerald-green wallpaper I'd chosen was throughout this room too. I stood in the small queue, waiting on my turn to use the only cubicle, observing the fancy golden taps and selection of Molton Brown soaps. There was no escaping the memories I had of him, especially here.

Eventually, I got into the toilet and sat down, placing my hands on my worried head. *I should just go, what am I doing here?* When I stood up again I felt a sudden gush onto my fanny pad. *Shit, I'll change this first.* I pulled my dress up and lowered my underwear to my knees. *Okay, so how do I do this again?* I reached over to my bag and retrieved the small, plastic sanitary towel pack and sat it on my lap while pulling the saturated pad off my pants. I glanced around the small cubicle. *Great. No bin. I'll have to wrap this in the new pad's packaging and take it home like Ash suggested.* I attempted this confusing and awkward process with great difficultly as there was nowhere to sit anything. With no other options, I lightly placed the used pad onto the wall while opening the fresh pad from the packaging. I made sure I stuck the new pad firmly to my pants, establishing a secure, comfortable seal before standing up. *Still have to get rid of the evidence.* The door chapped and I could hear the sounds of frustrated women needing to pee outside.

'One moment, please.'

Feeling harassed, I began to hurry, opening the empty poke to wrap and dispose of the bloody towel that waited patiently for me. I tugged on the pad sticking perfectly to the wall and with an almighty RIPPPPPP I tore not only the sanitary pad off but also the expensive wallpaper behind it. Before I could do anything, the entire strip of wallpaper was unleashed from the wall and crashed to the floor.

I gasped in horror at what I had done. *Fuck!!!*

My whole body froze. What was I going to do? *Think fast, Zara, think fast!* My heart was beating so hard I could hear it vibrate through my entire body. The crowd outside was growing larger and more impatient. With nothing else for it, I ripped the bloody pad from the mountain of paper piled up on the floor and shoved it in my handbag, then gathered the streams of emerald green into a corner of the cubicle and waltzed out, trying to look casual and inconspicuous. I washed my hands swiftly, smiling at some of the familiar faces waiting for their turn in the loo. Over the sound of the taps, I heard a dramatic gasp from the lady who went in behind me, and dashed through the door back into the hallway. After a frantic search around the room looking for my friends, I eventually caught a glimpse of a red trouser suit and rushed over.

Ashley and Raj were joking to one another as they read Tom's treatment menu.

'Guys!' I exclaimed in a hushed voice.

'Where were you? I was worried. God, Zara you have dust or something all over you, ' Ashley said and began flicking the evidence onto the floor.

'In the bathroom. We *need* to leave. Like *now*.' I flapped my hands in a panic, looking over my shoulder.

'Sure, Zara. Let's go.' Raj smiled and put his arm around me.

'I'd be happy to leave, the classical music vibe is giving me a migraine,' Ashley chipped in.

I lifted my champagne glass from Ashley and downed the bubbles before grabbing my friends' arms and ushering them out of the party. We headed towards the taxi rank, Raj constantly rubbing my back, offering me his way of support while I laughed hard, knowing the real reason I had to flee.

When I returned to my flat that night, I set my alarm for 8am, ready for my first shift in the clinic since my heartbreak. I laid out my clothes neatly for the following day before getting into bed and torturing myself with the Ageless Instagram posts from the party. I had got into the habit of scrolling through all their social media before bed and it got me wondering if Tom had even noticed my dress or new hair. He didn't seem too, which made me feel worse.

I knew it was time to start living my life again, no matter how much it hurt.

I was happy to return to the clinic and I felt surprisingly excited at the thought of placement on Monday. It was time to wake up and realise: I had lost Tom forever and no transformation would win him back.

Chapter Twenty-Eight

Between shifts at the clinic that weekend, I occupied myself reading up on the Law of Attraction. The fact that I could somehow change my life for the better and reach a peak state of happiness seemed unlikely, but I was willing to try anything to get some control back. I listened to podcasts, read books and began a gratitude journal in a notebook that was gifted to me a few Christmases ago by Ashley. I spent hours documenting things I wanted to change about myself— which let's face it, right now, felt like everything. I waited for signs 'the universe' would send me, hoping that one day I could get out of bed without having to swallow a handful of propranolol and sporting a dark cloud above my head.

Returning to placement was getting closer and looming over me, and although I added Jason on Facebook and we sent a few messages back and forth, I still felt nauseous about seeing Tom again. I explained to him that I had a bad break-up but didn't mention the names of the two doctors in question. I also couldn't believe that in only four more weeks I would be a fully qualified nurse. It was daunting.

The Sunday before placement, I attempted to get an early night. I tossed and turned at possible scenarios that could happen in the ward, letting my imagination run wild. *What if Harriette pulls me up in front of everyone? What if Tom has CCTV of my toilet escapades? What if my patient gets ill and nobody will help me?* My eyes were already wide for my alarm going off, and I questioned if I had even slept at all.

Peering outside my window, I saw a dry morning in Glasgow and decided to walk up the hill rather than jumping in a taxi as I had planned. When I was ready and had locked the flat behind me, I popped my head-phones on and continued to listen to Tony Robbins' *Unleash the Power Within* audiobook, desperate for posi-tive thoughts. As I approached the hospital, I took a deep breath. *Today will be a good day, please God make it a good day.* I walked through the main entrance, smiling at familiar co-workers who were still half asleep and en route to their allocated wards. I travelled upstairs to the changing room, and once I was in uniform, continued towards Ward Seventy-six for the handover. As I walked the ward corridor, I peered through the glass windows, keen to recognise some patients inside the rooms from two weeks earlier. When I got to the nursing station, I searched the colourful NHS uniforms until I saw Jason proudly sporting his royal blue tunic.

I approached him from behind, gently tapping his shoulder. 'Morning.'

He turned suddenly when he heard my voice. 'Oh, good morning, sweetheart! Here, I kept you a seat.'

He patted a small plastic chair at the side of him, and I sat down. 'You feeling better?'

'Yeah. I'm excited to be here,' I said, lifting a hand-over report from the desk.

'Have you done something to your hair?' Jason started running his chubby fingers through the ends of my newly chopped locks.

'Yes, fancied a wee change.'

'You suit it, love. New hair, new man.' He gave me a cheeky wink.

'Exactly! Jason, is Mr Grant still in?'

'Mr Grant, oh no he got discharged last Friday. He mentioned you specifically in his card though wee soul, *'a special thank you to Zara the wonderful student'* and all this. I'll show you it at some point today.' I smiled back feeling honoured and slightly emotional.

'Can we get on with this handover, please? Silence!'

The room fell silent at the sound of Anne's assertive tone and Maggie began to hand over the patients to the day team. I glanced over to Anne who gave me a polite, *'welcome back'* nod.

I listened carefully, understanding more of the report than I had the previous weeks. I was finally picking up abbreviations and taking fewer notes. The report concluded, and as always Jason and I had a five-minute catch-up to discuss the day's expectations and patients.

'Okay, so that last time you were here I gave you one patient for the entire day?'

'Yep, that's right,' I answered enthusiastically.

'Okay, today you have six. Do everything for them—their drugs, obs, dressings, ward rounds, et cetera. From tomorrow on you'll have the entire team of twelve. I'll help out when things need to be double signed et cetera, but it's your team from then on, Zara.'

My eyes expanded, trying hard to process the information.

'Oh, fuck. I'm not sure I'll be able to do all this.'

'Yes, you will,' Jason said firmly. 'Do you think I would pap my patients off to you if I didn't think you could do it? It's your team, Zara.'

I felt overwhelmed and out of my depth but strangely grateful that he trusted me with this.

'Okay, but if I need anything, you'll be there?' I reiterated Jason's promise.

'Of course. Today you can have rooms one to six. You better get going, I can hear Room Two buzzing already!'

He chuckled as my hands shook with nerves. *I can do this. I can do this. I can do this!*

I strolled into each room and introduced myself to my patients as confidently as I could. I began my shift administering medications and assist the frailer patients with washing and dressing. The majority of my patients that day were waiting on surgeries or scans and were pretty stable once I got their analgesia under control. The morning zoomed by, and before I knew it, lunch had arrived, and I had been too distracted by my workload that I hadn't given Tom or Harriette a second thought.

Jason passed me in the corridor with two trays of hot food. I was pushing a fully loaded sterile trolley of dressings.

'How are you getting on, Zara? Will we stop for lunch in an hour?'

'Yeah, fine thanks. Starting my wound care early but yeah that suits me.'

Jason's eyes drifted from me as someone caught his attention from behind.

'Oh, hi, Doctor Adams, how did the party go?'

My body instantly flooded with dread. I froze, gripping the trolley, resisting the urge to run away.

'Excellent night, thanks. Well, except for one thing I suppose.'

I turned around to face him, unable to stand still any longer.

'My bathroom was vandalised!' he exclaimed dramatically.

Jason gasped, and I followed a second behind.

'You don't know anything about that, do you, Zara?'

It took me a moment to realise I was being brought into the conversation. Tom was looking right at me, and his face was serious.

'Me? What? Of course not.' I tried my hardest to appear shocked while shaking my head in disgust.

'Yeah, the entire wall display was ripped apart. It must have taken some strength to do it, too.'

Or a fucking sanny pad, Thomas.

I struggled to look him in the eyes as my gaze slid guiltily to the floor.

'You know, Jason, some people can't see others happy. I pity them more than anything.'

264

I peered up at his aimed statement to find him staring down at me.

'Yes, I actually agree with you, Tom,' I said, feeling a burst of anger, 'but if some people were more honest, then perhaps everyone would have been a lot happier in the first instance.'

He looked taken aback. Jason stood dumbfounded at our cryptic conversation.

'Zara, can I speak to you for a minute alone?' Tom asked. Without waiting for an answer, he walked a few steps in front, opened the duty room door and gestured for me to enter.

I let go of my trolley and marched in confidently, feeling a build-up of rage beginning to simmer.

'Was it you?' he demanded as soon as the door was shut, pointing in my face.

'What?' I tried to give myself more time, avoiding the question. *What will I say? Shit. Shit. Shit!*

'Did you vandalise the bathroom at Ageless?'

'Of course I didn't!' I exclaimed, lying through my back teeth.

'It was you, or it was fucking Ashley. I bloody well know it!' He was pacing the floor, looking madder with each step.

'Don't flatter yourself, Tom, we don't care about your stupid clinic that much.' I shrugged and folded my arms.

'I thought you were leaving here anyway? It's uncomfortable for me, especially when Harri works here too,' he yelled.

I paused. *Who the fuck is he speaking to?*

265

'Oh, oh, I'm so sorry, Tom. Was it not uncomfortable for me walking up to your house draped in dolly fucking mixtures to find you with another woman?' I was shaking with anger. .

He stood opposite me, silent, his hands firmly on his hips.

'And tell me this: when you left me in your bed that morning to go to your conference, how quickly did you wait before having sex with Harriette? The same morning? That night? When exactly?'

'We waited,' he snapped back, attempting to shut me off.

'Oh, so you didn't do anything that day? Nothing at all when I was lying in your fucking bed? Eh? Eh? Tell me then?' I pushed and pushed him for an answer.

'We kissed, okay? It was only a kiss for fuck sake!' He laughed, trying his best to undermine me.

'Well, seeing you two together felt like a Glasgow kiss to me, Tom. Excuse me, I have work to do.'

I opened the door and slammed it behind me. Jason leapt back, still carrying his two trays of food, clearly startled out of his eavesdropping. He wasn't the only one; around him had gathered a small group of support workers and second-year students.

Flustered and still raging, I grabbed my trolley and started marching up the corridor. I heard Jason coming after me.

'That was the boyfriend? Like Dr Adams?' he whispered, nodding his head towards the duty room where Tom remained.

'Unfortunately, that was him,' I said, rolling my eyes. The adrenaline was still rushing through my body. *God, I needed that.*

Behind us, I heard the duty room door opening and a sheepish Tom slithering out. I glared back over my shoulder.

'Right, now I have that off my chest, I suppose I better get on with these dressings. Catch up with you in a bit.'

Holding my head high, I pushed my trolley on up the ward and headed back to work, leaving both Jason and Tom speechless.

Chapter Twenty-Nine

I woke that Friday morning after finishing my long week at placement ready to start an action-packed day at the clinic. Raj had booked clients in from nine till twelve, and then we were interviewing for Tom's position later that afternoon. Ashley had texted to remind me to wear something nice that morning, keen for me to impress another doctor. However, I was still caught up with my Sugar Daddy and wasn't mentally prepared for another arsehole in a suit with a devil dick to puncture my life. *Here we go again.*

I opted for a casual jeans day with a black cropped T-shirt. The top was too crushed with creases to wear normally, so rather than bring out the iron I pulled it to the side, making it tighter and smoothing out the wrinkles, then secured it with a bobble. *That's better.* I cleansed my face and added a little foundation and mascara. It was the first time I'd worn makeup since the party, and with my figure still reduced dramatically in size, I felt good.

I smiled, impressed at my reflection, and even participated in a mirror selfie before heading to work. I popped my earphones in and began the short journey to George

Square, keen to see my friends and get back to some form of normality, as well as potentially meeting the newest member of our team.

I was about thirty feet from the clinic door when my audiobook was interrupted by a notification.

I scooped into my denim jacket pocket and checked the home screen.

There was a new Instagram message—from Mark.

From fuckin' Mark?

I stared at my phone, not wanting to read it right away. *What does he want?* I wondered, and headed into the clinic.

'Morning,' Raj called out.

'Ashley! Ashley!' I yelled.

'Good morning, Raj, it's nice to see you too,' he muttered sarcastically.

Ashley bounced out of the staff room. 'What's wrong? Are you okay?' Her face was filled with worry.

'Yeah, I'm fine. Guess who's messaged me?'

She gasped. 'Tom?'

'No.'

'Harriette.' She beamed.

'Nope.'

'Eh . . . Anne?'

'What? Noooo.' I looked at her disapprovingly.

'For fuck sake, who?'

'Mark!'

'Noooo, as in the panty sniffer?' she exclaimed loudly while I began laughing, holding my finger to my lips for her to tone it down a little.

'I forgot about that.'

I turned to Raj, who was on the laptop at the reception desk, shaking his head at our revolting conversation.

'Get him to fuck, Zara. What did he say?' Ashley asked.

'I haven't even opened it yet.'

'Get it read and patch him for months as he did to you.'

I couldn't help but think Ashley was being a little savage. I'd felt a tiny bit of excitement when I got the message through, and that was a nice feeling to have again. I walked through to the staff room and hung my jacket on the hook, taking my phone back out from its pocket and reading the message.

Mark reacted to your story.

Ooft, you look lovely! How you been?

Hmmm, he liked what he saw. It took him long enough. I popped my phone back in my pocket not feeling the need to respond. It felt nice that someone actually appreciated my effort today though.

We had lots of clients booked in for Botox top-ups that morning. When they came in, I carried out their medical background check and endorsed other treatments that would enhance their features. Then I marked the sites Raj would inject with a small white pencil before leading them through to the clinic room. The morning flew by, giving Ashley and me less time to gossip than usual, but it was so nice to be back in the clinic with her.

'Has Tom spoken to you at placement yet?' she asked during a free minute.

'No. To be honest, I hardly ever see him.'

'That's good I suppose.'

We were opening boxes of stock that had been delivered earlier, and there was a pause as we both concentrated.

'So what are you going to do about Mark?'

'Nothing I don't think. I don't feel like I'm ready to speak to anyone just yet. But . . .' I bit my lip before I said it. 'I know this sounds ridiculous, but because I've been listening to Tony Robbins, I can't help thinking maybe it's a sign that Mark's messaged. Is that the risk I'm supposed to take?'

Ashley smirked over the boxes. 'He also says trust your gut. What does your gut tell you to do?'

'Nothing,' I replied, shrugging my shoulders.

'Do nothing then.' She pushed me warmly, making us giggle as Raj showed a client to the door.

'Okay, girls, the first candidate will be here in fifteen minutes! Are you ready with your questions, Zara?'

I clapped excitedly and ran over to him. 'Yes!' This would be my first time ever helping out on an interview and I was enjoying the new sense of responsibility.

'Where are we doing the interviews?' I looked around the room.

'I think here on the sofas? Be quite relaxing, less formal. What do you think?'

'Good idea, yeah, I agree.'

'Well, where will I go, guys?' Ashley asked.

'You can go home. Take a few hours off.'

'Seriously?' She jumped up.

'Yeah, two people is enough. I think.' Raj began repositioning the furniture so the sofas were a little further apart.

Ashley shoved the large stock boxes into the staff room for a later date and grabbed her stuff. 'So I can go now? You're sure?'

Raj laughed. 'I'm positive. Enjoy your day.'

'Bye then. Zara, pick a hottie.'

She left the clinic in an instant while Raj and I grabbed a drink of water each from the cooler.

'You do the talking, Raj,' I said. 'I've never done this before.'

He smiled. 'I will.'

We were sipping our water in comfortable silence when the door opened and a man in his mid-thirties walked in wearing a white shirt, trench coat and black tailored trousers. He had dark hair and glasses with a serious-looking face.

'Hi, afternoon. Am I too early?' He stood in the doorway.

'Not at all. What's your name?' I asked.

'It's Peter. Dr Peter Hogg.'

'Come on in, Peter, we were expecting you.' Raj beckoned him over to the seating area where he shook hands with both of us.

'Would you like a glass of water or anything before we start?' I asked, unsure if he looked nervous or stern.

'I'm fine. Thank you.'

'Okay, well. Peter, you've been shortlisted for today's interview so firstly congratulations. My name is Raj.

I'm the owner of the clinic. This here is Zara, my assistant—she pretty much does everything here except puncture anyone's skin!'

Raj looked towards me and I gave a little laugh at his praise. Peter's face remained still.

'So, Peter, tell us a bit about yourself.'

'Well. I'm an acting consultant in Forth Valley. I work in renal but ultimately would like to be a full-time aesthetics practitioner. I have five years' experience working in a clinic in Edinburgh and I'm familiar with all the treatments you provide, I checked the website.'

'Wow, you certainly have a busy life. What makes you stand out from anyone else?' Raj asked.

'Well, I'm confident, reliable, extremely professional and I like to come in, work hard and get results.'

He was saying all the right things but his face remained totally frozen and blank of any expression. *Maybe he's had too much Botox himself?*

I couldn't help but think Peter sounded like a boring bastard, to be honest, and within ten minutes, we were shaking his hand and showing him out the door.

'What did you think?' Raj asked when he left.

'Honestly? Boring.'

'Me too,' he admitted. 'When he said he's extremely professional all I thought of is how he would cope with the panty sniffing, Tinder date chats.'

I laughed hard at that, picturing Peter's face.

'Who's next then?' I asked.

'We have a Laura Elizabeth next.' Raj raised his eyebrows at me.

'Another woman? It's a yes from me,' I joked.

A few moments later, a casual older woman chapped on the door.

'Just push it,' I called out.

She entered the clinic looking nervous.

I could instantly smell an overkill of rose-scented perfume as she sat down beside us. As the pungent fumes hit the back of my throat, I tried to cough discreetly.

'Laura? It's lovely to meet you.'

I stuck out my hand to shake hers. Her hands were cold and dry, and as she spoke to Raj, I couldn't help but judge her funky outfit. She was wearing a large pleated skirt with trainers that looked like they'd just been through a 5K, camouflaged in mud and puddle splashes.

'So where do you work, Laura?' Raj asked.

'It's Laura Elizabeth. I'm a paediatric doctor. I work in the community with sick kids.'

This made me warm to her.

'And how long have you been doing aesthetics?' I asked.

'Not long, two or three months. I've completed the courses but haven't implemented the techniques as yet,' she admitted.

The two medics continued their conversation while I zoned out and thought about Mark. *Should I text him back?* He did upset me in the end, completely ghosting me then getting huffy at a little drunk text. God, I didn't know. What if this *was* a sign?

'Zara, any other questions?'

Raj and Laura Elizabeth were staring at me. I'd missed the majority of the discussion.

'No, I think you covered it,' I bluffed.

'Okay, I'll see myself out. Lovely to meet you all,' Laura Elizabeth added and left the clinic.

'Well?' I asked Raj optimistically.

'She's lovely, but not suited to this particular shop.'

'Raj! That's terrible.'

'Her trainers were manky. Plus, I have no idea why she went into aesthetics' in the first place.' He scrunched his face up in disgust.

'I even noticed them to be fair, and check out the nick of my top. Who's next then?'

Raj was engrossed in his phone, not listening to me.

'Raj?'

He flung his arms in the air, clearly frustrated.

'The final applicant for today has cancelled. Fuck, we're back to square one again. And yes, I noticed your top straight away—a bobble doesn't replace an iron, Zara.'

I stood waiting on him to calm down. He finally looked over and grinned when he saw my smiley face.

'What is it, Zara?'

'We could go get a drink since we're done for the day? I think we both need cheering up.' I fluttered my heavily mascara'd eyelashes at him.

'You know I don't drink.'

'Well, you can buy me one then! Do you want to?' I gave him a cheeky look and he rolled his eyes.

'Get your coat!'

We locked up the clinic and made the short, chilly walk, arm in arm, towards TGI's. I snuggled tightly into Raj's warm body as the wind blew out of my denim jacket. Through the huge double doors of the restaurant we could see groups of people waiting in the foyer.

'It looks busy, Zara.'

'It's fine, let's go in anyway,' I pleaded.

We walked to the front of the queue.

'Table for two please, mate,' Raj asked the waiter.

'Around a forty-five-minute wait, bud, that okay?'

'Is there room at the bar? It's only for drinks,' I added.

The waiter looked around the hectic restaurant.

'Yeah, I think you should be fine then. If you head in, turn left, it looks like there are a couple of empty bar stools up that way.'

He opened the door for us, and we entered the noisy, overpacked restaurant. The music was blaring, and the smell of honey-glazed chicken and wedges suddenly made my mouth water.

'You go get a seat, Zara. I'll nip to the loo,' Raj called out over the music.

I neared the bar and squeezed my way through several servers waiting for their trays to be filled. There were two unoccupied stools at the end of the bar. I made my way to them and sat down, glancing around for a menu. When I lifted my head, a young handsome cocktail waiter caught my eye. He was mixing a large shaker vigorously over his shoulder while his considerable muscles protruded through his black shirt. He had dark, tanned skin, a short, shaved head and was around 5ft 9, not as tall as I usually liked but holy fuck he was hot!

I stared, engrossed in his masculinity as he shook and chopped the life out of everyday objects that I never dreamed would turn me on. The once noisy room fell quiet in my head as I hummed the *Magic Mike* theme in my brain. He was fucking gorgeous. I continued watching him, my mouth halfway open in awe, when he turned and looked my way again.

'Do want a cocktail, lady?'

His broken English accent made my fanny flutters return in an instant. He sounded Spanish and I was hypnotised by his voice, nodding my head in response to his question.

'What one you want?' he asked.

I hadn't even looked at the menu I'd been so distracted by the handsome stranger.

'Eh . . . what do you recommend?' I asked, twirling my hair, trying my best to flirt with him.

'I'll make you the Pablo special, okay? One or two, are you with a friend?'

I'd forgotten all about Raj with the firework display happening between myself and Pablo.

'Just one, I'm with my boss. He'll have a Diet Coke or something boring.' I tried to make a joke, tittering away to myself.

Pablo turned away to mix the drinks.

'Would you like a bib, Zara?' Raj returned, raising an eyebrow at my chat with the server.

'He is fucking gorgeous!' I hissed. 'Great choice of seat if I don't say so myself!'

Raj was smiling uncomfortably. 'I'm sure I just saw Tom and Harriette leave,' he said.

'That could have been bad. Did he see you?' I asked, feeling a stabbing pain of anxiety.

'I think so. He definitely saw you and the child you were flirting with.'

I let out a howl of laughter.

'Too right, have you bloody seen him?' I gushed.

'Okay, one Pablo special for the pretty lady and one diet coke for the boss!' Pablo passed over an enormous fishbowl cocktail filled to the brim with orange and red alcohol, ice and straws.

'Wow. Thank you, Pablo.'

'That isn't for one person, is it? It can't be!' Raj was taken aback as I sucked ferociously at my beverage, tasting strong vodka and peach flavours.

'You like?' Pablo edged towards my side of the bar, waiting curiously for my opinion.

'I love it!' I answered, coughing a little. 'Very strong, though.'

'Yes, like Pablo.' He raised his bicep into the air, flexing his muscles firmly.

For fuck sake. He is a sexy wee bastard. My eyes followed him down the bar as he drifted away to serve other customers.

'Zara, what will I do about the interviews? I don't feel passionate about any of the applicants.' Raj had his head down, looking strained with worry.

'I know. Is there no one from the hospital that could step in? God, Raj, in a few weeks you'll be looking for my replacement too.'

'Zara, don't. I can't even think about that yet.' He took a sip of his drink, looking deep in thought. 'I need someone bright, chatty, trendy. Someone the clients will love and will actually look forward to seeing. Fuck, Zara, I need someone like you.' Raj gasped. 'That's it! That's fucking it!'

'What's it?' I seemed to have missed something between my mental undressing of Pablo and my immediate cocktail buzz.

'You could be my new aesthetics practitioner, Zara!' Raj's face was bright and full of hope. It looked like a weight had been lifted clean off his shoulders.

'Me?' I replied, shocked at the suggestion. 'Raj, I couldn't do that. I'm not a doctor.'

'You don't have to be, and sure you could, Zara— you're a quick learner! You know the products and the clients. You've seen me do the procedures a thousand times. You know exactly how the clinic runs. You would be utterly amazing.'

His voice was enthusiastic, but I doubted my ability. I didn't want to disappoint my friend, but I had trained to be a nurse for years. I was almost qualified, and in this placement I was finally enjoying the wards, and feeling like I was making a difference.

'I'm sorry, Raj. I honestly don't think I could. I don't have the confidence to inject someone's face, I just couldn't. Imagine I made a mistake? Hit a nerve?

Or ruined your reputation. I have a million people around me for support in the ward, but I'd just have me in the clinic,' I spilled.

His excitable grin plummeted rapidly, exposing a sad and disappointed look.

'No, forgive me. I just don't want to lose you. I understand you've been training for the hospital work for ages. I'm being selfish.' He patted my back.

'You're not! You'll find an amazing candidate. I know it.' I placed my head on his shoulder for support.

'I've more interviews in the morning, and I'll have Ashley to assist me this time. God help them.' He chuckled and took another swig of his drink.

'I better make a move soon, actually. I have so much on tomorrow now that I think about it. You want me to walk you home?'

I peered down at the gigantic bowl of alcohol that I hadn't made a dent in yet and attempted to lift it.

'There is no way I'm leaving this bad boy behind! You go. I'll see you next week.'

He stood up, looking uncertain.

'Are you sure?'

'Positive!' I smiled at him and went back to sucking the alcohol profusely through a handful of paper straws.

'Pablo, look after this girl,' Raj said and pointed above my head. Pablo stuck his thumb up. 'Zara,' he stuck a handful of notes in my icy cold hand, 'I'll get this,' and he left the bar.

I sat alone, sipping away on my drink, admiring the view, feeling more euphoric with every sip. Every so often, Pablo would catch my eye and smile over at me. His perfect white teeth beamed across the bar.

'Are you okay?' he called out.

I nodded, feeling tipsy.

'I'm great.'

He laughed and came over to me, drying a glass with a towel.

'So why is a young lady drinking alone on a Friday night? Where is your boyfriend?' His voice became more sultry as he leaned over the bar towards me.

'Well, I was recently dumped. For another woman. So I will just have to get used to drinking alone, I guess.' I threw my hands wildly into the air as the alcohol pushed through my veins, and he dodged out of the way.

'Wow, no lady should drink alone. I finish in ten minutes, and if you like I could join?' His large dark eyes stared across the bar at me, waiting on a reply.

What the fuck? Did he just ask to join me? I looked at him, gobsmacked. *He probably feels sorry for you, Zara, don't get your hopes up.*

'Yes, wow, of course, I'd love that,' I replied excitedly. 'Can you keep an eye on my drink first? I'm going to use the ladies'.'

I slid my bottom carefully off the seat and made my way through to the bathroom, holding the walls for support as I did so. As I sat in the cubicle expelling an extra-large pee, I wondered: *Was Pablo flirting with me? Should I try and pull him? This could be the best rebound any girl has ever had if I pull this off—a hot, muscly, Spanish cocktail maker*. I felt my old fanny twitch return as I finally thought of another dick besides Tom's.

I swaggered outside and washed my hands, observing the mirror as best as I could with double vision. *You scrub up not too bad, Zara, not too shabby at all.* When I returned to the bar, I was surprised to see Pablo sitting on the barstool previously occupied by Raj, sipping a cold Budweiser.

'Is that you finished then?' I asked, hopping back onto my stool.

'Yes. Finally! Tell me your name please.' He turned his head closely, invading my personal space. I could feel his beer breath hit off my skin.

'Zara,' I replied, giggling like a horny schoolgirl.

'Well, Zara, I don't know why any man would ever leave you for another lady,' he said.

I smiled, feeling flattered.

'Well if you saw her you would understand, Pablo, trust me. She had long blonde hair, she's very tall and she's a doctor.'

He tutted, unimpressed.

'I prefer brunettes.' He shrugged.

'Where are you from, Pablo?'

'Barcelona. The most beautiful city in the world I think. You would fit in very well there,' he said and took a swig of his drink. *Was this sexy hunk of spunk coming on to me?*

I felt an overpowering amount of sexual desire as I gazed at this fit, hot, young man so coolly drinking his beer from the glass bottle. *Maybe this is a sign?* I had to take risks!

282

Buzzed from the alcohol and with butterflies in my stomach, I turned to the exotic waiter and asked, 'Do you want to go back to mine?'

Pablo didn't acknowledge my question. Instead, he continued to gulp down his Budweiser, holding it firmly, high in the air. An overwhelming feeling of cringe washed over me as I waited, praying for an answer. I instantly regretted my bold proposal. *Why did I have to ruin this? Of course, he doesn't, Zara, look at him!*

But when he eventually finished his beer, he jumped up off the stool and faced me.

'Come on then, Miss Zara, show me your house.'

Chapter Thirty

Pablo and I strolled towards my flat together after fleeing the bar. My heart was galloping at the notion of potentially having sex with someone new, someone *else*, but I somehow continued to question his intentions. *Maybe he doesn't want to have sex with me? Perhaps I've imagined this passionate night of flirting solely in my head. Does he really feel the same? Or did he just feel sorry for me boldly asking him to come back to mine? Shit, maybe he's going to rob my house—he is a stranger after all.* My head was spinning with possible outcomes of how tonight would unfold and I began to panic. *Calm down, Zara,* I told myself, but the fresh air was only making my boozy brain fuzzier. Pablo just followed my lead, slowly and calmly, looking much more comfortable with a late-night booty call than I was.

The walk fell silent at times, and my eyes remained down, fixated on the shadows cast across the dark pavement as I tried to think of what to say next. Hearing the dulcet tones and dirty laughter of women staggering to the clubs, we glanced at one another and exchanged a smirk. I watched them from afar strut across the road in their tiny skirts and high stilettos and couldn't help but think Pablo would be best suited to one of them. But he kept his warm smile and sexy eyes on me the entire time, not appearing to be intrigued by their ten-foot legs and vaginas on show.

As we approached the flat, I began to wonder how untidy it was. After all, I was certainly not expecting company. Maybe I could keep him waiting in the hallway until I tidied up.

As we walked up the stairs to the flat, I turned to Pablo and said, slowly making sure he understood, 'Pablo, my house is a bit messy, I'm afraid I wasn't expecting any company tonight.' I pulled an exaggerated face to help explain my words and he broke into laughter.

'I no mind about mess. I want to see your bedroom though, okay?'

I turned to the handsome Spaniard, who was smiling at his mischief. *Okay, this cunt understood perfect English, and I was definitely about to get my hole tonight!* I unlocked the front door, giggling and scanning the room for anything too embarrassing to leave lying around.

'Please, have a seat. I'll be one minute.'

I steered him to the sofa and like Usain Bolt tore through the flat, stacking up mouldy plates and cutlery that had been accumulating for a few weeks. With bravery, I sniffed a pile of underwear that was on the floor, trying to establish what was clean and what was nasty. Next, I moved into the bathroom, pulled my unmentionables to my knees and forcefully scrubbed my vagina. I splurted a dollop of Exotic Foam Burst in my hands and smothered my muff in an instant. The pleasant fragrance quickly filled the room, and I was pretty confident this would mask any unappetising odour for my Spanish prince. I glanced at the furry bush I was sporting and concluded it would have to stay. My pubes had gained radical volume and shine from the unexpected hair wash. Still, with insufficient time to trim back the hedges then shave into the wood, I regrettably made do pulling up my underwear, spider legs and all.

Well, I hope you like au natural, Pablo.

I returned to the living room, where Pablo was sitting casually with his arm along the back of my sofa.

'So sorry about that. Would you like a drink?' I asked.

'No, thank you. I want you to come to sit.'

Pablo's dark eyes gazed suggestively at me. He leaned forward and grabbed my hands to pull me onto the couch beside him, almost losing my balance as I did so. My heart pounded rapidly as he brushed his strong dark hand over my face and into my hair, tightly gripping the ends.

'Come here, baby,' he said, and I was suddenly aware of his large, soft, juicy lips on mine.

We were kissing passionately, and I could taste his warm, tender tongue wrap around mine. *Jesus Christ.* My fanny was banging as hard as my heart. His fingers were still entangled in my hair and I could feel the bristle of his stubbly chin brush off mine as things got more intense. His hands started to wander, grabbing my tits as he bit my lip. *Jesus, I'm moving to Europe!* Things were progressing at a rapid pace, and Pablo was caressing every part of my body.

I managed to stop for air and panted, 'Bedroom.'

He agreed, not wanting to take his tongue out of my mouth but eventually standing and grasping my hand for me to show him the way. My face felt wet, shiny and tender from stubble rash, but I hadn't felt this alive for weeks.

I hopped on my bed while Pablo pulled his black shirt over his muscular abs and shoulders and threw it to the ground dramatically. He crawled towards me with pure desire in his eyes, stopping just short of my face. He grinned mischievously before tugging on my jeans to get to the honeypot. I laughed but suddenly felt hesitant as I looked down at my strong pubes protruding through the sides of my underwear. He didn't seem to care about the extra foliage though and within a second both my denims and underwear were whipped off and lying on the floor. He lowered his body and edged forward. I closed my eyes and felt a heavy, warm breath between my legs. *Fucking yesssss! He's a licker!*

He started off slow and gentle, his fingers stroking me at the same time. I looked down to see him munching away at me while I wondered how on earth I got this lucky. His talented tongue knew precisely how to please. I was gasping and moaning, my back arched in pleasure as the handsome man hit every nerve ending again and again, continuously stroking and sucking my clit. Eventually, he came up to my level, snogging my face and sharing my juices as he discreetly inserted his dick inside me. *Wow.* I suddenly felt full as he leaned over my trembling body, pushing in and out of me.

He was leaning on both my arms with his strong frame, pinning them down above my head. I could feel myself cum over and over again as he went deeper inside of me. He was squeezing my tits hard, grinding up and down, biting my ear and grunting until he eventually came.

'Fun?' His accent seemed even more suggestive as he lay naked alongside me. He was panting and moist from sweat. I had never seen a more handsome naked man in my life.

'Yes! So much fun,' I gushed. I was still catching my breath. 'Would you like a drink?' I asked, always striving to remember my manners.

'I'm not finished with you yet, you not go anywhere, okay?'

I turned, shocked and pleasantly surprised. 'Okay, I'll leave the water then.'

'I want to drink your juice, yes?' He pointed down towards my enormous growth, and I felt myself blush at how untamed I'd let her go.

'Really? Fine with me.'

He began sliding down under the duvet for round two. I beamed as his eyes met mine, back between my legs.

'You real woman, Zara. I like that.' He pointed to my bush, looking impressed.

'Thank you, Pablo.' I gave him an awkward thumbs-up and he went to work, caressing my clit repeatedly for the rest of the night.

The following morning, the high-pitched screech from Pablo's alarm startled us awake at the crack of seven. He jumped out the bed, finally giving me the chance to examine his massive dick as it swung effortlessly between his thighs. He retrieved his phone and silenced the alarm, then came back to bed, hovering over my naked body.

'Good morning, beautiful.' He pecked my dry lips.

'Morning.' I stretched and sat up while he started getting dressed, searching the room for lost objects.

'I need to go. I work early today and go for a run first.'

'Yes, of course. On you go,' I insisted.

'I had a lot of fun last night. Like *a lot*.' He winked across the room at me.

I blushed, feeling insecure as my makeup had perspired off my naked face and I could only imagine how bad I looked in the morning light. I pulled the covers aside to stand and walk Pablo to the door when he came closer.

'Stay in bed. It's too early for you, baby. Have more sleep.'

God, I love how he tells me what to do!

I swung my legs back into bed and watched him button his shirt, feeling proud of my latest accomplishment.

'Can I leave my phone number, Zara? Call me if you get lonely.'

I placed my hands over my mortified face.

'Yes, of course, although I must admit I don't normally do this casual sex thing, Pablo.'

'Well, I'll sit it here, and if you like, you can call. Pablo would like that.' He pulled a rolled-up napkin from his pocket and sat it on my dresser.

'I was going to give last night. But I didn't have to in the end up.' He shrugged his shoulders and smiled.

'Thank you.' I stuck my thumb up assertively. *Why the fuck do I keep doing that?*

Pablo shuffled towards me, leaned over and kissed me once more.

'Bye, baby.' He turned around and walked out, giving me one last look at the door.

As soon as he was gone, I began hysterically laughing at myself.

You still have it, Zara! You still fucking have it!

I was just about to turn Alexa on to full victory mode songs when I heard a loud chap at the door. *So much for 'stay in your bed, Zara,'* I thought.

I glimpsed around the room, wondering what Pablo could have forgotten. I couldn't see anything, but the room was untidy and smelt like a fishmongers. I discovered my dressing gown lying in the corner and swung that around my shoulders, moving towards the front door.

'Back so soon?' I called out, turning the door handle.

'It felt like a long time to me.'

My hand slipped off the grip at the sound of a deep posh twang as I gazed into the hallway where Tom was standing.

'Hello.' He stood with a large bouquet of flowers, wearing his most expensive suit.

'Tom?' I was in shock.

'I'm sorry to wake you. I just had to see you. I wanted to come over all night last night after seeing you and

Raj in the pub, but I didn't want to rouse you.' He faced the stone floor, struggling to make eye contact.

I'm fucking glad you didn't.

'Come in.' I pulled the door open wide, allowing him to enter my untidy home while I pulled my robe tighter, trying to conceal any suspicious smells or nudity.

'House is a bit of a tip. Come sit down if you like?'

'These are for you.' He handed me the bouquet; a beautiful bunch of multicoloured roses.

'Thanks, I guess, but what for?' I was still astonished he was here.

'I was such a dick. I'm so sorry. It's you I need to be with, Zara. I miss you. Harri knows about everything. I've come clean.'

'I don't understand, Tom.' I took a few steps back, trying my best to filter the information.

He began rubbing his eyes, looking traumatised.

'Zara, I love you. Please forgive me. Please. I miss your smile, your laughter, your clumsiness, and silly sense of humour. I am completely in love with you, I'm just sorry that it took another woman for me to realise it.'

I had waited so long to hear him say those words. I couldn't help the warmth that flowed like honey through me at the sound of them.

'I love you too,' I whispered and looked down at the floor. What the fuck was happening? My mind was spinning like a kaleidoscope, and I felt like I couldn't breathe.

He came towards me like he was going to kiss me.

'No, wait, stop.' I held my hand up and took a step back. 'You can't just walk back like nothing happened. You hurt me so badly.' I was crying now. I felt dizzy and out of control, shaking my head in disbelief. This was all too much.

Then, I felt his tall figure wrap around me. I inhaled his scent, the smell that I had missed so much, and within a second, I felt whole again. I squeezed my arms around him tightly, completely entangled for several minutes, not saying a single word.

My eyes were shut tight, terrified to open in case this was all a dream.

Eventually, he spoke.

'You know it's still early. We could go back to bed for a proper cuddle?' He raised my chin so I was looking right into his face, his eyebrows raised suggestively.

My heart pulsated, remembering the night of passion I'd just had with Pablo.

'If we're really going to do this, I'd rather take things slow, Tom.' I tried my hardest to seem mature. I couldn't have sex with two people the same morning, could I?

'I understand, let me hold you on the sofa then. God, I've missed you.'

We took a few steps back towards the couch and sat down together. I rested my fragile head on his chest and shut my eyes. It was the closest I had felt to anyone, ever. *I can't believe he came back.*

'You know you're a fantastic nurse, Zara. You're very well-liked on the ward.' He stroked my legs as he spoke.

'Really? Awk, you're just saying that. But thank you. I do love it there.' I smiled, doubting him but still enjoying the compliment.

'I'm sure Anne could keep you there when you get your official registration if you liked.'

'Maybe.' I shrugged. 'Tom, promise me you will never do that again to me. I was broken.' I lifted my head off his chest and faced him.

His eyes looked sad, like he was full of regret. 'I promise. You will never understand how sorry I am, Zara. I'll make it up to you, I promise.'

'Mmmm . . . you promise? Will you spoil me?' I raised an eyebrow, and he rose quickly, throwing his jacket to the floor.

'Shall I show you?' he said. He knelt to the floor in front of me.

Oh shit, is he about to do what I think he is? But he's not a licker. What the fuck is he doing? I held my dressing gown tightly.

'No, don't do anything. I want to wait.' I was lying and desperately craving his cock but was so unclean from last night's antics.

'It's not for me; I promised I would make it up to you,' he whispered, trying hard to prise my knees open. Fuck, I hadn't even douched after last night's shag fest.

'Honestly, no need. I haven't shaved, Tom. I'm sorry.'

'Zara, I don't fucking care. I understand you've been cooped up in here and sex was the last thing on your mind.'

I looked down at the man I loved in the position I had craved for so long, and finally thought *fuck it*. I opened my legs to a bearded, sticky, matted bush. My clit was still enlarged and highly sensitive from Pablo, and it looked like an angry cyclops throbbing for his tongue. I sat back, trying not to look at my bits and felt Tom rummage around with his tongue until he eventually found what he was looking for. He was going for it too, munching and diving, biting my lips and gnawing on them like a dog eating beetroot while I moaned.

'Mmmmm, you taste so bloody good, Zara,' he groaned, and although the compliment was sweet I couldn't help but think it should have been passed to Pablo—after all, it was probably the remainder of his jizz Tom was devouring.

Still, I managed to relax and enjoyed the concept of Tom finally between my legs, so much in fact that I came pretty quickly. *Jesus, I am a sweaty smelly mess.* I wasn't even sure who or what I smelt of, but an overpowering smell of sex filled my flat. *I'll need to start burning the Yankees early today.*

Tom sat beside me after my orgasm, looking pleased with himself, discreetly wiping the pubes from his mouth.

'Did you enjoy that?' he asked, cockily rubbing his hard-on.

'Yes, but stop, no more!' I laughed, trying to act sensibly. *It would not be very ladylike of me to pump both men in a matter of hours.* I tied my gown shut again to try and tame his beast, and opted for a cuddle instead.

'Tease!' He laughed. 'What's been happening at the clinic then?'

'Nothing, still busy! We had interviews yesterday. Trying to find the new you.' I touched his nose, and he pretended to bite my finger.

'There's only one Dr Adams though, isn't there, Zara?'

'Yes.' I rolled my eyes jokingly at him. 'Oh wait till I tell you—when Raj and I were out last night, he asked if I wanted the job, like he would train me up.'

Tom let out an almighty laugh.

'You're kidding,' he said.

'No, what's up with that?' He was quick to find the idea funny, and I felt offended.

'Nothing's up with it at all, just seems Raj is getting a little desperate.'

'Desperate? Asking his friend who's nearly a qualified nurse and has worked there for three years? I'm sorry, I'm confused.'

'Why are you defensive? Lighten up. It's just that it's a highly skilled position and the fact he's willing to train a nurse, then . . .'

Is this cunt being serious?

'Oh, so you don't think I could do it? I said no by the way, but it's nice to see I'd be supported if I changed my mind.' I folded my arms, feeling huffy, and backed away from him on the sofa.

'Ohh, Zara, don't be like that. He's asked his fucking receptionist to be his latest medic—who, by the way, isn't a medic, is a bloody nurse! I'm not getting at you.

It's Raj I'm getting at. He's asked too much of you!'
When I didn't move, he sat up and opened his arms.
'Come here.'

He waited for a few seconds, but I still didn't move.

'No, I'm not happy,' I replied sternly.

'Oh here we go again, Zara, it didn't take you long,
did it?' he said, his voice rising and irritated. 'What
makes you happy? Like seriously, what do you actually
do that makes you happy? Because I've been dying to
know.'

What makes me happy? What makes me happy?

I was about to answer him, full of wit, when all of
a sudden I had it. Everything made sense. I laughed
out loud but felt overcome with emotion at the same
time. *Yes! This is it.* I felt invincible, like I finally knew
what to do. I began screaming with pure joy, waving
my hands to the sky.

'Zara, what the hell are you doing?' He looked on,
puzzled.

'To answer your question, Thomas, I'm happy when
I'm with my friends. I'm happy at the clinic working
with Raj and Ashley, or when a patient gets discharged
from hospital and simply says 'thank you'. I'm happy
getting chatted up by a stranger in a bar. I'm happy
speaking to my sister, spending time with my niece
and nephew or when it happens, ever so occasionally,
making my mother proud. But most of all, I'm happy
spending time with people who believe in me, and,
Tom, you really don't. I'm sorry, you haven't made the
cut. You need to go now; I need to be somewhere.'

He stared at me, looking bewildered.

'Sorry? You're acting mad.' He continued to sit on my couch, trying to understand how the situation had slipped from his grasp.

'Leave now. Go, go, go.'

I pushed him off and ushered him to my door, feeling a spark come alive in me that was never there before. Adrenaline blitzed through my blood like lightning; my feet couldn't stay grounded from jumping with joy. *Finally, I've had my breakthrough!*

'Shut the door behind you, I need to get ready.'

I rummaged around the floor looking for something clean to wear. I had to get out of this sex pit. I heard the front door slam shut and knew Tom was finally gone, but I didn't care. Eventually I found an abandoned pair of jeans and fished the used knickers out from the ankle before shoving them over my naked body. I tore open the wardrobe and grabbed a white hoodie off the hanger, throwing it on over my bed head, and made for the front door. A pair of sliders lay in the hallway and I managed to slide my feet into them while flip-flopping down the stone staircase.

It was almost 9am on a rainy Saturday morning. Lots of morning joggers were sprinting up and down the city streets. I stood on the pavement and inhaled the fresh damp air.

Well, here goes!

Like a flash, I bolted straight past the morning commuters with the broadest smile I had ever worn. The cool breeze was wafting up my hoodie, and I could feel my tits bounce with every sharp thump. *I should seriously have worn a bra,* I thought, but no tit jumping would put me off my mission. I carried on, crossing busy roads and holding my hands up in apology to the cars that I almost crushed, until I finally reached my destination—Individualise.

I burst through the door to see Ashley immediately glance up from the computer in shock.

'Where's Raj?' I asked. I was panting for breath and my flipflops had bounced off my feet.

'He has an appointment through the back. What's going on, are you okay?' Ashley's face was puzzled as she stared at my mismatched outfit.

Oh no, the interviews had started. I took the deepest breath and marched towards the clinic room, throwing open the door. Raj jumped as I entered and stood up from his desk, where he was interviewing an older woman.

'Zara?' he blurted.

'Raj, I'm so sorry to burst in like this when you're interviewing but I had to see you.' I turned to the interviewee. 'I'm so sorry for the intrusion,' I said, then carried on frantically spilling my guts to Raj. 'Everything has suddenly become clear to me. This is my risk; this is where I'm supposed to be. This is my breakthrough! I want the job, Raj— no, I need it! I was too scared to realise it before. Please say you'll think about it. I could work here and the ward like you do, I'm sorry I didn't give it a chance, but I know now I can seriously do this.'

'Zara, wow, wow, slow down.' He smiled and came closer.

'I know this lady is probably far more qualified than I ever will be, but I'll work so fucking hard, you have no idea.'

He carried on walking towards me and wrapped his arms around me.

'The job's yours. This place couldn't function without you.'

He held me as I finally broke down with happiness. *I've done it.* The relief was pouring out my body as I jumped up and screamed.

'Thank you, Raj. You've always believed in me.' I felt happy tears fall from my eyes.

'Oh my God, and I'm sorry.' I broke away from Raj's hold to acknowledge the candidate in the room. 'I'm so sorry for the dramatic interruption, I'm sure you'll find the perfect clinic to be a part of.'

She nodded, looking no less confused at the commotion.

Raj began to laugh. 'Zara, this is a client. I was doing a consultation. Interviews were at eleven.'

I gasped as the client joined in laughing with Raj, and he returned to his desk to carry on with his work.

When I revisited the shop floor, Ashley was wiping away her tears of joy. She'd clearly overheard the whole thing.

'So, what the fuck happened, Zara?' She shook her head as she examined my untidy ensemble in confusion.

'Well firstly, Mark texted, then I had a rebound with a complete stranger, and then Tom showed up at my door to tell me he loved me, all within twenty-four hours.' I shrugged, not quite believing it myself.

'So, which one did you pick?' she asked.

'Well, I chose me, I guess.'

Chapter Thirty-One

It's funny how I searched my entire life for someone to complete me, and in the end, the only person I needed was myself.

Six months after my revelation, I can confirm that I am an official graduate, qualifying with distinction in my nursing degree. I had a wild party to celebrate with my friends and family, and we hired a certain cocktail waiter for the occasion.

I'm currently working part-time at the hospital, keen to maintain my nursing skills, as well as spending three days a week in Individualise. I pinch myself at how lucky I am to have friends like Raj and Ashley, and every day I appreciate the opportunities I have because of them.

Following weeks and weeks of intense teaching and private courses, Raj subsequently moulded me into a fully-fledged aesthetics nurse. He taught me every trick and skill it takes to be working independently, and I can safely say I'm as confident with these procedures as I am with wiping my own arse. Ashley has marketed my brand religiously, and as a result, my clientele has expanded so vastly that I can no longer take on new clients! Like, what the fuck? I've been asked to speak at the next big aesthetics' conference and exhibition about my experience of climbing the ladder from receptionist to sell-out. I realise now that things like this didn't happen to me until I made them. I made my own luck.

Financially, I kind of have my shit together! I now get two wages! And believe it or not, I've been known to keep some money in the bank to last the entire month. I'm still living in my mother's flat but will eventually look for my own place. This place is central and, let's face it, it holds a lot of memories for me.

Tom's clinic moved from Blythswood to Possil as he desperately couldn't keep up with the payments. He's struggled to replace Harriette as she never wanted him back after his declaration of 'love' to me. I see him occasionally in the corridor at work and acknowledge him with a smile but we haven't spoken since the morning he was booted out my flat.

All in all, I seem to finally have my life in order. Well, for now, anyway. I'll never say never to romance. I mean, let's face it, if some hot bastard from Clydebank with a six-pack and a twelve-inch cock wants to come and sweep me off my feet, then I won't resist, but I'm not obsessed with looking anymore. I've finally realised that I don't need someone else to make me happy—I just need me, my friends and my family.

That's not to say I'm off Tinder—I still have fucking needs. However, my profile has had a significant revamp of late.

Name: Zara Smith
Age: 30
Location: Glasgow
Interested in: Males
Zodiac sign: Leo

Biography: *My name is Zara! Hectic work life and not looking for anything too serious! I enjoy work, spending time with my friends and the occasional cocktail, looking for a commitment-free relationship with no strings attached!*

Ping.

I pull out my phone from my coat pocket and glance at the screen—new Tinder notification.

Mark: *Did you know, nearly three per cent of the ice in Antarctic glaciers is penguin urine?*

I smile at my phone, feeling witty and curious.

I mean, who can ignore an interesting penguin fact? And I suppose meeting up with one old friend won't rock the boat too much, right?

Acknowledgements.

I'd firstly like to thank all of my incredible *Sex in the Glasgow City* blog readers. Not only did you encourage me to write this novel, but you shared my journey with the utmost support. Building a following with you by my side was a genuine pleasure, and I hope this book has met all of your expectations.

I'm grateful to Rhea Kurien and all at Orion for contacting me and showing such passion for my work. I remember that phone call like it was yesterday, and it was one of the proudest moments of my life to be approached by your fantastic company. Thank you for having the time and patience to explain the crazy publishing process to me. I can't wait to see what the future brings.

To the talented Rosie McCafferty for proofreading my work and not only embracing my filthy mind but encouraging it! You were more offended by a misplaced apostrophe than a bit of erotica, and Zara's journey wouldn't have been the same without your guidance. You picked me up when I had doubts, and I will be forever thankful to have found you. Rosie, you are so talented and deserve more praise than I can ever give you!

Lisa McCafferty, you supported me in my final days before publication with last-minute edits, and I'll be forever appreciative. If it weren't for your crazy hen weekend and breaking my hand in Ibiza, I wouldn't have had time off work to start blogging! This process started with you – however painful that it was.

To my friends and colleagues in ward one, you gave me instant support from the day I published my book. The past year of working through this pandemic has made me realise how essential teamwork is, and I couldn't have gotten through it all without you. Especially Rae, Maggie, Karen, Samantha and Amy – you were the first to buy the book and read it within a day! You guys are not only great friends but fantastic nurses who have been my rainbow this year.

To Mum, Dad, Arlene, Andy, Les and Joyce, for supporting me and being proud even when I broke the news that I had written a steamy novel. Please never ever read it, but know I'm eternally grateful to have you all standing in my corner.

To my soul mates, Lisa Scott, Lisa Massey, Sasa Scott and Emma Grant, you have filled my life with complete hilarity, love and friendship. Thank you for allowing me to publish your dating disasters throughout the years without sending me a lawsuit! Your honest and frank guidance made you my first proofreaders, and your advice meant more to me than anyone else. You really are my biggest fangirls, and I love you all forever.

Lastly, but most importantly, thank you to Olivia Rose and Gracie. The first people I told about this project and the unconditional key to my heart. Thank you for being big dreamers and believing in me. Always remember that anything is possible if you are brave enough to take the risk. My journey is for you, my darlings. Girls really can do anything, and this is proof!

Lots of love and eternal gratitude,
Sophie x

Credits

Orion Fiction would like to thank everyone at Orion who worked on the publication of *A Glasgow Kiss* in the UK.

Editor
Rhea Kurien

Contracts
Anne Goddard
Paul Bulos
Jake Alderson

Editorial Management
Charlie Panayiotou
Jane Hughes

Production
Ruth Sharvell

Design
Rabab Adams
Joanna Ridley

Nick May
Clare Sivell
Helen Ewing
Jan Bielecki
Henry Steadman

Finance
Jasdip Nandra
Afeera Ahmed
Rabale Mustafa
Elizabeth Beaumont
Sue Baker
Victor Falola

Marketing
Helena Fouracre
Lynsey Sutherland